Last Tango in Brooklyn

KIRK DOUGLAS

Last Tango in Brooklyn

WARNER BOOKS

A Time Warner Company

*To Michael, Joel, Peter, Eric
and Cameron and Kelsey Anne*

"Do not complain about growing old—
not everyone is granted that privilege."

FILIPINO PROVERB

ACKNOWLEDGMENTS

A great deal of this book is very close to my heart and personal experience. I know what it feels like to confront old age. I know what it feels like to recover from an accident and find that the aftereffects—the lessons that came out of the trauma—linger for years, and compel one to take a new view of life. I know what it is like to work with a gym instructor who is a minimalist and who believes in the mind/body approach to exercise. That person is my personal trainer of twenty-five years, Mike Abrums, who served as an inspiration for much in this book.

But there is also a lot here that was not familiar territory, and I owe an enormous debt of gratitude to the people who helped me get acquainted with their worlds. There were many experts I consulted in the medical field, but I must single out Dr. Alfredo Trento, director of heart transplantation at Cedars-Sinai Medical Center; Dr. Phillip

Koeffler, director of hematology and oncology at Cedars-Sinai; and Geoffrey Visbal, head of surgical research at the Loma Linda International Heart Institute. I must also mention Drs. John Stevenson and Ronna Jurow, who didn't mind being pestered by medical questions; Frank Garcia, who introduced me to the secrets of the morgue; and medical librarians Ellen Green and Joanne Kennedy, who helped me understand the day-to-day realities of their work.

I am very grateful to Rachel Levitsky and John Greenbaum, who, along with other members of the Human Outreach Mobile Exchange, showed me the shadowy world of Coney Island, the world inhabited by the homeless. And especially to Tommy Jones and Knowledge and the other homeless people who shared their stories and lives with me.

I want to thank John and Jesse Holland for contributing their memories of growing up in Brooklyn, and Gene Sarro of the Ballroom Workshop, whose tango instruction tapes helped me to translate the special magic of the dance into words.

But most of all, I want to acknowledge my gratitude to Ursula Obst. Since my first book, *The Ragman's Son*, through the writing of *Dance with the Devil* and *The Gift* and now this novel, she has been my editor and much more than that. She has guided me—cajoling and badgering if need be—to get the best out of me. Thank you.

Last Tango in Brooklyn

1

Her eyes, milky with age, opened wide in horror as she looked from the rocky riverbank into the swirling waters below. "But Ben, you know I can't swim," she pleaded, clutching his shirtsleeve with her bony hand, the blue veins standing out against the transparent, liver-spotted skin.

"You have to try, Betty." He pulled his arm free of her grip. There was no contest between her fragile, disease-ridden body and his muscular, well-maintained one, even if they were exactly the same age.

"I can't!" she protested, shaking her head so hard that her stringy gray hair fell over her eyes.

"You must," he insisted.

She started crying softly, resigned to his command, "Whatever you say, Ben."

He kissed her on the cheek. And then, with one forceful motion, he pushed her into the water. She flailed helplessly as the rugged current picked up her emaciated frame and sucked her down.

She came up, the top of her head breaking the surface of the water just barely, and immediately disappeared again. He could still save her if he jumped in—he was a strong swimmer—but he made no move, staring blankly at the spot where her head had bobbed up. The current was swirling so rapidly he couldn't make anything out. Finally he saw her. Her whole head came up this time—she gulped for air but got a mouthful of water. Then the river pulled her down for the last time, sweeping her toward the deadly cataracts.

Suddenly overcome with the realization of what he had just done, he screamed, "Betty!" but he knew she could no longer hear him. His wife of forty-seven years had disappeared for good.

He woke up covered with cold sweat, gasping for air, as if he were the one drowning.

This was the third time he had the same nightmare since Betty died a year ago. Marion said it was part of the normal grieving process and the swirling waters represented an ablution of the survivor's guilt. Bullshit, he thought, he knew damn well what it meant. But how could he ever explain it to her? How could he ever describe to Marion her mother's terrible final moments?

He was sorry he had even mentioned the nightmares to her. He hated the pinched look on her face as she peered at him through her wire-rimmed glasses, delivering her "professional assessment" in that condescending, doctor-to-patient tone. She might be a licensed psychologist, but she was still his daughter, and he wasn't going to let her patronize him with her psychobabble.

The last time they talked she had given him a whole lecture on the perils of "trying to run away from grief." He was no fool, he knew what was behind it—Marion was only trying to make him feel bad because she was ticked off that he was selling the house.

Not that he could blame her all that much. She liked coming back here, especially now that she was divorced. For her, the cozy clapboard Victorian, tucked behind the parade grounds in Flatbush, represented happy childhood memories. For him, it was just an empty cavernous space without Betty. He wanted to leave it behind—he would take only the good memories with him.

The problem was that he had not thought out where he would move after the house was sold. The real estate agent said that in today's market it would be a slow-go. But it sold immediately, and now he had less than a month to pack up and move before escrow closed.

Oh God, what would he do with all this junk?

He looked around the room that Betty had redecorated about ten years before. White and pink—frilly, feminine. He never told her that he hated all those flowers and flounces.

If Marion didn't want it, he'd give all this stuff away to the Salvation Army: the overstuffed sofas, the uncomfortable straight-backed chairs, and all those knickknacks. There had to be a truckload of those itty-bitty things that Betty had bought in the last few years before her death. He never figured out why. Maybe it had something to do with her Alzheimer's. Well, he'd just get rid of it all. He'd buy something new—something his own—for the new apartment. Leather. That's it, nice rich leather, like the kind he had chosen for the equipment down at his gym. But he'd better get a move on finding a place. It wasn't going to be easy with all the yuppies leaving Manhattan and descending on Brooklyn. Would there be time to apartment-hunt today?

He checked his watch—not this morning. His first client was due at 8:00 A.M. That would be Milt, his old friend, the movie agent. He had a half hour to get ready.

He took a quick shower, then, still in his robe, he headed for the kitchen to fix his usual breakfast: an omelette made with the whites of four eggs and one yolk, one slice of toast, no butter, one glass of skim milk. Funny how life was—even in the midst of the worst traumas and upheavals, you still clung to the small routines. Here you were, having just passed your sixty-ninth birthday, your wife dead, your house sold, the future a bleak blank in front of you, and you still made breakfast as you had for most of your adult life, you still took a shower, brushed your teeth, combed your hair, like nothing had happened.

Breakfast eaten, the dishes rinsed off (to prevent "coagulation," his pet peeve) and stuffed into the dishwasher, Ben laid out his clothes for the day: neatly pressed khakis, tailored to show off his slim hips and flat stomach, a blue-and-green-striped polo shirt that fit snuggly over his muscled chest and arms, and green socks to match. Snappy.

As he dressed, he glanced in the mirror. Staring back was a well-weathered face with gray marble eyes, framed by a steel-gray mane of hair that matched the carefully trimmed mustache. That face belonged to an older man (a good-looking older man, but older, it was a fact), yet the body did not, not by a long shot. He had a dozen clients at the gym—Wall Street brokers young enough to be his sons—who looked at him with envy. Well, your body

4

couldn't do it alone. If you didn't exercise regularly, watch what you ate, get the proper amount of rest, and cut down on the vices—cigarettes, coffee, alcohol—by age thirty-five it would be written all over you.

Quickly now, he finished dressing, topping off the outfit with a navy blazer, and hurried out. On his way to the garage he noticed that the lilac bush was almost ready to pop open its blooms. He loved lilacs and lilies of the valley—all those fragile flowers that bloomed so briefly each spring only to die as soon as May had passed. He remembered when he had planted them all . . . the cherry tree and the apple. . . . He wouldn't be picking their fruit this year. Not letting himself get maudlin, he revved up his sporty Camaro (his one personal vice) and sped off, circling Prospect Park on the West Side, to reach his gym in Park Slope, on the corner of Union and Seventh. It was a ten-minute drive, a half-hour walk—and whenever possible he preferred to stroll through the park—but he might be driving around looking at apartments later, so it was better to have his car handy today.

BEN'S BODY BUILDERS—3RD FLOOR said the sign over the entrance. The plural in "builders" was meant to refer to the equipment, since Ben was the sole instructor. He believed in personalized training. No assistants.

Ever since he opened the gym, Ben always had a steady following of committed clients: bodybuilders (of course), jocks, actors needing to keep in shape. But in the last ten years, with the philosophies he had preached long ago finally taking hold among the baby-boomer generation, his business swelled with a new type of exercise freak—the stressed-out yuppie. He actually had a waiting list now.

5

They were attracted by Ben's program of moderation (they were never the type to buy into "no pain, no gain," which Ben had always maintained got you only temporary gain, and permanent pain) and they loved it that a fifteen-minute pit stop at his gym was all that was required. Happily, they forked over fifty dollars per daily session and considered him cheap.

Ben bounded up the steps, taking three at a time, and unlocked the door to the small waiting room, which purposely was not equipped with chairs, but which had plenty of reading material pinned to the cork-covered walls. There were articles clipped from newspapers and magazines about diet, exercise, disease—all, naturally, supporting Ben's thinking on these matters—and a whole section that he called "spiritual food for thought." Ben was a great believer that body and soul worked in tandem. He smiled as he tacked up: IF YOU HAVE ONE LEG IN YESTERDAY AND ONE LEG IN TOMORROW, YOU ARE PISSING ON TODAY.

Finally, he unlocked the door to the gym itself, a thirty-by-forty-foot room with a mirrored wall and carpeted floor that was furnished with various exercise devices, a treadmill, a stair climber, and several types of weight-lifting stations.

He turned on the stereo and popped in a cassette. He had an eclectic collection to suit the tastes of his clients: big band music, classical, country and western, and some rock. A throbbing beat filled the room. Bam, pa-pa, bam, pa-pa, bam . . . then the voice of Phil Collins: *"Oo-oh, think twice, it's another day for you and me in paradise . . ."*

"If this is paradise, I'll try hell." Milt came in puffing. "Your elevator is out of order again."

"I didn't turn it on—you're supposed to walk."

"I'll walk in here, out there I ride." Milt pulled off his jacket to reveal a short, chubby body, which always reminded Ben of a basket of fruit—the torso was like a pear, the bald head like a rosy apple. Why Milt shelled out money for a session at the gym Ben couldn't fathom, since he was clearly a hopeless case. But Ben was glad he did, because it was fun to start the morning chatting with his best friend. What Milt lacked in body he made up in spirit—he was always in a good mood, had a joke or an amusing anecdote to tell. Behind his large horn-rimmed glasses, the brown eyes always sparkled with merriment as if hiding some funny little secret.

"Look at you, Milt!" Ben grabbed Milt's love handles. "A spare tire is only good for rafting."

"Ouch, that hurts." Milt's plump face scrunched up in mock anguish. "You're suppose to get me in shape."

"Fifteen minutes a day of exercise will get you in shape only if you stop eating that *hazzerei* Sarah feeds you."

"Yeah? Well, I see you stuffing yourself every time you come over for dinner."

"Miltie," Ben grinned, "that's just so Sarah doesn't get a complex about her cooking."

They both laughed. Sarah's terrible cooking was their special in-joke.

It was actually what led them to reestablish their boyhood friendship after Milt—who had spent thirty-five years as a very successful Hollywood movie agent—moved back to Brooklyn. Sarah, pushing Milt to look up some old friends, insisted he invite Ben and Betty over for her famous (or "infamous," as Milt put it) pot roast, to be followed by a friendly game of bridge.

Sarah was originally from the Bronx, and she had

wanted to go back there when Milt decided to retire and return "home" to New York. But even Sarah's Jewish will-power could not turn back the clock on the Bronx, so she settled for Brooklyn—if moving into a Brooklyn Heights townhouse with a garden on the promenade and a view of Manhattan could be called "settling." And Milt never did retire, because his agency, Famous Artists, offered him a "troubleshooter" post in their New York office.

Pot roast and a game of cards became a weekly rou-tine—pleasant enough socializing for the two couples. They enjoyed reminiscing about the good old days when Ben and Milt were kids and rode the roller coaster at Coney Island or sneaked into Ebbets Field to watch the Dodgers play. Sometimes it made Ben sad, thinking how easy boyhood friendships were, so uncomplicated—you told your best friend your darkest secrets. As you got older it was so much harder to be open, to trust people. A year passed before that unforgettable moment of male bonding took place between them that made Milt his best friend once again.

It happened one evening, after dinner, as the wives were clearing the table and getting ready for a game of cards, and Milt and Ben were catching a breath of fresh air out on the balcony.

Milt turned to Ben, his brown eyes communicating an-guish, and whispered, "I think I'm gonna puke." He rubbed his ample tummy.

"What is it?" Ben asked, alarmed that Milt might up-chuck right then and there, down onto the promenade.

But Milt took a deep breath and recovered his compo-sure. Then he glanced back into the living room, where the wives were chattering away. "I gotta tell you something I never told anybody in my whole life," he announced solemnly in a low voice.

"What?" Now Ben wasn't sure if Milt was serious or about to deliver one of his jokes.

"I hate Sarah's pot roast."

"You do?" Ben looked at his friend wide-eyed. Hadn't he just witnessed Milt devouring a second helping with great gusto?

"One day it's gonna kill me." He slumped down on the chaise longue. "But don't breathe a word of it to her—she makes it at least once a week. If she finds out I hate it, it'll destroy her."

With a wry smile, Ben squatted down next to Milt. Conspiratorially, he whispered back: "I gotta tell you something, Milt."

"You hate it too?"

"Worse."

"Worse? What's worse?"

"I hate playing cards."

"But you and Betty play a couple of times a week."

"I know—it's torture."

They both looked at each other and broke out into laughter. The more they laughed, the more hysterical they became, till tears were streaming down their cheeks.

Sarah popped her head out onto the balcony. "Must be one of Milt's dirty jokes," she grumbled to Betty, which only made Ben and Milt laugh harder.

From that moment on, their friendship became special. It was like in the good old days, when they were kids.

"What are you grinning about?" Milt now asked in a slightly exasperated voice, beads of perspiration forming

9

on his forehead as he moved up and down on the stair climber.

"Oh, just remembering . . ."

"Yeah—the good old days when one was young and didn't sweat, even when fucking." Milt slowed down his pace and wiped himself off with a towel.

"I bet you miss Hollywood with all the women and romance." Ben changed the cassette on the stereo to a tango.

"There ain't much romance," Milt scoffed as he started curling two ten-pound dumbbells, the next step in his exercise routine. "All those stars fucking around—that's just publicity."

"No fucking?"

"Oh there's plenty, but not between the stars."

"Well, who's getting it?"

Milt winked at Ben. "The agents."

"Come on—guys like you?"

"Yeah! Stars compete with each other—for the best lines, the close-ups, the right light. They hate each other."

"They do?"

"Sure. Those gorgeous women come home after a day's work, and the last thing they want to see is one of those gorgeous guys. They're too upset. They take a bath, put on their nightgowns, but they can't sleep. They call their agents."

"No shit?"

"No shit. The agent's gotta go over. He holds her hand, cuddles her, reassures her—fucks her. And she's grateful for it."

Ben shook his head, turning up the tango music a bit. "You agents get ten percent of everything."

"Anything to help a client."

Ben laughed.

"You know—" Milt dropped the weights to the floor, making Ben wince. "I wish there had been a way to bank some of those fucks back then—so you could draw on them now . . . like a pension."

Ben shook his head. "Milt—you have sex on the brain."

"Well, when you can't do it, you like to talk about it."

Ben didn't respond.

"Hey, boychik—do all your muscles still work?"

Ben gave him a wry grin. "They haven't invented a Nautilus machine for that one. As soon as they do—I'll order three, one for me and two for you, Milt."

"That seems fair." Finished, Milt whipped off his sweats and reached for his street clothes. "I better get going—Michaelson's in town."

"Michaelson?"

"The bozo who heads up the agency."

Milt pulled out a fresh shirt he had brought along in his briefcase and put it on in front of the mirror. In the back he could see Ben swaying to the tango beat, lost in the music. He spun his imaginary partner around and put her into a deep dip.

"Reminds me . . ." Milt sighed, "when you and Betty got first prize in that dance contest on Coney Island. When was that . . . 'forty-five?"

"A long time ago, that's for sure. Too bad they don't dance the tango anymore." Ben's voice was wistful.

"I guess the last tango was in Paris."

"What?"

"Didn't you ever see that movie—with Marlon Brando?"

"No, Betty never liked going to the movies."

"Too bad. It's playing at the Plaza, where they show the old classics."

"I know the place."

"You ought to go."

"Might do that. I was thinking of going apartment-hunting tonight, but what the hell."

"*Last Tango in Paris*—you'll love it."

Ben wasn't sure. He never liked Marlon Brando, but how bad could it be if it had the tango in it?

2

The sharp teeth of the electrical saw made a grating, rasping sound. The acrid smell of burning human flesh filled the air. Ellen felt queasy, but she clenched her teeth and forced herself to watch.

Richard's rubber-gloved hand held the saw steady as it cut through the wide bone at the center of the rib cage, tiny splinters flicking off to the sides. The assisting surgeon's hand was right behind his, holding the electrical wand that scorched the blood vessels shut to prevent hemorrhage. The absence of blood made the rib cage look like a turkey breast about to be stuffed on Thanksgiving morning. Ellen almost giggled behind her mask, but then she reminded herself that there was a real live person under the green tent of surgical drapes. The reminder also brought on another wave of nausea.

Now Richard started to crank up the bar on a stainless-steel rack that resembled some medieval torture device. Ellen looked away, pretending to be interested in the numbers flashing on the monitors above the operating table, but she could not avoid hearing the noise—the excruciating crunch of the ribs being forced apart. Her knees buckled, and she grabbed the anesthesiologist's arm. "You okay?" he whispered from behind his mask.

"Who? Me? I'm having a great time, can't you tell?" she whispered back.

The anesthesiologist chuckled softly and without a word shoved a stool under her.

"Thanks."

She sat down, taking deep breaths, feeling the face mask being sucked in against her face.

"Where is it?" Richard's tense, Austrian-accented voice echoed in the tiled room.

"Helicopter just landed on the roof—should be here at any moment," one of the nurses answered.

"All right, let's proceed," Richard said.

Ellen forced her eyes open as Richard's scalpel cut through the tubes leading to the heart. But when his hand went in and plucked out the now limp mass of flesh like a hunk of beef in a butcher shop, she nearly fainted.

"Go get a drink of water," the anesthesiologist suggested. Gratefully, she seized on the excuse to leave the scene for a while. It would be terrible if she fainted or upchucked her breakfast right in the operating room. This was a good time for a little break; Richard seemed too busy to notice she was gone.

In the hall outside, she leaned on a surgical cart and pressed her forehead against the cold tiled wall. Her stomach had almost returned to normal when she saw an orderly come hurrying out of the elevator with a red-and-white Igloo cooler in his hand. He brushed past her as he knocked on the door of the operating room.

The door opened and a nurse eagerly grabbed the cooler from him. It was just a plain plastic picnic basket, quite small really, with room enough for only a couple of sandwiches and sodas. But that was what the new heart traveled in—stilled only for a few hours by ice and saline solution.

Ellen knew everything there was to know about heart transplants. As a medical librarian, she was up on the latest in high-tech organ surgery, but she had never watched one before. Attracted to medicine since high school, she had discovered in the first semester of pre-med that she couldn't stand the sight of blood. Becoming a medical librarian had been a way to keep her hand in a field she loved without being subjected to the daily gore of it. She would never have come in to watch this, or any other operation, if the surgeon was not her lover.

After a few minutes, she composed herself enough to go back in, determined—no matter how queasy she got—to get through it.

She opened the door, took a deep breath—for insurance—and approached the operating table. The cavity of the patient's chest was now empty. Here was a man without a heart, all his arteries clamped off and attached to plastic tubes leading down to the floor where a computer-controlled cardiopulmonary bypass machine whirled his blood around, inserting molecules of oxygen and sending it back to his body. That mass of spinning cylinders was now his heart and lungs.

"So what do you think about it so far?" Richard's question, directed at her, startled Ellen.

"Fascinating," she managed. Her normally husky Lauren Bacall voice—considered one of her sexiest features—had changed to a strangled rasp from the strain of keeping her gag reflex at bay.

"Are you all right?"

"Oh sure."

Gina, the surgical nurse standing next to Richard, shot him a glance. Ellen caught the exchange—what was that supposed to mean?

She felt like such an outsider—a foreigner in a strange world—not able to understand this silent language of the eyes that seemed to exist between doctors and nurses in the operating room.

Gina now placed the cooler on the table near Richard and removed the cover. The assisting surgeon reached into the ice with both hands to pull out a large plastic bag filled with more ice surrounding a glass jar. He discarded the ice bag and took off the lid. Something was swimming inside. Richard's hand scooped it out.

My God! Ellen gasped inwardly. She knew what was in the jar, but the sight of it resting in Richard's palm astonished her nevertheless. This was a human heart! She had just seen one plucked out of the patient's chest. But this one was different—this was a healthy heart, waiting to beat again. For that body on the table this heart meant the difference between life and death—for real—and it had arrived so unceremoniously, in a beat-up Igloo cooler.

Richard picked up a scalpel and began deftly to trim some tendrils off the sides. Ellen was amazed. She had done that herself many times when trimming excess fat off a

16

piece of meat she was about to barbecue. Nothing special about the technique.

He placed the heart into the chest cavity and picked up a pair of long tweezers holding a crescent-shaped needle and thread. He began sewing, the assisting surgeon tying the knots after each stitch. Gina kept scooping up ice and dumping it on the heart, whispering something to Richard from time to time.

Ellen felt almost relaxed now, though her legs hurt from standing. How long had it been? Three hours. She shouldn't be this tired—it must be the tension.

As Richard continued to sew, connecting the tubes of the new heart with the severed tubes in the chest, the thought again flicked through her mind that this activity, like trimming the fat, seemed so everyday, so mundane. She had seen her mother use the same motion hemming dresses. Such ordinary actions to such an extraordinary end—saving a life, cheating death.

Now Richard snapped off the clamps and motioned to the technician controlling the heart-and-lung machine. The anesthesiologist also jumped up. This was the crucial moment. Would it work?

The new heart, which had been without blood for hours, stirred. Then it leaped, a weak, spastic movement, and then it leaped again. It looked to Ellen like a small hungry animal gulping for air, except that this creature was gulping for blood.

Gina held out the electric paddles, but Richard waved them away. "This is a thirsty heart," he said, his eyes smiling, "it does not need stimulation." His precise English gave him such an air of distinction. He turned to Ellen. She knew he was smiling broadly behind his mask. "That is it."

"Miraculous," she said breathlessly.

"Now that you have seen it, you should be able to do it," he chuckled.

"And if you see it twice," Gina chimed in, "you can teach it." There seemed to be a sarcastic note to her voice.

Ellen had an impulse to rip off Gina's mask and expose the twisted smirk she was sure was there. But she just stared back coldly into Gina's eyes, which were framed by heavy black mascara to make the most of her large brown eyes. Cow eyes, Ellen thought, instantly feeling guilty for being so stupidly jealous.

She envied Gina, who got to stand here, day after day, next to the man Ellen loved, helping him perform miracles.

"Damn!" That was Richard. Something was going wrong. From the top valve, a small trickle of blood was beginning to ooze out.

"Better zip it fast," the assisting surgeon said, reaching in with the tweezers.

Ellen shot a questioning look at the anesthesiologist.

"Don't worry," he reassured her, "just a loose stitch, happens all the time. They'll stop the leak in a jiffy."

But the feeling of nausea was beginning to return. "Looks like you're almost finished," Ellen said more loudly than she intended. "I should get going."

"Don't you want to help us close up?" Gina chirped.

"No, I have to get back to work." She moved quickly toward the door as if afraid someone might stop her.

"Glad you came," Richard said, intent on the opened chest cavity. "I'll see you for lunch."

The thought of food made her gag, and without answering him she bolted from the room.

* * *

Out of the surgical gown, back into her street clothes and feeling somewhat more composed, Ellen walked down the hallway of Saint Joseph's Medical Center. It was 9 A.M., peak action time for Coney Island's (Brooklyn's, for that matter) busiest hospital, but Ellen was oblivious to the nurses, doctors, and orderlies rushing past her. What a miracle she had just witnessed, and her lover was the miracle worker—the famed Dr. Richard Vandermann, *the* man at the forefront of transplant surgery, the riskiest of all medical disciplines to master. Today he had impressed her more than ever.

In five days it would be exactly eight months since he had walked into the medical library and changed her life. She had been working late that evening, getting research together on a rare form of breast cancer for the hospital's chief oncologist. Her back was bothering her as usual, so she got up to stretch and was in the middle of touching her toes when she heard an accented male voice behind her.

"I was looking for the library, but I see this is the gymnasium."

She straightened up with a jolt and whipped around to face the voice. It belonged to a tall, slim man in his early forties with sharply chiseled features, a slightly aquiline nose, blue eyes, and short, curly, blond hair. Nordic. Very nice.

"May I help you?" she asked, deciding not to react to his lame joke.

"I am Dr. Vandermann," he pronounced his name with the emphasis on the last syllable. "I just arrived here from Stanford—to head up Cardiology."

So he was the one. The hospital had been abuzz for months in anticipation of his arrival. A former disciple of Christiaan Barnard and more recently an associate of Norman Shumway (the near mythic originator of many transplantation techniques), Dr. Vandermann was considered quite a catch for Saint Joseph's. His expertise would qualify the hospital for this highly specialized field and bring in millions of insurance dollars. Reportedly a bidding war had ensued among several hospitals eager to get him on staff. It was rumored that to win him over, Saint Joseph's had had to cough up a six-figure salary plus perks, practically promise him an eventual promotion to chief of staff in a couple of years, *and* offer him his own research lab—to be outfitted for baboon experiments, the cutting edge of transplant medicine. Clearly, Dr. Vandermann had high ambitions. And he was handsome to boot.

Bet all the female nurses in CCU are in a tizzy, Ellen thought. Dr. Thorne, the former head of Cardiology, was short and fat with thinning hair and hanging jowls.

"It must be some change for you—from sunny California to grimy Brooklyn."

"I have not been here long enough to notice."

"You're lucky. Take my advice. Go out on the street only at night, that way the dirt blends in."

He laughed. A sexy laugh, straight, white teeth.

"Did you need something from the library?" she asked, feeling his eyes appraising her. Involuntarily, she straightened her shoulders, stretching out her five-foot-six tomboy frame. She knew men found her attractive. She looked a great deal younger than thirty-four with her smooth, round face, large hazel eyes, and shoulder-length, dark brown

20

hair, though he couldn't see her best feature—her long, slender legs—under her slacks.

"Would you give me a complete list of all available books and articles on heart transplants?"

"Forget the instructions?" she quipped.

"No, I have those tattooed on the back of my hand."

She laughed. He had a good sense of humor.

"Actually, I have being doing heart transplants for many years, and I'm writing a book about my experiences. I need the list for my bibliography."

She motioned him over to her computer. "Let's see what we've got on MedLine." She adeptly punched in the codes for the data bank. The screen lit up as her fingers quickly danced over the keyboard.

"This is it—a list of books and journal articles on the subject. I'll give you a printout."

"Excellent. And thank you."

"No problem."

"You are very quick with that computer."

"Hey, researching books and periodicals doesn't require much computer training. It's knowing what to look for that counts."

"Where did you go to school?"

"Columbia—pre-med and after I dropped out . . . two years in a master's program, library science."

"You are perfect."

"Perfect for what?"

"I am looking for someone familiar with medical terms who is also an expert with the word processor."

Ellen made a face. "What? You offering me a typing job?" What a put-down.

"Please don't get insulted—it is more than that," he smiled, revealing his strong, white teeth again. "I need someone to help me with research and to organize my notes."

She tore off the long list from the printer and handed it to him. "Why are you writing a book on transplants? Isn't there enough already on the subject?"

"Are you asking a question or answering it?" His wry smile said he liked bantering with her.

"Sorry."

"That's all right. The answer is, I want to write a book for the general public . . . to encourage people to become donors. Right now we can only take the hearts of the brain-dead—"

"What about your baboons?"

"Hm . . . news travels fast. Unfortunately, to date no baboon transplant has been successful, but I am hopeful that my experiments with transgenics . . . that means—"

"I know what transgenics are," she broke in. "Interspecie gene transfers. The hottest thing in medicine. The only way you can prevent the human body's rejection of an animal organ—in theory, that is."

He raised his eyebrows, clearly impressed with her knowledge. "Perhaps soon, not only in theory. However, until such time when baboons can become viable donors, cancer patients are much better prospects. But, there is still too much fear the organs might be taken from people before they are truly dead."

"You can't blame them. Those folks would have to be taken into the operating room to die, so you can snatch their hearts at the moment they take their last breath. That's ghoulish."

"I know it *sounds* ghoulish, but it is *not*." His steady gaze gave her a slightly uncomfortable feeling. "Wouldn't you give your heart to save another person's life if you were dying without a chance for recovery?"

He was so fervent. Ellen bit her lip. "I suppose, but I don't know what I'd do, really."

"That's why I am writing this book. To convince people to think of organ donations not as giving something up, but as giving."

"That sounds noble."

He stiffened.

She corrected herself quickly. "No, I mean it. And yes, I'd be glad to help you."

"Thank you. We will talk more after I get settled." He stuffed the printout in the pocket of his white coat and turned to leave, but he stopped at the door. "Would you like to see a heart transplant?"

"Oh God . . . I'm no good with blood."

"Well, who knows, I might help you get over your squeamishness."

She knew, watching him walk down the hall that day, that it would be exciting to work with him. And perhaps it was inevitable that they should become lovers. After an evening filled with work and creative tension, it was great to end up in bed with him. But she was also genuinely impressed with his dedication. He was always actively searching for potential donors, trying to persuade families of the comatose to disconnect life-support equipment and donate the organs so some other, vital people could live. On his office wall, he had a chart that showed how many patients in the United States were waiting for hearts—the number was usually over 2,000. Most of them wouldn't make it. Most of them would die while waiting for someone else to die—someone younger, stronger, with a heart that could live again.

It had taken her all this time to force herself to watch one of his operations. And the experience, as uncomfortable as it was, turned out to be quite incredible—well worth every bit of the discomfort. And yet . . .

And yet the strongest image that stayed with her from this dramatic day was that of Gina's eyes locking with Richard's over the pulsating heart.

Stop it, she told herself. That woman was only doing her job.

She knew that she could never do what Gina did. She was not tough enough. She might come across that way with her no-nonsense, straightforward style, but really she only spoke her mind, and people mistook that for toughness. Right now she wished she really could be tough, instead of feeling jealous that Gina shared something with Richard that she never could.

"They don't pay for daydreaming around here, girl." The teasing drawl came from behind. Ellen turned around to greet the smiling, chubby face of her best friend, Goldie. An operating room nurse, Goldie—whose real name was Beatrice—had often been kidded about her strong resemblance to Whoopi Goldberg. (She could easily have passed for the comedienne's sister.) The nickname stuck. Now no one dared to call her Beatrice—only her husband got away with that.

"They don't pay for anything around here, Goldie. I asked for one of those ergonomic chairs to help my bad back—they told me to buy it myself."

"What do you expect—they don't care about your back.

It's a Catholic hospital—we work for peanuts to keep the pope in his fucking gold dresses."

Ellen laughed; she loved Goldie's down-to-earth sense of humor. It was a trait they had in common.

"How are you and your boyfriend getting along?"

"I just watched him do a heart transplant."

"You? You can't watch blood from a pinprick!"

"I was queasy the whole time—but I got through it."

"Come on, I'll buy you a cup of coffee to celebrate."

"Just what I need—some of that cafeteria acid. No thanks."

"Well, keep me company while I have some. I had a rough morning, too—a triple bypass with old fumble fingers Fineberg. And saints be praised, the patient lived."

Giggling, Ellen followed Goldie's wide hips to the cafeteria, where she opted for a Coke, hoping it would settle her stomach.

"So, girlfriend—now that you've passed the test, is lover boy gonna move in with you?"

"I don't think so, Goldie. Not yet."

"Ya'll been screwing long enough—how long is it gonna take him to make it semipermanent?"

"Please, Goldie, don't you start getting sarcastic about my love life."

"Sorry, honey." Goldie was stuffing a large frosted danish into her mouth and had to pause to swallow. "I'm just trying to make you get real. Sometimes you act like a small-town girl on ether."

"I am a small-town girl."

"Yeah, but who the hell is he? Dr. Been-Around-the-World-So-My-Shit-Don't-Stink Vandermann?"

That was funny. Ellen couldn't get mad.

"Ellen—*he* doesn't deserve *you*."

"Thanks, Goldie, but enough, okay?"

"Okay, okay. But I still don't understand what's holding the boy back."

"Oh, lots of things."

"That explains it," Goldie washed the danish down with a large gulp of coffee.

Funny or not, sometimes Ellen wished Goldie was just a touch less pointed in her commentary.

"You're not getting any younger, you know," Goldie continued. Once she got onto a pet peeve (and Ellen's ill-managed love life was one of them) she was hard to divert to another subject. "Thirty-four is close to the wire if you wanna have kids."

"I don't know if I want to have kids. I know I'm *suppose* to want to, and I think they're cute and all, but somehow I can't imagine myself doing this family bit—kids, house in the suburbs, picket fence, station wagon . . . I'm just not ready for that yet."

"You're not ready, he's not ready . . ." Goldie shook her head. "But meanwhile you better find another roommate for that expensive apartment of yours."

"And fast." Ellen sighed. "It's been three months since Sharon moved out. I'm getting desperate scraping that twelve hundred together all by myself."

"Two bedrooms, two baths, in Park Slope . . . if I could leave my old man, I'd move in with you."

Ellen stopped listening—she was staring over Goldie's shoulder at Richard coming into the cafeteria with Gina, whose red hair, no longer contained in the surgical cap, was cascading sexily down her shoulders. They were both laughing at some private joke.

Goldie turned around. "Well, if it isn't Dr. Right and Silicone Sally. I hate that bitch."

Ellen burst out in throaty laughter. At times like these she forgave Goldie for everything.

Just then, Richard saw them and waved. He whispered something in Gina's ear and came over to their table.

Goldie got up, draining her cup. "Well, I'd love to stay, but I gotta go. No, no, please don't insist, Dr. Vandermann-n-n-n." And with a giggle, she moved toward the door.

"What was that all about?" Ellen asked, not getting Goldie's joke.

"She misspelled my name on a chart—one *n*—now she's making up for it," he said, sitting down opposite her.

"Ahh." Ellen nodded.

The waitress placed a coffee cup in front of Richard and smiled coyly. "Black, no sugar, right?"

"Right." He returned the smile with a glistening display of teeth.

"Do you have to seduce them all?" Ellen asked.

"You are silly." Richard reached over and put his hand over hers. "Have you recovered yet?"

"I think so, but never again."

Richard chuckled. "Well, at least now you know how I spend my days."

"I'm more interested in the nights." She gave him her most seductive look. "Like tonight?"

He sighed. "I only wish I could."

"Why not—what's wrong?"

"I have to fly to Miami tonight."

"Miami?"

"A dying baby—looks like the parents will give up the heart, but they have a lot of questions. I know I can convince them."

"Is Gina going?" Ellen couldn't stop the question from rushing out.

"That is what she gets paid to do."

Ellen forced a smile. "Of course. Hope all goes well."

She went back to the library with mixed feelings. Okay, so he was a wonderful man, doing all sorts of amazing things to save lives. But why the hell with that bimbo? She took a deep breath, commanding her mind to snap out of it. This kind of thinking was petty and selfish—all she cared about was that he wouldn't be spending the night with her.

She was disappointed, but that was no reason to go home and sulk. She just wouldn't let herself dwell on it. She was a modern woman—she could go to the movies alone and have a *good time*. Well, maybe . . . She'd try, anyway.

She had passed the Plaza on her way to the subway. What was playing there? Something with Marlon Brando, an actor she loved. Oh yeah, *Last Tango in Paris*. She had always wanted to see that. The evening wouldn't be a total loss—she'd spend it with Brando.

3

Ben parked his car on Seventh Avenue and walked around the corner to the dilapidated structure that was the Plaza, a theater known for its daily showings of oldies but goodies. Once the rage with nostalgia buffs, the Plaza had, in the last few years, lost to Ted Turner and his box of coloring pens. It still held on, though the battle scars showed, the most visible being the weathered marquis, which read like a jigsaw puzzle waiting to be filled in:

M rlon Brando

in

L ST TANGO IN P RIS

When Betty was alive, they rarely went to the movies. Betty preferred more sophisticated entertainment—the theater, the opera. So they compromised and went nowhere.

What a silly thing marriage can be, Ben thought, too much togetherness. You have to have the same friends, do the same things, and sometimes you end up doing things you both hate, just because it's expected of a married couple.

But oh how sweet, when you are passionate about something in common. They had both loved ballroom dancing, had competed as partners in high school, and had continued their winning streak when he came home from the war. He often joked that he married Betty to keep winning dance contests. They sure were good together. Come to think of it, they probably danced together more than they made love. It was a favorite pastime—to go out to a restaurant with a good band and dance through the night. When the discos came into vogue, their kind of dancing places became hard to find—even Lawrence Welk went off the air—and you had to drive to south Jersey or up to one of the old resorts in the Catskills.

Then Betty got "sick." Of course, they didn't know at first that she had a disease, just that she started to become impossible, and often created some embarrassment in public. Time stood still for those eight years as she battled demons too horrible to imagine, and he watched helplessly.

It's all over now. It's all over. He repeated the words to stop himself from reliving it again. Betty was gone; he was still alive. So get on with it, he ordered his mind.

"Would you like to buy a lucky chance?"

The voice coming from below startled Ben. On the sidewalk against the wall of the movie house sat a middle-aged bearded man dressed in a tattered pea coat, sweatpants, and laceless sneakers of unrelated origins. His very grimy right hand was reaching in Ben's direction, holding out a scrap of paper, while the left stroked a little mouse peeping out from beneath his lapel. "Would you like to buy a lucky chance?" he repeated.

There was a smile on the man's face, an expression of . . . of . . . what could you call it? Kindness? Ben smiled back—it was hard not to. "How much?"

"Whatever your conscience commands," the man said solemnly, then added, "but nothing under a quarter."

Ben peeled off a dollar bill.

The man started to say something, but his words were cut off by a racking cough. He handed Ben the piece of paper. On it was scribbled in crayon: *God bless you.*

"I told you to take care of that cough!" a stern female voice admonished from behind. Ben turned to see a young woman approaching, whose cheerful face and laughing hazel eyes belied the sternness of her tone.

"Hiya, Miss Ellen." The bum clearly knew her.

"Are you taking those pills I gave you?"

"Sure are."

"You don't want to get pneumonia."

"Sure don't."

"All right, Jello. See you Sunday." She waved.

Jello waved back. "You can count on me."

What the hell was *that* all about? Ben was curious as he followed her to the ticket booth. Patiently, he watched her digging through her purse.

She was growing more agitated by the second. "Oh God," she sighed, "I'm short a dollar. Wouldn't you know it? Just what I need today!"

"Miss—you're holding up the line," the pimply-faced cashier whined. "Are you buying a ticket or not?"

31

"No, I'm sorry," she said dejectedly, stepping away.

Ben quickly pushed a twenty-dollar bill through the ticket-window slot. "Allow me—I just hit a lucky chance."

"Oh no, I couldn't." She seemed embarrassed.

"Please. I'm not gonna let you end up like your friend over there—begging on the street." He motioned to the cashier. "Two tickets, please."

"Senior ID?" the kid asked.

Ben's jaw tensed. "Two regulars."

"Sure thing, man. Just trying to help ya."

"Well, don't try," Ben snapped. For five years, he had not been able to admit that he was entitled to a senior citizen discount, and resented it when someone implied he should take it. He handed one of the tickets to the girl.

"Thank you," she said with a smile, and extended her hand. "My name is Ellen Riccio."

"Ben Jacobs," he replied, surprised at the firmness of her handshake.

Walking into the theater, Ben couldn't help wanting to satisfy his curiosity. "How do you know him?"

"Who?"

"The chance seller." He motioned with his head to the man, who was now getting up and moving away.

"Oh, Jello—he is one of my regulars."

Regulars? She must be one of those social worker types that travel around in vans dispensing medicine and food to the homeless. But her manner and attitude didn't say bleeding heart. Oh well, appearances could be deceiving.

The curtain was already going up as he followed her inside. She chose one of the rows in the middle. Ben hesitated a moment, then elected the same row, but left a couple seats empty between them.

The theater was sparsely populated. Directly behind him a yuppie couple munched popcorn, and over to the left a group of leather-clad punks raucously agitated about something, but they simmered down when the movie started.

Ben was immediately disappointed. "I thought it was supposed to be a musical," he muttered loud enough for Ellen to hear. She threw him a surprised look. The yuppie couple snickered.

For a moment he thought of leaving, but then he became absorbed by the film. It sure had a socko sexy beginning. He was riveted watching a beautiful girl walking through an empty apartment and then bam, next thing you know, clothes still on, she was making it on the floor with a total stranger.

He looked over at Ellen—she was the picture of intense concentration: big eyes fixed on the screen, her teeth biting down on her lower lip.

Now the punks were letting out loud whistles at the sight of bare-breasted Maria Schneider saying something to Marlon Brando in a thick French accent. Ben strained to catch the words, which sounded like: "I'm a rhed rhriding ood and yoo ze woolf. What strhong arhms yoo haf."

"What'd she say?" Ben muttered to Ellen.

"What strong arms you have," Ellen replied in a loud whisper.

Ben looked back to the screen as Brando was saying: "The better to squeeze a fuck out of you."

"What'd he say?"

"The better to . . . ah . . ." she stammered. "The better to squeeze you."

The yuppie guy guffawed and popcorn came spitting

out of his mouth, a kernel hitting Ben's shoulder. Ben moved over one seat closer to Ellen, who flashed him a weak smile and turned back to the movie.

One steamy scene followed another. But you couldn't call it porn. Ben was not versed in artsy European flicks, but he realized that this wasn't some self-indulgent tribute to kinky sex. This movie was deep, in ways he couldn't quite follow. He listened attentively as Brando tried to convince the girl that she would never find a man to love: "You want a man to build you a fortress, to protect you . . . so you don't have to feel lonely. . . . But you are alone, you're all alone and you won't be free of that feeling until you look death right in the face. . . . And then maybe—maybe then you'll be able to find him."

Maria Schneider said plaintively: "But I find this man, it's you, you are that man."

Out of the corner of his field of vision, Ben noticed that Ellen's big brilliant eyes were brimming with tears. Just like a woman. He wanted to lean over and remind her, "Hey, it's just a movie," but decided against it.

A few moments later, he felt like apologizing for his thoughts. Marlon Brando was speaking to the corpse of his dead wife, laid out for the funeral service. Memories of Betty's death came flooding back with such force that for a second he couldn't separate the images in his mind from the images on the screen. He closed his eyes, gripping the arms of his seat tightly.

Then, it passed.

And finally, the tango. The title didn't lie altogether. Ben leaned back in his seat and watched the tango contest on the screen. It wasn't the same dance he knew at all—this was exaggerated, stiff, with mannequinlike figures looking ridiculous.

When the lights came on, he stood up to follow the sparse audience shuffling up the aisle of the theater. Then he noticed that Ellen was sniffling. "Are you all right?"

"Why did she kill him? She loved him. He loved her. Why did she kill him?"

"Take it easy—she didn't kill him."

"What? He died right in the last scene."

"No, Brando made a bunch of more movies after that."

Ellen smiled. "You're right, I have to remember it's just a movie."

"And a bunch of bull."

"Well, it was supposed to make you think."

"I didn't come to think—I came to see a musical."

Ellen burst out in a peal of throaty laughter.

As they left the theater, they saw the three punks out on the street playing some sort of gross game, spitting kernels of popcorn in each other's direction. The one with a red bandanna wrapped around his head seemed to be winning.

Ben took Ellen's arm to guide her out of the jerk's way, but their path was suddenly blocked. Red bandanna shoved the popcorn box practically into Ellen's chest. "Want some?"

"No, thank you," she said, startled.

"How about your old man?"

"Get lost." Ben barreled passed them into the street, his arm around Ellen for protection.

"Keep your socks on, grandpa," chortled his companion, the short, tubby one.

"Little shits," Ben snapped, quickly adding, "forgive my French."

"Nothing to forgive."

Ben looked back in the direction of the three punks, who were muttering among themselves. Red bandanna was looking right at him.

"I better drive you home."

"Oh no, that's really not necessary, I live just a few blocks away."

"Then, if you don't mind, I'll walk you."

"Oh, there is really no need, believe me, they're harmless."

"Please, indulge me."

"Okay, then." She smiled, glad for the company after all.

They walked across the street, taking the scenic route along Prospect Park, which was awash with the fragrances of spring flowers and freshly mowed grass. There was something intoxicating about the smells at this time of the year, Ben thought. As they approached the tunnel leading to Long Meadow, he broke the reverie. "Do you know how to tango?"

"God, no."

"Too bad. I won a few prizes doing the tango."

"You did?"

"Before you were born—but back then dancing was art, people don't dance like they used to."

He hummed a few bars of a tango as they entered the tunnel, the arched walls amplifying his voice. "I've loved this place ever since I was a kid. See how it's paneled in wood, all those slats—that's called tongue-in-groove. See the workmanship?"

"Yeah—they don't make tunnels like they used to."

Ben shot her a glance. Was she making fun of him? The wry smile on her face said so.

He smiled back sheepishly. "Okay, I'll cut out the older is better stuff." He stopped. "Look! Look at the initials people carved here." He pointed to one that said *JT loves SL, 8-25-51.* "JT? I wonder who that was? Jack? He must have done the carving."

"Does he still love Sue?" Ellen enjoyed playing along.

"I wonder if he's even alive . . . he might be dead, they both might be dead. . . ."

"Is it difficult?" she asked abruptly.

He looked at her. "Is what difficult?"

"The tango."

"Oh, no—it's really very simple. It's based on just five steps. Look . . ." And he straightened himself up, bent his arms gingerly around an imaginary partner, and lightly stepped over the octagonal pavement tiles. "Slow . . . slow . . . quick, quick . . . slow . . ."

From down the tunnel, the loud sound of hands clapping reverberated harshly. "Not bad for an old geezer," said red bandanna, his pals following, still munching popcorn.

"I told you," said Ben sternly, "I want *you* to get lost."

"We don't care what you want," red bandanna countered. "What does *she* want?" He grabbed Ellen and pulled her forward. "You want Brando to fuck you in the ass, babe?"

With lightning speed, Ben sent his fist smack into the punk's mouth and sent him sprawling against the wooden paneling. The box of popcorn went flying out of his hands, spraying kernels all over the pavement. The short one with the long hair and earring jumped out from behind and wrapped his arm around Ben's neck in a choke hold. Without an ounce of strain, Ben grabbed him by the hair with both hands, doubled over, and flipped him off onto the pavement. As the third one moved in, Ben's foot shot out in a side-kick, catching him in the groin.

Speechless, Ellen just stared.

"Let's go." Ben took her arm, stepped over red bandanna, whose mouth was bleeding all over the pavement, and didn't even look back as he led her away, groans of pain echoing in the tunnel behind them.

"Shouldn't we call the police?"

"Why? They won't be attacking anybody for a while."

Ellen shuddered. "All that blood. I can't stand to look at it."

"Something tells me you're not a nurse."

She smiled weakly. "No, I'm a medical librarian. And I prefer books without pictures."

He chuckled.

Ellen looked at him—he was showing no sign of exertion, and yet he had just single-handedly done in three young men.

Seeing the expression on her face, Ben grinned. He knew he had impressed her and he liked how it felt. "I'd say that calls for a celebration," he said. "You like chocolate?"

"I love it."

"Me too—it's my secret vice. I give in to it once a month . . . ah . . . not counting special occasions like this one."

"Well, you sure earned it. It ought to be my treat, but I still don't have any money."

"Don't worry about it. The place I have in mind—Café La Fontana—plays opera. You can sing for your supper."

"That's not a bad idea. Considering how I sing they may pay me not to."

"I'd like to see that."

"You shouldn't tempt an Italian to sing opera—nasty things happen."

"Oh, I remember now—your name is Italian, isn't it? Riccio, right?"

"Memory like an elephant."

They were laughing and bantering like old friends by the time they got to the café.

"Two decaf cappuccinos and two large pieces of your Sinful Temptation Torta," Ben ordered, settling into a booth in the corner.

Ellen sat down opposite, sizing him up in bright light for the first time since they met.

"What's the matter?" he asked, feeling her eyes studying him.

"Where did you learn to fight like that?"

"The war—I was in the marines."

"Vietnam?"

"Nah—the real war—WW Two."

Quickly Ellen tried to calculate, 1943 subtracted from 1993 was fifty years ago—my God, how old could he be? He didn't look much over fifty, yet he was an adult back then. So he had to be close to seventy. She started to giggle. "Guess you won that fight, too."

"Yep."

"You always win, don't you?"

"Usually," he said not too modestly as the waiter placed two brimming mugs on the table, and two pieces of velvety smooth chocolate cake.

"You ever get hurt?"

"Once." He raised the sleeve of his finely tailored blazer. A long ugly scar ran across his well-muscled forearm. "I learned by this one. I never lost again. But it was pretty nasty when it happened. The blood—"

She grimaced, "Don't tell me any more."

"Sorry, I forgot." He bit into the chocolate, savoring it, letting it roll around on his tongue. This sure was turning into a nice evening. Opera music, which he had barely tolerated when he came here with his wife, sounded good tonight. Ellen was lip-synching along with Placido Domingo, not at all self-conscious. He liked this girl—she was lively, with a good sense of humor, and she really was quite attractive. "What hospital you work at?"

"Saint Joseph's—down in Coney Island."

"That's a bit of a commute from Park Slope."

"Oh, I don't mind, it's only twenty minutes by subway."

"You're not from Brooklyn."

"How did you know?"

"Subway."

"I don't get it."

"We natives call it 'train.' "

"Ahh—forgive me. Train it is."

"So where are you from?"

"Amsterdam."

"Holland?"

"I wish. But no, it's a little mill town upstate, near Albany."

"Never heard of it."

She took a deep breath and rattled off: "Amsterdam-NewYork-served-by-two-railroads-and-the-barge-canal-boasting-among-its-many-industries-the-manufacture-of-rugs-carpets-buttons-and-brooms."

"You sound like the chamber of commerce."

"I sound like my Uncle Pete. He used to be the mayor of Amsterdam. Won the election playing the accordion."

"Don't tell me—opera."

"What else would an Italian play?"

They finished the cake and coffee.

"Thank you," Ellen said as Ben paid the check. "For the chocolate, the movie, and for one hell of a dramatic evening."

"You're welcome." He bowed gallantly as he opened the door for her, and they walked out onto the street.

"I'm just sorry you never got your musical."

"Oh, I enjoyed the movie anyway, even if some parts were kind of phony."

"Phony?" she seemed surprised. "Like what?"

"Come on—a beautiful young girl meets a man in an empty apartment, barely looks at him, and the next thing they're going at it? That doesn't happen in real life."

"Oh, I don't know about that. Brando could probably walk into any room and make love to any girl he finds there."

"Nah, I don't believe it—he's too fat."

"Not in that movie."

"You kidding? Didn't you see his hips, his rear end?"

"He looked sexy to me."

"He should take better care of his body. If I had Brando in my gym, in six months he'd have a fine physique."

She didn't say anything.

Not wanting to make himself obnoxious by pressing the point too far, he changed the subject. "You know the moral of that movie?" he went on. "The trouble people can run into looking for an apartment. I have to remember that—I'm looking for one now."

"That's a coincidence." They had stopped in front of her building, a well-maintained turn-of-the-century brownstone.

"What is?"

"I'm looking for a temporary roommate."

"You are?"

"Just for a couple of months, until my boyfriend gets up the nerve to move in."

"Maybe we can make a deal."

"Great," Ellen said, looking at him directly.

"No, no, I was just kidding."

"I wasn't. Six hundred bucks for a private room and your own bath. You wanna see it?"

He looked at her quizzically. "You serious?"

"Sure am—but it's only for a couple months."

"You know, I have a daughter about your age, and if I found out . . ." he wagged his finger at her, "that after knowing a man for only a couple hours she proposed he move in with her, I'd spank her."

"I figured you were the old-fashioned type—that's why I suggested it. You're safe."

"That's an insult."

She laughed. "Well, think about it. If you warm up to the idea, come by and look the place over. I'll be home all weekend."

He hesitated, but just for a moment. "Okay, I'll think about it," he said.

4

Ben came to slowly, feeling lazy and relaxed. He'd had a good night's sleep—no disturbing dreams of Betty, thank God. He raised his eyelashes halfway. Pitch black all around. Like the poet said: The fingers of dawn had not yet pried the lid of darkness.

He enjoyed beating the alarm clock, waking up gradually like this, luxuriating in the feeling. As always, he guessed the time. 6:17. Then he opened his eyes to check the large digital clock glowing on the bedside table—6:22. Five minutes off, not bad. He was constantly amazed how close he came, sometimes he guessed it exactly.

He stretched out. It was Sunday, the gym was closed, no need to get up. He could just languish in bed, let his thoughts drift. That lovely young actress in the Marlon Brando movie ... beautiful boobs, but she should develop her pectoral muscles or they would soon begin to droop.

That would be a shame . . . maybe he should send her a note prescribing the correct exercises. Milt could forward it to her. Then he remembered that it was an old movie. Probably too late.

He smiled to himself. That was some evening. . . . He remembered so clearly Ellen's profile in the darkened theater . . . she got so emotional about the movie. . . . What a strange girl she was . . . friendly with bums . . . but also full of life, witty, funny. Marion ought to be more like that, instead of always serious, uptight, talking as if she were a walking textbook on psychology. Was that why her husband left her? It sure wasn't fun to get a dose of her sour side. Ellen seemed just the opposite: cheerful, spirited, even a bit mischievous.

Of course she was joking about the apartment. But then again, she did invite him to look it over. Maybe . . . nah, ridiculous.

A few hours later, he was driving down the quiet streets of Park Slope. The long shadows cast by the rising sun stretched out in front of the shops, barricaded at this hour by iron shutters. The Brooklyn *Daily Bulletin*'s classified section, with various housing possibilities circled, lay on the seat beside him. Time was drawing close; he better settle on something this weekend, even if it was temporary.

Temporary. . . . Ellen had said she was looking for a temporary roommate . . . separate room and bath . . . that was practically like having your own studio apartment. . . .

Why not go to see it? What's the worst that could happen?

He found a parking spot a block from her place and walked up to the brownstone. He pushed the button opposite her name. Almost immediately, her warm voice came through the speaker: "Who is it?"

"Your bodyguard," Ben said. "I've come to check your security system."

He heard a throaty laugh. "Third floor," she directed. Then the buzzer sounded to release the door latch.

He felt a tinge of excitement as he walked up the stairs. Her door was ajar. "I hope I'm not disturbing you." He came in tentatively. "I know I should have called first . . . but you did say come by. . . ."

"Oh, I always mean what I say." She was in the kitchen busily wrapping something.

He looked around. He was standing in a large living room with a view of the tops of the trees on the street outside. The furniture was an eclectic hodgepodge, well-worn but comfortable looking, a large red oriental rug dominating the center of the room. One feature you could not ignore was the books—the walls were covered with them, and more sat on various tables and shelves.

"How about a cup of coffee?" she called out.

"You got decaf?"

"Sorry, no, I need the wake-me-up stuff."

"Okay, but with lots of milk, no sugar."

"Coming up, as ordered," she chirped.

She seemed happy to see him, or did he imagine it?

She poured out a cup. "Would you like a bagel?"

"Bagel? You Jewish?"

That throaty laugh again. "Can't a Gentile like bagels too?"

The kitchen was small, but clean and neat, painted a cheerful yellow. The round oak table in the middle was piled with food—apples, bananas, coffee cake, and mounds of sliced bagels with cream cheese.

"Oh my God—I don't think I can eat more than ten or twenty."

"One is all you get, the rest are for my regulars."

"Regulars?"

"You know, Jello and the boys."

"Jello . . . oh yeah, the chance seller. Your friend with the rat."

"It's not a rat, it's a mouse."

Ben munched on a bagel (nice and doughy, fresh) and sipped his coffee (not good, but drinkable) as Ellen continued her packing. She was making up brown lunch bags—two bagels, an apple or banana, and a piece of coffee cake in each.

"Where's my room?" he asked boldly.

She didn't blink. "Oh . . . let me show you."

"You were serious?"

"Of course. But remember, it's a temporary arrangement—for a couple of months."

She took him down a short hallway. "This is it." She opened the door. Like the living room, this one also faced the street and had a bay window with a seat built in. The room was quite large; he was surprised.

"That door," she pointed, "is your closet, and this one the bathroom."

The closet was more than he needed. The bathroom, small but clean.

"There is no tub, just a shower. Do you mind?"

"Perfect for me."

"This used to be two studios, but the previous tenants

fell in love and made it one apartment. It's rare to get two bedrooms, two baths."

"I wouldn't know—it's been a while since I shopped around for an apartment. Not since I first got married. . . ."

"You divorced?"

"No, my wife died."

"Oh. I'm sorry." Her voice had real sympathy in it.

"This place is very nice," Ben said. He could imagine himself here—watching TV in that big armchair in the living room, making breakfast in that sunny kitchen.

"Six hundred a month. But I gotta have two months up front."

He looked at her directly. "You're *really* serious?"

"Yeah! How many times do I have to tell you—I mean what I say."

"Well . . . I'm not sure."

She let out a sigh of exasperation. "Okay, but listen—" She checked her watch. "I gotta go. You can sleep on it, let me know tomorrow." Hastily she started loading the lunch bags into one large cardboard box.

"Where do you have to go with that?"

"Coney Island."

"How you get there?"

"By subway—oops—" She flashed him a grin. "I mean by train."

"I'll give you a ride."

"You will?" She seemed surprised and delighted by the offer.

"Can't think of a better way to spend a Sunday morning."

* * *

47

As his Camaro sped along Coney Island Avenue, Ben looked over at Ellen sitting next to him, nearly obscured by the cardboard box on her lap.

"Boy—that's a load to carry alone. Can't you get your boyfriend to help you?"

"Oh, he did once or twice." Ellen sighed. "But his heart wasn't in it. He thinks it's all a waste. He says that giving the homeless things they ought to work for only encourages them to do nothing. I stopped trying to convince him."

"Why do *you* do it?"

"Well, I used to volunteer with an organization that goes around in a van and feeds them. Then, I got involved working on a book with this doctor. . . ."

"Your boyfriend?"

"Yeah, him. Anyway, I didn't have the time anymore. But I felt so guilty. Especially about this one group. They're . . . different. They've found their own quirky ways of coping with life."

"Coping? They're homeless."

"It's their way of surviving." She looked at him earnestly. "It could happen to any of us, don't you think?"

"I . . . I'm not sure. . . ."

She was silent for a moment, then she said softly, "My father died on the street."

Ben turned to her. She was staring through the window pensively. Something told him not to ask questions; he himself appreciated people who didn't pry. Instead, he changed the subject.

"You know Brooklyn?"

"Well, I don't get a chance to see much of it from the train."

"In that case, let's take the scenic route. I'll be your *cicerone*."

"You know Italian?"

"I was with the marines in Salerno."

"And I'm glad you were." She smiled wryly.

It pleased Ben to see her in a happy mood again. "But there is no place in the world like Brooklyn. You name it we got it: Russian Mafia . . . Hasidic Jews—"

"Oh yeah, those weird guys in the black hats and long coats."

"The weirdest of them is a ninety-year-old rabbi named Schneerson. He's had a stroke and can't talk, and they think he's the Messiah. Go figure."

"Wasn't there a big protest about them a little while ago, when the rabbi's limo hit a little black girl?"

"Right. . . . And this is their section. See? Garlick's Funeral Home . . . Yabakoff's Memorial Chapel. The best way to know where you are in Brooklyn is by the signs."

"Well then, we must be in Mexico." Ellen was pointing at a sign that read: MOSHE'S OLE—WHEN YOU COME TO US YOU KNOW YOU'RE HOT. "Or," she giggled, "maybe the French Quarter of Hong Kong." She pointed to another that read: WOK'S KOSHER CHINESE CUISINE.

Ben laughed. "Now, in honor of your heritage, we'll cross over to Bensonhurst and then we can take Stillwell right down to the beach."

"I hate to tell you this, Ben. But I know how Italians live."

"Not how they live in Brooklyn."

"Okay." She was enjoying this Cook's tour.

"Guess where we are now?" he asked as they passed

WOK THE ROK—THE BEST IN ITALIAN-CHINESE CUISINE. Wok was obviously an enterprising sort of guy.

"Chinatown?"

Ben laughed as he turned into a residential section of narrow row homes with postage stamp–sized lawns, but each sporting at least one oversized plaster statue. Swans were very popular, next came lions and pink flamingos, but blue Holy Marys won the contest hands down.

"We've got lots of Holy Marys in Amsterdam, but nothing like this."

"I told you—Brooklyn is something else. Take Coney Island—haven't been there in years, but when I was a kid that was a world of magic for me, especially the Thunderbolt—"

"That's where we're going!" she broke in.

"Really? Is that roller coaster still there?"

"What's left of it."

"So the old monster still lives. Wait till I tell Milt."

"Who's Milt?"

"My best friend. He was a little timid when he was a kid, scared to death of the Thunderbolt. But you couldn't become a man if you didn't ride it. I remember the day Milt decided to do it—if I sat next to him."

Ellen peered at Ben over the box. A big smile lit up his face; he looked boyish reliving the moment.

"So we rode it together. When we got off, I said: 'How did you like it?' He couldn't utter a sound, and there was a big dark wet spot around his crotch. The other kids were merciless. The whole way home on the train, he had to keep his arms crossed over his pants."

"Oh, poor Milt." Ellen's voice said she felt the little boy's humiliation.

Her concern made Ben laugh. "Don't worry—he lived."

* * *

When they got to the beach, the area was deserted and they had no trouble finding a place to park right at Fifteenth and Surf, near the boardwalk.

Ben was amazed at how seedy and run-down the place had become. The only thing unchanged was the ocean. Foamy crested waves still rolled in against the wide, sandy beach, which was dotted with early morning joggers and dog walkers. The smells of brine and decaying ocean life mingled with the pungent smell of hot dogs.

"Gee, Nathan's Hot Dogs are still here!" Ben exclaimed. "You don't know how good that makes me feel."

"We'll have one."

"Are you crazy?" Ben made a face.

"Why?"

"Have you ever seen how they make a hot dog?"

"Can't say I have."

"It's gray meat scraps ground up together with a whole lot of red dye. It's disgusting and bad for you."

"Oh, no—you just spoiled something I love. Thanks." Her tone said she was mocking him a little bit, but Ben wasn't paying attention.

Without a word, he advanced slowly along the chain-link fence topped with barbed wire that enclosed the ferocious roller coaster of his youth. Thunderbolt. Arched against the blue sky, it looked like the skeletal remains of some prehistoric monster.

"I can't believe it," he muttered.

Ellen could tell that lots of special memories were rolling through his mind; she didn't say anything as she led the way through a hole in the fence and pointed out the narrow path through the scraggly stand of last year's weeds.

She turned to him, but Ben had drifted off. "No, no, it's this way!" she called out.

He didn't seem to hear her as he walked on over crumbling boards to the weather-beaten turnstile covered with ivy. He pushed his way through, the rusty joints grating and rasping, then giving way with a long, anguished squeal. In front of him, on rusty tracks, stood a frayed chariot rotting away. He sat down on the dilapidated seat.

"Ellen," he said in a low voice as she approached. "This glistened once. . . . The colors were so bright . . . red, yellow, blue. . . ."

As he described it, Ellen could see it: a place vibrating with life, a roiling cauldron of humanity, kids having fun at an amusement park, screaming with joy and fear.

He took a deep breath and shook his head. "Who could have imagined the Thunderbolt would ever die—"

"Hey! Got a ticket?" a voice from the sky interrupted them.

They craned their necks to see someone's feet dangling from the highest peak of the curved spine.

Then a large nose and a pair of sunglasses peered over the edge. "No free rides!"

"Sunny!" Ellen obviously knew him. "What are you doing up there?"

"Catching my Vitamin Ds."

"He does too much crack," Ellen muttered, then yelled, "Jello home?"

"Last I checked," the answer came back, then Sunny disappeared from view.

Ben shook his head and followed Ellen. She picked her way through the debris in the center area, which was encircled like a cage by the carcass of the roller coaster. He wondered what kind of world she was leading him into.

As they approached a pile of trash at the far end, Ellen called out: "Wake up, everybody! Breakfast's on the table!"

Ben looked at her, puzzled—nobody was there. And then a piece of dirty carpeting thrown over a large cardboard box started to move; a plastic bag hanging from it was pushed aside and a pair of eyes peeked out. The trash all around was stirring now, and from beneath it people were emerging. These seemingly random piles of debris were dwellings! This was an urban development built from the haphazardly discarded objects of an uncaring civilization.

They came forward—a tattered bunch of human beings who smelled like the trash they had just crawled out of—as Ellen dispensed the lunches from the box that Ben held. With great civility, she introduced everybody. They had peculiar nicknames: Choo-choo, Knowledge, Caruso, Flyer, Squeegee.

"Ben, if you don't mind, hand out the rest of the food," Ellen said, as she moved toward a refrigerator box covered with plastic, "and save some for Sunny."

"Oh, you'll never get him down," said the one called Knowledge, who wore thick glasses with a cracked lens. "Not as long as the sun is shining. He thinks he's Icarus." He turned to Ben and continued in the tone of a professor delivering a lecture. "Icarus was the Greek who flew too close to the sun and the wax on his wings melted."

"How do you know about Icarus?" Ben asked.

Choo-choo laughed with his mouth full. "That's why they call him Knowledge—he went to college."

"Why do they call you Choo-choo?" Ben asked.

"Trains are my specialty."

By this time, Ellen had roused the occupant of the refrigerator box, who emerged rubbing his eyes. Ben recognized the chance seller from the movie house.

"About time you got up, Jello," Ellen chided good-naturedly.

Jello muttered something in greeting, then took a bagel and divided it in two. One half disappeared in his mouth, the other he started to break into little pieces, which he placed on his shoulder. A mouse immediately peeked out from the folds of his scarf and snatched a crumb.

One of the men had made coffee in a tin can heated over Sterno, and Ellen poured it into the plastic cups she'd brought along. She filled one for herself and another for Ben, who was watching with fascination as the mouse returned over and over to snatch the crumbs lined up on Jello's shoulder.

"He sure has an appetite," Ben said.

"Junior never gets enough," Choo-choo chortled.

"Junior?"

"His correct name is Jello Junior," Ellen interjected.

This struck Ben as very funny.

"Don't laugh," Jello spoke with a note of indignation. "I have no other children. Junior will be my heir"—he spread his arms around—"to everything."

Now the others laughed, too.

"Don't be ignorant, y'all," Jello scolded. "When a man works hard his entire life, builds up his legacy, he wants his heir to enjoy the fruits of his labors."

"What labors might they be?" Ben asked indulgently.

Jello stood up now. He clearly had read Ben's question

as a challenge. "Everyone here serves a vital function in the city." He puffed out his caved-in chest. "Caruso and Choo-choo, to cite one example, sing on the train, making an unbearable experience at rush hour more pleasing to the commuting public. . . ." Jello paused to clear his throat, but, instead, convulsed in a fit of coughing.

Ellen looked at him, her eyes full of worry, but said nothing. The others waited respectfully for him to continue. He was obviously the leader of the group. Ben was surprised how articulate he could be.

The coughing exhausted Jello, and he sat down on the ground, motioning Ben to sit near him. He gently petted the mouse with one finger, as if to reassure it.

Not wanting to dirty his good clothes, Ben grabbed a box to use as a stool.

"Hey, don't you sit on that box!" The angry voice belonged to the one called Flyer.

"Huh? Why not?"

"Because that box fell off a Federal Express truck," Flyer said. "There is a brand-new radio inside."

"There is?"

"No, it's empty." Flyer winked at him conspiratorially. "But you gotta act like you believe or you can't make nobody else believe. And then you can't sell it."

Ben examined the box—it was properly labeled, priced, wrapped in plastic bubble paper. "You sell empty boxes? How?"

"Does Macy tell Gimbel?"

"Oh, give him your spiel, show the man how hard you work," urged Jello.

"Well," said Flyer, wetting his lips, enjoying the spotlight. He took the box under his arm and, acting out his riff, furtively looked up and down the imaginary street. "I pick a crowded spot in Manhattan, Forty-fourth, Forty-fifth, when I spot a vic—"

"A vic?" Ben interrupted.

"A victim," Knowledge filled in.

"I rush up to him." He nudged himself up against Ben. " 'Brand-new radio, how much will you give me, man?' " He lowered his voice to a whisper and hissed in Ben's ear, " 'Got it off a FedEx truck an hour ago.' "

"And this works?" Ben asked.

Flyer nodded. "You know you got the right vic when he says, 'I give you twenty.' Nobody buys hot unless they've got larceny in their heart. Now here's where the art of the sale comes in: 'You crazy?' " Flyer delivered the question in a voice strangling with indignity. " 'Look at the price, man. Six hundred bucks! I gotta have eighty.' When I get the guy up to fifty, I look around real worried, then I cave in. 'Okay man, you robbin' me, but I need the money.' " With a big smile he added: "And when I get it they don't see me no more."

Everybody laughed, enjoying Flyer's routine even if they had heard it before. Ben was impressed. "You deserve an Oscar nomination."

"And how!" Jello spoke up. "But the best part we never get to see."

"How's that?"

"That guy—when he gets home and opens that empty box—we never get to see how it changes his life."

"Huh?"

"That's right. He won't be so greedy next time. An honest man doesn't fall for con games. An honest man walks away."

Ben nodded, impressed by the logic. He was enjoying this odd band. "How about you, Jello? You have other games besides chances?"

"Games?" Jello spat out the word, clearly offended. "I don't play, I work."

"That's right," Choo-choo interjected. "He's got the most important job of all—he's the boss of the Bobs."

"Bobs?"

"That's what Jello calls his campaign: 'Bums on Every Block.' Get it?" Flyer nudged Ben. "Bobs for short."

"And I'm always looking for new recruits."

"To do what?"

Jello placed his cup down, moved closer to Ben, and with exaggerated patience said, "Bring cheer to the city. When people see us, they forget their troubles, they feel better, just thinking they're not us. Very important function."

Ben laughed, delighted.

"You laugh, Ben, but New York needs more of us. You want to be a Bob, Ben?"

"Me?" It was all so nutty, but in a way it made sense.

"My instinct tells me you're interested."

"What would I do?" Ben grinned, playing along.

"Ahh," said Jello, "I have just the spot for you—Wall Street, outside the World Trade Center." He eyed Ben's neatly tailored outfit. "You'd look just like one of the Salomon Brothers. But I'd give you dark glasses, white cane, tin cup. You'd stand tall and erect—" Jello stopped to cough, then continued: "All those greedy brokers and bankers—their cold hearts beating 'more money . . . more money . . . more money'—they'd pass you and for a brief moment forget all about it. I'd bet you'd collect, too."

Ben laughed.

Ellen, who had been listening quietly, happy to see that Ben was enjoying such a lively conversation with her favorites, smiled broadly at him. "Ben, I think Jello's offering you an opportunity to make a unique contribution to society."

"Room and board comes with the job." Jello's arm was pointing in the direction of a pile of carpeting. "And we have a vacancy."

"Hard to resist." Ben winked at Ellen. "My second housing offer today, don't know which to take."

"Take my advice," Jello declared. "This is the better offer."

"Now there's where you might be wrong." Ben grinned.

Suddenly, he knew that he didn't have to sleep on it— he would move in with Ellen.

5

"Are you crazy?" Sarah, arms akimbo, greeted Ben at the door, her plump face, usually cheerful, scowling with indignation.

"Let our guest in, Sarah." Milt was standing behind her, eyes twinkling with merriment. Having learned long ago that in a difference of opinion with Sarah it was best to concede defeat early, he enjoyed someone else squirming under her righteous onslaught for a change.

"What's so crazy about it?" Ben shot back defensively as he came in and took off his jacket.

"Moving in with a young girl you don't even know is *not* crazy?" She wiped her hands on her apron, a disdainful gesture.

"Please, Sarah—" Sometimes her Jewish-mother attitude got under Ben's skin, but he didn't want their usually pleasant weekly dinner to deteriorate into a fight. "You know I'm in escrow on the house. I gotta live somewhere until I find the right apartment. It's just for a couple of months. That's all."

"Well, *I* consider it none of my business" (everything was Sarah's business), "but *you* should worry—for your own protection."

"My own protection?"

"Don't you read the papers, she might have AIDS!"

Milt cleared his throat, strangling laughter. "Sarah has a point." He motioned Ben to sit down.

"Now stop it. She's not my girlfriend, just my landlady."

"Landlady, huh?" Sarah sputtered. "If Betty were alive she'd turn over in her grave." Dismissively, she spun on her heel and marched off into the kitchen.

And just in time, because Milt was about to split a gut from holding in his laughter. He exploded in hysterics, which he tried to muffle with both hands over his mouth.

He had barely managed to quiet down when Sarah burst out of the kitchen, looking like she'd been continuing the argument with her pot roast. "Promise me one thing, Ben." It was a demand, not a request.

"Okay, Sarah, what?" Ben sighed.

"Not a word about this to Brenda."

Ben looked blank. "Brenda?"

"Your bridge partner this evening."

Ever since Betty died, Ben had been subjected to a long procession of bridge partners, mostly widows from the neighborhood whom Sarah tried to foist on him. They came in all shapes and sizes, with big bank accounts and small ones, but with one goal in mind: land a husband. Clearly his new living arrangement would detract from his eligibility and put a crimp in Sarah's campaign to marry him off.

"I won't say anything," he agreed, "if *you* promise to drop it."

"Why should I care that you lost your mind?" Still in a huff, she returned to the kitchen.

Milt burst out in peals of laughter again.

Ben shook his head. "She thinks it's crazy and you think it's funny."

"I think it's great." Milt wiped the tears from his eyes. "And I bet she's a looker, hey boychik? Nice knockers?" He cupped his hands to his chest.

"Cut it out, Milt. . . . She's a nice girl, works at Saint Joseph's Hospital."

"Oh, she's a nun?"

"Not funny."

"Okay Ben, okay." Milt put his hand on his friend's shoulder. "Seriously though, if you want me to check her out, I know everybody at Saint Joseph's—that's my hospital."

"Your hospital?"

"That's where I send all the agency's 'indisposed' clients—if you know what I mean. You can count on those nuns to keep their mouth shut. And regular generous donations don't hurt, either."

"I bet it costs you."

"It does, but it's worth it. They saved my ass more than once."

"You never told me."

"Well, it's hush-hush stuff. . . . If the *National Enquirer* ever got a hold of any of this . . . *oy!*" Milt rolled his eyes.

"Nah—they wouldn't care; they make up all their stuff anyway."

"You got a point."

"So what secrets are you carrying to your grave?"

"Okay, I'll tell you one." Milt's gleeful expression said it was going to be a good one. "This involved one of our most important clients, though back then, she was just a starlet, and if it weren't for the nuns, she'd never be a star today."

"Who?"

"I'm sworn to secrecy, but the initials are KB—you figure it out."

"KB? You don't mean . . ."

"Yep—that's who I mean. She was fucking one of the studio execs, and right in the middle, the poor guy drops dead."

"That's what happened to Nelson Rockefeller."

"So they say—but there's a twist to this story."

"What?"

"Get this—she rolls him off her, and there he is, deader than a doornail," Milt paused for effect. "With a stiff prick pointing at the ceiling!"

"What?"

"Inflatable penis."

"What's that?"

"Boychik, at your age you should know about these things. The guy was impotent—he had one of those implants that you can pump up with air. But she couldn't figure out how to let the air out."

"So what happened?"

"She had the presence of mind to call me. When I got there, we managed to get him dressed, except that he was still pointing to the ceiling, right through his zipper."

"It wouldn't go down?"

"No. I didn't know how the thing worked either."

"Holy shit."

"No kidding. But when I got him to Saint Joseph's, Sister Clarita did it."

"A nun?"

"Yep. She worked a miracle."

Now Ben was laughing, too. Despite a bumpy start, it promised to be a good evening.

In the dressing room at Madison Square Garden, Don Arnold was fastening his corset over his bulging beer belly. It wouldn't do for the Southlands' answer to Elvis to start looking at the peak of his career like the King did just before his ignoble end. And 20,000 adoring fans would notice every fold in that skintight outfit.

"That's right, Don, sucko la gutto," Joe, the opening-act comic, called out.

The makeup and wardrobe people waited for Don to laugh before joining in.

"What's so funny, darling?" Dawn—Mrs. Don Arnold— swept into the dressing room, giving her husband a peck on the cheek. He pressed his meaty hand to her butt. "Now, now, darling," she chided, adding in a loud whisper, "not in front of everybody."

They were an odd couple: he, poor white trash from the wrong side of the Mason-Dixon Line, now uncomfortable as a megastar; she, a society debutante of Rockefeller-Astor lineage, pushing her way into the movie world using both elbows and her husband's fame.

"Hello, Sam." She greeted Don's agent with a regal smile, but pointedly ignored Joe, who started to leave.

"Warm them up good," called out Don.

"When I get through with them, they'll be red-hot," the comic answered. Going out the door he waved to Dawn, "Have a good evening, Mrs. Arnold."

She didn't seem to hear him as she studied her lips in the mirror.

"Can't you even say hello to him?" Don turned to Dawn, his movement smearing the eyeliner the makeup man was trying to apply.

"Didn't I?"

"You just don't like him, huh?"

"No."

"Well I like him, he does a great job."

"That's all that matters," Dawn said coolly. She moved toward the bathroom. "Listen, hon, I feel sticky—I'm going to take a quick shower."

"Hard work on the set today?" He turned to her again; the frustrated makeup man was close to losing it.

"Well, we had to finish the scene in Grand Central Station. . . . They won't let us shoot there again."

"So the picture is coming along?"

"Well, they say the rushes are fabulous."

"Have you ever been in a film where the rushes were bad?" Sam chuckled.

Dawn didn't acknowledge the comment as she disappeared into the bathroom, and soon the noise of the water running was heard.

Sam turned up the volume on the intercom system, piping the show into the dressing room, and Joe's jokes boomed over the loudspeaker: "The pope arrives in New York and this big white limo is waiting for him—"

Don rolled his eyes. "He's still telling that one."

"And it still works," said Sam. "By the way, I'm gonna

have Milt Schultz and his wife come to the show Friday night."

"Who's he?"

"Our troubleshooter on the East Coast, an important man in the agency."

The dresser handed Don his jacket. "Honey!" Don called out in the direction of the bathroom door, where the shower had stopped. "I'll see you after the show!"

"Wait a minute," Dawn came back in, a thin robe clinging to her damp body. She put her arms around his neck and in a breathless voice cooed, "When you sing 'I'm So Excited,' think of me."

He moved to kiss her, but she turned her face away. "Don't mess up your makeup."

She pressed her body against him provocatively. "More coming later."

"Save it baby, save it," Don leered.

She broke away. "Don, tell your guys to clear out of here—I want to rest for a half hour."

"You heard the lady," Don commanded, and the makeup man, the dresser, and the agent all filed out, followed by Don himself.

When the door closed behind them, Dawn turned off the lights and, still in her robe, stretched out on the couch.

Over the loudspeaker, Joe, the comic, was announcing: "And now, ladies and gentleman, here he is, the man you've been waiting for, the one and only . . ." his voice strained above the roar of the crowd, "Don Arnold!"

Dawn sighed. The partially opened bathroom door let a sliver of light into the darkened room. She untied her robe, exposing her naked body as the throbbing tempo of Don's opening number picked up:

Tonight's the night we're gonna make it happen
Tonight we'll put all other things aside
Give in this time and show me some affection
We're going for those pleasures in the night

She couldn't repress the smile on her lips as she heard the doorknob turn softly. The dark silhouette of the comic appeared in the doorway. He locked the door behind him.

Saying nothing, she brought her left hand to her breast and started playing with the nipple, while her right moved down to her crotch. Joe was breathing rapidly as he watched her. Slowly, he unzipped his pants.

Don's voice filled the room now:

I'm so excited
And I just can't hide it
I'm about to lose control
and I think I like it

Roughly, he mounted her. "You bitch, you love to hear his voice when you're fucking."
"Yes, yes."

I want to squeeze you, please you
I just can't get enough
And if you move real slow
I'll let it go.

"Fuck me, fuck me . . ." she whispered.
The crowd was going wild, hooting, clapping, shouting requests. Teasing them, the orchestra went into a medley

of Don's hit songs, giving him a chance to catch his breath between numbers and fix his makeup. The dresser offered him a tumbler of water (vodka on the rocks). "Thanks," Don muttered. The hairstylist moved in, but Don waved her away. She was insistent, however—urgently, she grabbed his sleeve and whispered something in his ear.

Don's face went white. The tumbler crashed to the floor, and he raced down the hall to his dressing room.

"Hey, Don, hey, Don . . ." cried out the agent. "What the hell?"

But Don was out of sight. A few seconds later, the crash of a door being kicked in resounded through backstage.

He caught Dawn sprawled nude on the couch, legs spread apart, and Joe scrambling into his pants.

"You son of a bitch!" He took a swing at the comic, who deftly ducked and like a penguin scurried out of the room with his pants bunched down around his ankles.

"Don, I can explain." Dawn jumped up, wrapping the robe around her.

"Explain this!" His clenched fist came crashing into her face. Blood spurted out of her broken nose. She tried to get away from him, but he grabbed her by the hair. "Resting, huh?" And he smashed her again.

"Stop it!" Sam ran in just as Don's fist made contact for the third time. He tackled Don at the midrift, momentarily unbalancing him and giving Dawn enough time to escape into the bathroom. "Jesus, Don! The concert!"

Sarah dealt out a fresh deck of cards. "You know, Ben, Brenda's husband was a wonderful man."

Oh boy, thought Ben, she's selling this one on the merits of her dead husband. But he smiled politely at the middle-aged woman across the table who was peering at him over her cards.

"Left her very well off, didn't he, Brenda?"

"Oh yes, oh yes." Brenda was a woman of few words.

"Brenda has a lovely apartment in—" The ringing of the phone interrupted her. "Let the machine pick up," she commanded, but Milt had already lifted the receiver.

"Ben," Sarah chirped, "would you mind taking Brenda home when we finish?"

"Of course not."

"You must see her place."

"What!" Milt was shouting on the phone.

They all turned in his direction.

"You gotta keep it quiet, Sammy," Milt was saying. "No ambulances! Just drive her down to Saint Joseph's yourself."

The person on the other end was obviously arguing with Milt, who was losing his patience. "A broken nose is not brain damage . . . okay, okay . . . no, not the emergency room. The side door on Seabreeze . . . I'll meet you there."

"Now what?" sighed Sarah as Milt hung up.

"That crazy singer Don Arnold."

"Those show people are impossible," Sarah informed Brenda.

"What happened?" Ben wanted to know.

"Well," said Milt, putting on his jacket, "while he was onstage singing 'My Way,' she was in the dressing room doing it her way—with the comic."

"Disgusting!" Sarah muttered.

"He caught her and beat the shit out of her."

"Please don't talk that way in front of company," Sarah

reprimanded, leaning over to Brenda apologetically: "Holly-wood talk."

Milt headed for the door. "She's in the middle of shooting a picture. I gotta fix it up quietly."

"I'll go with you." Ben got up.

"No, no." Sarah placed a restraining hand on Ben's arm. "You promised to take Brenda home."

Ben thought he heard Milt's amused cackle as the door slammed behind him.

6

Ellen was usually early for work—she disliked rushing, lateness, the anxiety that came with it—but today she came in a full hour ahead, intending to catch Richard between operations. She missed him after their week-long separation. She hoped he got the baby's heart he was after. Such triumphs put him in a very good mood, and she wanted him in a good mood when she told him that her new roommate was a man. Of course, Ben wasn't anyone to be jealous of, not like a man her age, but Richard had "Old World" ways of looking at some things.

She stepped off the elevator on the surgery floor and saw a familiar form moving toward her down the long corridor—a tent of black cloth topped off by a white ball, a face as pale and round as a moon, framed in a white headdress.

This was Sister Clarita, the Sisters of Pity's only holdover from the old days, still wearing the full habit, still adhering to the old values of service, worship, poverty, chastity, and obedience that the modern nuns had almost abandoned.

Sister Clarita stopped her voyage. The orderly pushing a gurney behind her stopped also. "Hello, my dear."

Ellen suspected that Sister Clarita had identified her as a lost lamb—a lapsed Catholic—and took special care to speak to her whenever they ran into each other.

"What are you up to, Sister?"

The nun motioned to the body lying on the gurney, the face completely encased in bandages. "An unfortunate horseback riding accident. Her face was badly disfigured, poor thing, but Dr. Smothers is a magician."

"You're the magician, Sister. The best nurse here."

"I can only pray. God decides the course of all things," the nun replied modestly.

Ellen looked at the inert figure on the gurney.

"She's still under anesthesia," Sister Clarita explained. "But it should be wearing off. I'm taking her to a *private* recovery room."

Ellen raised her eyebrows.

"Yes." Sister Clarita nodded conspiratorially. "Another Jane Dolphin."

"Oh."

Jane Dolphin was the hospital's code for its special clients, those whose names were never recorded. Sister Clarita—who could be counted on to take all their secrets to her grave—was usually assigned private duty.

The figure moaned slightly.

"Oh my, I better hurry—she's coming to."

"See you later, Sister."

The nun walked away rapidly, the orderly trotting to keep up with her.

Ellen wondered who this Jane Dolphin was. Somebody famous? Or the daughter or wife of somebody famous?

When she reached Richard's office, she found Gina sitting at her desk, filing her nails. How did a nurse get away with nails this long? The hospital had to have rules about this sort of thing. Gina looked up and forced a smile. "Hi."

"I'd like to see Dr. Vandermann."

"So would I—but he hasn't arrived yet."

"Isn't he back from Florida?"

"Oh yes, *we* came back last night." Did Gina stress the word purposely, or was it Ellen's imagination? "He just isn't in yet—had a consultation in Manhattan."

"Would you tell him I'm looking for him?"

Gina nodded, continuing to file her nails.

The sound grated on Ellen's nerves. "I'll be in the cafeteria if he gets here in the next half hour."

"Ready for another operation?" The question was delivered with a snide smile.

Yeah, a frontal lobotomy, yours, Ellen wanted to say, but decided it was wiser to ignore the question and just walk away.

"Are you nuts?" Goldie almost knocked over her cup of coffee.

"Calm down," Ellen said softly, "the whole cafeteria is looking at us."

Goldie started to laugh. "Girlfriend, you *are* nuts! First you're feeding bums in the park, now you're setting up a geriatric ward in your apartment. Maybe you can get Sister Clarita to help you—"

"I'm sorry I told you."

"He'll end up becoming a patient, and—"

"Please, Goldie, he may be old, but he's not an invalid. He's very fit and a real gentleman."

"Of course, an old-fashioned kind of guy. Opens the door for you and thinks every woman was put on earth to be his maid."

"He's not like that."

"No? How do you know? You said he was married for forty some years. I bet his wife was the little woman—cooked, cleaned, picked up his socks, and he sat on his ass drinking beer and watching football."

"That's a scene from your house, Goldie."

"And what a royal pain that is. But I'm *married* to the guy, I sure as hell wouldn't have him as my roommate."

"But how else can I pay the rent? Especially with what the therapist costs me."

"Oh God, I do not get you—why do you waste money on a shrink?"

"Because he's helping me."

"How?"

"Well, he's helping me with my bad back, making me realize that it's psychosomatic."

"Psychosomatic, how?"

"I'm spineless."

"Jee-zus Christ!"

"No, it's true. He's right. I'm spineless because I have the ugly duckling syndrome."

"Now I've heard everything—you pay a man two hundred dollars an hour to tell you you're an ugly duckling?"

"No, no, Goldie, you don't know the story."

"Sure I do, the ugly duckling turned into a swan."

"No, it didn't. It didn't *turn* into a swan—it was *always* a swan, it was *never* a duckling."

"Oh I see, you're not a duck, you're a swan. I think he's full of crap."

"Who are you vilifying now, Goldie?" It was Richard.

"Don't look at me, Doctor, I don't even know what the word means." Goldie's exasperation with Ellen was still in evidence.

Richard eased himself into the empty chair, squeezing Ellen's hand under the table.

Goldie caught it and cast a look in Ellen's direction that said, "Aren't we getting lovey-dovey." But Ellen's expression warned her not to make a joke of it. Instead, Goldie smiled sweetly at Richard and quipped in her usual irreverent way: "Didn't we meet like this just a few days ago, Doctor, or is it a recurring nightmare?"

Richard laughed. "I thought Dr. Fineberg holds that honor," he teased her.

"This morning the honor belongs to Dr. Smothers. He lost the needle twice while sewing up that movie star."

"What movie star?" Ellen was thinking of the body on Sister Clarita's gurney.

"Dawn . . . what's-her-name . . . the wife of that singer. Which reminds me—I told Sister Clarita I'd give her a hand in recovery, better get a move on." Goldie stood up.

"Why is she here?" Ellen was curious.

"The poor thing was riding in Central Park and was kicked in the face by her horse." Goldie rolled her eyes to indicate how much she believed that story. "The footprints of his patent-leather shoes are still visible. See ya."

"That Goldie . . ." Richard shook his head.

"My best friend."

"I like her too, although I must admit, sometimes her . . . ah . . . *ethnic* sense of humor evades me."

74

"How did things go in Florida?" Ellen changed the subject.

"Oh, Ellen." He furrowed his brow and she waited for him to continue. "It was tragic. A young couple with an anencephalic baby—"

"Without a brain?"

"Just the brain stem . . . but the parents—a rarity—were willing to donate the organs of this child who could not survive the week to any other baby that needed it. You see why I had to rush down there."

"I understand, Richard. I'm proud of you."

"Nothing to be proud about, I'm sad to say. The courts stopped me."

"What do you mean? How?"

"Your American judges say a doctor may not remove vital organs if there is independent respiratory and cardiac function."

"But wasn't the baby going to die anyway?"

"That is the tragedy." Richard's voice was full of indignation. "She had no skull, no brain, couldn't see or smell or hear. She died while we tried to appeal the decision."

"How terrible."

"But what is worse, the little baby waiting for a heart upstairs died too." Dejectedly, he stared into his coffee.

Ellen felt a strong wave of sympathy for him. "Richard, when you become chief of staff maybe you can change things."

His head snapped up. "Ellen, in America judges with no medical training have all the power." He paused. "But becoming chief of staff will be an important stepping stone for me. . . ."

Ellen waited for him to continue.

"Someday, when I get the money, I will have a hospital of my own in a different country—in Europe or Africa. I'm sick and tired of these senseless, hair-splitting arguments over individual rights, over fetal rights, over baboon rights, and all the other nonsense I have to endure here. I want to save lives!"

When Richard talked in that impassioned way, Ellen felt a tingling sensation over her whole body. "You know," she volunteered tentatively, "everything you are saying should be in your book."

"It will be," he said with determination. Then relaxing, he leaned back in his chair and smiled. "Enough of my rantings. Now tell me what you've been doing in my absence."

"Oh, nothing much, but . . . I did manage to line up a temporary roommate."

"Good. Who is she?"

"It's not a she—it's a he."

"Oh." Richard took a sip of coffee. "You are joking, of course," he said evenly.

Oops, thought Ellen. She had suspected this might not sit too well with him. "His name is Ben Jacobs, and he's a very nice old guy—a widower. He'll help pay the rent while he looks for a permanent place of his own. I think he'll be an ideal fill-in until I can get somebody more permanent."

Richard narrowed his eyes. "A strange man, whatever his age or marital status, is hardly an ideal roommate for a young woman." His sarcasm was palpable.

Ellen felt herself losing her patience. Who the hell was he to disapprove of what she did? She was the one who was struggling to pay the rent, she was the one who was broke.

"You're right!" She set down her cup with a bang. "You move in with me, I'll tell him the deal's off."

Richard reached over and grasped her hand. "You know why I cannot do that."

"No, I don't know why."

"Ellen, I haven't been here a year yet. This is a Catholic hospital—"

"But you're not a priest and I'm not a nun."

"Please, the board of directors is old-fashioned. And they make decisions for key appointments."

Ellen didn't answer.

"I don't think we should move in together until . . ." he paused, "we get married."

Ellen held her breath. She raised her head and looked at him. She opened her mouth but couldn't say anything. This was the first time he had mentioned marriage.

7

The clock in the gym's waiting room said five minutes to nine when Milt, huffing and puffing as usual and cursing Ben for not turning on the elevator, squeezed the claxon horn to announce his arrival. At exactly nine o'clock, the client, now inside making a racket with the barbells, would be leaving. Ben only took one person at a time for a fifteen-minute workout, which, he insisted, was all anyone really needed to keep fit. Milt had often tried to convince him to set up classes of five to ten people for a half hour and make more money, but Ben refused to listen. He had his own way of doing things and that was that. And he was never diplomatic. He'd poke his clients, pointing out—none too gently—where the pockets of fat were accumulating. Milt had been the victim of this kind of treatment much too often. He had heard it a thousand times: "If you don't burn up what you take in, Miltie, it turns to fat—like here (poke) and here (poke) and here (poke, poke, poke). . . ."

"Stop it, Ben—I'm not trying to make the NFL," Milt would defend himself.

"My point exactly. Did you see John Madden on TV? Used to play for the Eagles before he coached the Raiders, remember? The guy's a blimp now, 'cause he still eats steak for breakfast like he did when he was playing, but he's only making commercials—sitting down! Soon, you're gonna look just like Madden!"

"What am I supposed to do—destroy Sarah by refusing to eat?"

That kind of statement would usually make Ben throw up his hands in defeat and quit—at least till next time. He'd hear it again today, Milt was sure. He sighed and walked over to the bulletin board—he liked discovering what new food for thought Ben had put up there. Here was one: WALK, DON'T RUN, the headline read. Milt put on his glasses to read the story, which could easily have been written by Ben, judging by its message. "Experts are re-examining how much exercise is enough and concluding that less is more. . . ." The article reported on a medical study that found lengthy strenuous exercise—such as taught in most aerobics classes by inexperienced instructors—was detrimental to health, and concluded that a shorter workout conferred more health benefits without risk of injury.

Milt was not quite finished reading when the gym door opened and Ben's last client emerged. Milt was surprised to confront not a Wall Street type but a fat woman—and not just fat, but obese.

"Good to see a new client who looks worse than me," Milt quipped as she disappeared down the stairs.

"Oh, no, she's not new—been with me five years."

Milt raised his eyebrows. "I was just reading the bulletin board and thinking you've been finally proven right, but she certainly kicks the hell out of *all* your theories."

"No, she doesn't. She's lost eighty pounds."

"Yeah. Where?"

"Listen, her problem is not a physical one, it's emotional. I'm working on that."

"Okay, Dr. Freud." Milt picked up two ten-pound weights and started his curls. "Following in Marion's footsteps, I see."

"Don't be such a smart-ass. You know the emotional aspects of a person go hand in hand with physical fitness."

"Yeah, I guess you're right." Milt completed his curls and moved over to the stair climber. "When I came back from Hollywood, I had to get rid of a lot of tension."

"You're still tighter than a drum."

"Well, geez boychik, look at the shit I gotta deal with. Like that whole Don and Dawn fiasco."

"What's the latest with that?"

"You should see the tabloids: DON DECKS DAWN in ten-foot letters. They've stopped production of her movie, it's costing everybody millions!"

"He beat her up that bad?"

"Could have been worse—just broke her nose, but it takes a while for the black-and-blue marks to go away. Meantime, the crew sits waiting—"

"Come on, Milt!" Ben interrupted him. He was wise to Milt's trick of talking and slacking off. "Raise your legs higher."

Milt ignored him. "When do you move out of the house?"

"Tomorrow—I'm almost all packed."

"Sarah will never forgive you. You spoiled her scheme to move you in with Brenda."

"Well, Brenda does have a lovely apartment."

"So you thinking it over?"

"If I could get rid of Brenda."

Milt laughed as he stepped off the stair climber and paused to wipe his sweaty face.

"Come on, Milt—start your sit-ups."

Milt didn't exactly spring to the task. "What about Marion?"

"Haven't told her yet."

"Coward."

"Just waiting for the right opportunity."

"When will that be—when hell freezes over?"

"I said start your sit-ups and quit being cute," Ben snapped, irritated. Milt's gibes were hitting too close to the truth—he was not anxious to get into an argument with Marion. "I'll tell her tonight when she comes over to help me finish packing."

Ben fidgeted with the key before he turned it in the lock. This would be the last time he'd come home from work like this, open the door, walk in. Tomorrow the movers would come and pick up everything to be put in storage; he was taking only a bureau, bed, night table, and lamp to Ellen's.

Soft violin music from the stereo greeted him as he crossed the threshold. Marion was already here; he hadn't noticed her car outside.

She was standing at the dining room table preoccupied with wrapping Betty's good china. Her back was toward him. At five-foot-nine she was quite tall, and her blonde hair was cut boyishly short. From a distance, she might have passed for a young man—a basketball player, maybe. Too bad she wasn't one. He had often wondered what it would be like to have a son. The thought always made him feel guilty. How narcissistic could a man get, wanting to see a mirror image of himself. But still, it might have been nice; it sure would have been different.

She turned, slightly startled. "Father, I didn't hear you come in."

"Marion, there was a time you used to call me Dad. What's with the 'Father' stuff?"

"The words are synonymous." Her tone was cool, professorial. "A father is a dad who is older and deserving of more respect."

"Thanks for the explanation." He made a face, but came over and kissed her on the cheek anyway. "Did you find much stuff you can use?"

"Mom's china. Certainly your landlady wouldn't appreciate it. She's quite young, isn't she?"

So she knew—from Sarah, of course. He didn't answer her as he headed for the kitchen.

"*Why* is it such a secret?" She followed him.

It annoyed Ben that she so easily put him on the defensive. "No secret. Just nothing to talk about. A temporary arrangement—tides me over for a couple of months until I find a place of my own."

"But she's half your age, Father."

"So are you, Marion, so are a lot of people."

She scrutinized him through her wire-rimmed glasses. He hated that look. It made him feel like a little school boy, guilty of throwing a spitball.

"Knock it off, okay? She's my landlady, not my lover."

"Then why didn't you tell me?"

"News travels faster with Sarah."

She let out an exasperated sigh and stomped back into the other room.

He poured himself a glass of cranberry juice and sat down. What had happened to Marion over the years? She had been such a happy, uncomplicated child, crawling into bed with him and Betty and sleeping with her tiny hand clutched around one of his fingers. Sometimes to tease her he would pull it back and sleepily she would grope around to find her support line.

But as she grew up she became a pain in the ass, always so serious—so different from him, from Betty. "You sure they didn't give us the wrong baby at the hospital?" Ben used to ask, but Betty maintained that Marion was very much like him, even if he didn't see it.

Maybe Betty had a point, maybe Marion had inherited all his worst traits—in triplicate. Where he was headstrong, she was overbearing; where he was opinionated, she was intolerant; where he was quick to anger, she'd come out punching, not with her fists but with her sharp intellect, using it sometimes in ruthless, mean-spirited ways.

He was glad when she found a husband and moved to New Jersey; they didn't have to see each other that often and Simon defused the tension between father and daughter. But the marriage had lasted only seven years; they never had any children, though Betty told him that Marion wanted very much to get pregnant. What went wrong?

Marion had divorced Simon right after Betty's death. Ben always wondered if that emotionally stressful event had provoked the split. Or did all those years of Betty's deterioration simply take their toll? They had to affect Marion deeply.

A sudden wave of pity for his daughter overcame him. She was his child—he loved her. If only she didn't bug him so much, calling every day, preaching. Well, it was probably her way of trying to help him deal with his grief. Maybe that was the way she dealt with hers.

How much worse would she feel if she knew how Betty really died?

The alcove in Richard's bedroom—which he jokingly called his office—had become Ellen's home away from home now that the final draft of his book was nearing completion. The big window looking out across the river toward Manhattan offered a mesmerizing view of the city's imposing skyline. Just now the setting sun, hiding behind a low layer of clouds, backlit the skyscrapers to make them look like gargantuan tombstones—a graveyard for giants.

"This view never ceases to amaze me," Ellen said.

"Hm?" Richard was shuffling through some handwritten notes. "It costs enough."

It sure did, but Richard didn't have to pay for it. This suite, in a Brooklyn Heights residency hotel, was one of the perks (which also included a leased Mercedes-Benz) that Saint Joseph's had given him to sweeten his move to New York. The other doctors in the hospital were understandably jealous. But Ted Grabowski, Saint Joseph's administrator, was no fool. An average heart transplant brought in a quarter of a million in insurance revenue, a complicated one twice that.

"Aah, I found it." Richard looked up from his notes. "Ready?"

"Get set . . . go!" she chirped, her fingers poised over the portable computer in her lap. This was the only way she could work without her back killing her.

Richard leaned back in his chair, propped his long legs on the desk top, closed his eyes, and started to dictate: "At this very moment, a fifty-year-old scientist, one of a dozen of the world's genius experts in genome sequencing—" He opened his eyes. "Make a note to get some specific information about his accomplishments."

"Will do."

He closed his eyes again. ". . . the father of three teen-age girls, is taking labored breaths, unable to rise from his bed, because his weakened and enlarged heart has almost stopped beating. The United Network for Organ Sharing has given him top priority—the next available heart that matches his blood type and body size will be his. He has already waited a month. In a few weeks, the maximum time that a human heart can be made to pump by medication will have run out. He will die."

"Richard, that is so . . . dramatic."

"Thank you," he muttered and, not breaking concentration, continued: "This genius whose expertise is essential to society will die, but others, useless burdens, will live. Consider that U.S. prisons are filled with inmates who have taken a life or many lives and who will give nothing back to society when they are finally executed. One of them could donate his heart now; one of them could save this man's life."

A sharp intake of breath from Ellen made Richard open his eyes again. "This shocks you, Ellen?"

"Isn't that the Kevorkian view?"

"So?"

"But the possibilities for abuse would be enormous."

"We cannot leave it all in God's hands, Ellen." He got up abruptly and started pacing the room. "Do you not see? I have to say this." When he was irritated, his Austrian accent always became more pronounced.

"I understand, Richard, honestly." She couldn't stand it when he lost his patience with her.

"No one wants to face these things. I must force them."

"Well, it's bound to make the book controversial. That should get you a lot of publicity . . . and help sales."

His anger seemed to leave him as quickly as it came. "I hope the publisher agrees with you when we submit the manuscript next month. I want the book to come out before the board's annual review."

"Is that when they select the new chief of staff?"

"Correct."

"But . . . but . . . the board is so conservative—won't controversy hurt your chances?"

"Just the opposite. More hospitals will be aware of me and bidding for my services. They will have to promote me to keep me."

"I adore your arrogance." She laughed.

He raised his eyebrows. "I am stating a simple fact. In the ten months that I've been here, my heart transplants have brought in over twelve million dollars. No other doctor can point to this kind of revenue."

"You're right. They can't afford to lose you."

He smiled broadly, seductively, then walked around her chair and began to rub the back of her neck. The movements of his hands were slow, deliberate. "Ellen, this book will prove very important—in many ways." His fingers pressed more firmly into her skin.

"Keep doing that, Richard, and your assistant will quit for the night."

"Fine, then we shall continue tomorrow."

He spun her around in her swivel chair to face him, and knelt down in front of her, his hands resting loosely on her thighs. "Ellen, how can I thank you enough for the help you have given me?"

"I can think of a way." She giggled.

"Hmm . . ." His eyes locked on hers. "I can, too." And he firmly pulled her out of the chair, picked her up in his arms, and carried her into the bedroom.

8

Ben felt himself slowly waking up, his drowsiness lifting like the morning fog warmed by the rising sun. What time could it be? 5:47? He opened his eyes and was startled for a moment. In front of him slatted shutters let in the morning light. Oh, yes—Ellen's apartment. So strange to wake up someplace new after all these years. Unsettling. He turned toward the nightstand—now on the right, not the left. The familiar face of the digital clock said 6:26. Not so good at guessing time in this new environment.

Probably early for her. She must work nine to five, and with a half hour for travel, that would mean she didn't have to get up till seven-thirty or eight. If he took a shower now, would the running water wake her up?

He got out of bed and opened the shutters. The building faced south so the morning light came in at a slant. He turned to survey the surroundings in his new "home." Who would have thought that going to see a movie would lead to this?

He had arranged the room as best he could, but there was not much to arrange, really: the bureau in one corner, the bed against the wall, his clothes in the closet. It didn't take him long when he came here yesterday afternoon, so he sat down and waited for Ellen to come back from work.

But she didn't show up. He turned on the TV, eventually fell asleep. She must have come in very late because he didn't hear her.

Now he decided against making breakfast—he'd get something on his way to the gym. Maybe Milt would meet him at the Happy Days Diner on Montague.

He was a bit disappointed—he had looked forward to introducing Ellen to his omelette. Well, too bad.

Milt belched. He had eaten too much and too fast. Ben was right—three eggs were two too many. Being late on the day of the "Big Meeting"—Ron Michaelson, the smug yuppie heading up Famous Artists had flown in from Hollywood for this one—wasn't helping to settle his stomach, either.

The elevator of the Chrysler Building zoomed too fast to the fortieth floor. Milt belched again.

When he slinked into the conference room, Michaelson—casually attired in a hip Armani suit and striped Turnbull & Asser shirt—was already speaking. All the agents, obediently arranged two deep around the twenty-foot-long mahogany table, seemed to be hanging on his every word.

"We can't afford gaffes like this." His icy condemnation could be felt around the room as he focused on Sam. "It's your job to keep things like this from happening."

Poor Sam, thought Milt, Michaelson must be talking about Don Arnold.

"I watched him like a hawk, Ron. It happened so fast. . . . I pulled him off . . . he was gonna kill her . . . I . . ." Sam stammered. "I got him back onstage—"

"It shouldn't have happened in the first place." When Ron got excited he stood on the tiptoes of his expensive Italian shoes. "At least you had the presence of mind to call Milt instead of the police. And Milt—"

Oh shit—what's coming now? Milt wondered.

"You didn't manage to keep it out of the tabloids, but I'm not sure that's bad. It might be good for his image—the wounded bull striking out blindly. . . ."

Wounded bull? What the hell did that mean? But Milt wasn't about to ask stupid questions.

"But we're lucky the story didn't make the mainstream press," Ron continued. "Don's at the peak of his career and we've got to keep him there as long as possible. He's worth millions to us."

"What about Dawn?" That came from Frank, who had the misfortune of representing her. He must have been sorry as the words left his mouth because Michaelson's eyes—like steel drills—were now aimed in his direction.

"I don't give a fuck about Dawn. She's just a society whore with no talent—she'd be nothing if she wasn't Mrs. Don Arnold." His voice assumed a malevolent tone. "The only reason we're still representing her is that we don't want her to hurt the studio."

That's a novel approach, thought Milt, a talent agency more concerned about the studio than the client.

"Milt—"

Shit. "Yes, Ron."

"I want you to look after Dawn personally, make sure she gets back to work as soon as possible—"

"Well, Ron, I ain't Jesus—I can't heal her with the wave of a wand."

"Heh, heh, heh." Michaelson liked the joke. "Too bad we don't represent Benny Hinn."

The other agents chuckled politely.

"You can do it if anybody can, Milt. We don't want World Pictures to lose a dime more than it absolutely has to. This can't affect our deal with the Japanese."

"What deal, Ron?"

Michaelson didn't answer right away. He looked around the table, making sure he had everyone's undivided attention. His face was gradually lighting up as he measured the level of anticipation in the room. To underscore the drama, his left hand toyed with his ever-present worry beads.

Milt remembered, a few years back, when Michaelson had taken his wife on a trip to Greece and had become convinced that playing with worry beads takes away inner tension and gets rid of anxiety attacks. Somehow though, as near as Milt could tell, it wasn't working too good on Ron.

"Mr. Osamu Hashikawa of Hashikawa Electronics will be in New York in a couple of weeks to finalize a deal I have worked out ..." he paused, the worry beads clicking, "to buy out World Pictures for five billion dollars."

The intake of breath in the room aggregated into one loud gasp. Even Milt was impressed—no wonder Michaelson was more concerned with the welfare of the studio than of Dawn.

"The commission to the agency ..." Ron was glowing

91

now like a schoolgirl at her first dance, ". . . will be no less than ten million."

"Ron!"

Everyone turned to young Bill, one of the newest associates. He reminded Milt very much of what Ron looked like when he first came to Famous Artists—back when he was running out to get coffee for the last head of the agency.

"Yes, Bill." The worry beads kept moving.

"Well . . . ah . . ." the young agent fumbled, "that's great, Ron, but this will be the third movie studio bought out by the Japanese—"

"That's right. Ovitz will be pissed I beat him out on this one."

Everyone laughed loudly. They all envied the success of Creative Artists, and no one was more envied than Mike Ovitz, its head and Michaelson's nemesis.

But Bill forged on. "There is a danger—"

"*What* danger?"

"The Japanese will be influencing what kind of movies America produces."

"How could they influence movies?" Ron had a rigid smile on his face, but the worry beads were doing double time. "Miniaturize them?"

Another group laugh. Only Bill wasn't laughing.

"We'll make the movies, they'll just put up the money and say, 'Ah soo.'" Ron bowed in Japanese fashion. The group laughed again.

Milt looked around the room—all these young fellows so pleased with themselves, each of them making more money than they'd ever dreamed of. And there was more to come, a lot more. How things had changed since he had first started with this agency—God, he hated to remember—forty years ago.

"But if the deal goes through—" Bill started in again.

Milt wished he was sitting next to the young fella so he could shut him up; at this rate he was gonna lose his job before the meeting was over.

But Bill continued as if unaware of the consequences. "Aren't we going to be accused of a conflict of interest?"

"Ovitz was accused of the same thing—didn't hurt him one bit."

"Yes, but—" Bill obviously had a suicidal impulse. "We would be getting a commission from the new owner of the studio, at the same time that we get commissions from our clients working for the studio."

This one hit too close to home. Ron's worry beads fell to the floor. Everyone was silent as he bent down to pick them up. When he lifted his head, his face was beet red and the veins in his throat stood out like ropes. "They'll own the studio. They won't make the movies." He was rapidly losing control. "There's *no conflict of interest!*" he yelled. "You dumb shit!" He threw the worry beads on the table and stomped out of the room.

Gradually, not saying much, the agents filed out.

Milt picked up the worry beads and walked over to Bill, who, feeling the ostracism of the others, was looking very confused.

"Good luck, kid," Milt pressed the beads into Bill's palm. "You'll need 'em."

With a bag of groceries in his arms, Ben climbed the steps leading to the brownstone, reached to press the bell, then remembered that he had his own key.

He was annoyed that it was so difficult to find a place to park around here. That's the first complaint he'd make to his landlady.

"Ellen!" he called out as he entered the apartment.

No answer.

The note that he had left tacked to her bedroom door was still there. He knocked (just in case), then cracked the door open and peeked inside. No sign of life. Obviously, she hadn't come home the night before. He had been so quiet this morning, tiptoeing around, and she wasn't even here.

He took out the carrots, string beans, celery, and lettuce for his dinner and left them on the kitchen counter, then put away the rest of his groceries, being careful to store the eggs, skim milk, and yogurt on the left side of the refrigerator, the space she had cleared out and assigned to him. The right side, her side, was nearly empty—only two Snickers bars, a tin of onion dip, a jar of peanut butter, and the heel left over from a loaf of bread. He smiled to himself—he'd have to teach her how to eat.

He turned on the faucet and stuck the head of romaine under the running water. He'd make a nice salad, big enough for two. But what if she came back late, or didn't come home at all again? What was he knocking himself out for? The hell with it—he'd go over to Milt's instead. He dialed the number, hoping Sarah wouldn't be the one to pick up and nag him about Brenda again.

"Hiya, sweetheart." Milt's cheerful voice came on the line.

Ben could never get over the speech mannerisms that Milt had picked up in Hollywood, men addressing each other like lovebirds.

"Let me take you and Sarah out for dinner tonight," Ben offered, the usual cue for him to get invited over.

"Boychik, we'd love to have you, but we're just on our way out."

"Where to?"

"Madison Square Garden—to watch over Sam."

"Sam?"

"Yeah, the poor guy who has to watch over Don Arnold."

Ben chuckled. Milt sure moved in a crazy world. He could hear Sarah in the background yelling at Milt to get off the phone or they'd be late.

"I gotta go—can't miss the new girl comic who replaced Joe. See you at the gym tomorrow."

A little disappointed, Ben went back to his lettuce. Outside, dusk was settling in. The leaves of the tall maple tree brushed against the glass of the window. He made a mental note to trim the branches—maybe this weekend when he had the time—then remembered he had packed away his clippers. Oh well, it wasn't his tree anyway.

He switched on a few lights and placed the dripping wet lettuce in the spinner to dry.

It had been a long, hard day, and Ellen's aching back knew it better than any other part of her. The fact that she hadn't slept so well over at Richard's last night, and then had worked nearly eleven hours straight—interrupted only once by a short coffee break with Goldie—didn't help matters either.

No use dwelling on it; she'd be home soon. She walked out into the hallway. Even though it was after eight, the hospital looked just the same as when she had come in that morning. It always surprised her how little the atmosphere changed from shift to shift. There were fewer outsiders now, the offices were closed, but the corridors were brightly lit as always. It was perpetual day here. It was as if the hospital denied the existence of night. It was as if the hospital denied the existence of death. The hospital lived round the clock dedicated to the pursuit of life, its preservation at all costs. Death meant its mission had failed. And one didn't dwell on failure here.

The thought depressed her, and she was glad to step outside. It was a cool summer evening, with a brisk breeze coming off the water. She zipped up her jacket as she turned up Ocean Parkway heading for the BMT stop.

The screeching of the approaching train made her bound up the steps, taking two at a time. She jumped on just as the doors were closing.

There weren't many other passengers, so she had a choice of seats. She put up her feet and relaxed. Most people hated public transportation, but she loved it. She never tired of watching the strange mixture of humanity—well-dressed men with briefcases rubbing shoulders with Hispanic women in their hand-me-downs. The New York subway was a great equalizer; in here they were all the same, just passengers.

The train squealed, careening on the rails above the streets until just before Prospect Park, where it descended underground.

After the Brooklyn College stop, she saw two men—one small and skinny, the other tall and skinny—working their way through the cars, singing a cappella. Choo-choo and Caruso. Ellen grinned. She had lucked out. They sang very well in a complicated harmony jiggling a cup full of change like a tambourine: *"Hey, Mr. Tambourine man play a song for me, I'm not sleepy and there is no place I'm going to. . . ."*

She quickly pulled out two quarters from her purse and deposited it in their cup—they bowed, acknowledging her, but did not stop singing. She knew she shouldn't give them money—the strong whiff of alcohol breath told her where the quarters would go—but she couldn't help herself. The song communicated a strange mixture of sadness and joy that got Ellen straight in the heart.

"Yes, to dance beneath the diamond sky with one hand waving free, silhouetted by the sea. . . ."

Reluctantly, she exited at Seventh and Flatbush. The clatter of the departing train obliterated their serenade but she could see them through the window, still singing their hearts out as they receded into the darkness of the tunnel.

She came out onto the street and glanced up at the Plaza. Marlon Brando was no longer there. Now the marquis read:

Gloria Sw nson

in

SUNSET BOULEV RD

Didn't they ever have enough letters for a complete title?

She walked down Seventh Avenue, singing the rest of the verse to herself: *"Let me forget about today until tomorrow. . . ."* The song had invigorated her somehow. She felt light, happy. Things were really coming along with Richard. She was sure now that he would move in with her before they got married. Married! Wow, what a feeling! The thought filled every pore of her body with helium—she felt she could float right up and touch the sky.

She wished now she hadn't made the deal with Ben. It was a stupid thing to do. Why was she always so impulsive? What would this get her—a few months' rent? It would have been better to borrow the money than get into an uncomfortable situation over it with Richard.

Maybe Ben wouldn't be there when she got home. Maybe he didn't move in. He had seemed very uncertain at first, maybe he'd had second thoughts. Probably not—he did give her an extra month's rent when she gave him the key.

Keeping her fingers crossed that her wish had come true and Ben had reneged on the deal, she ran up the stairs and flung open the door. No dice—tango music filled the air. How corny!

Ben was at the kitchen counter, turning the crank on a round plastic contraption.

"Hi," he said cheerfully.

"What are you doing? Making ice cream?"

"This is a spinner. I'm drying lettuce."

"You dry lettuce—with a machine?"

"Yeah, I don't like it soggy."

She watched him transfer the lettuce to a large wooden bowl filled with all kinds of vegetables and start tossing them.

"Would you like some?"

"I don't eat rabbit food."

"Yeah, you eat junk food, I saw." He motioned with his head toward the refrigerator.

"Stay on your half of the fridge, please."

"Thanks for making me feel so welcome." He sat down

at a table, ready to eat. "Pull up a chair—there's enough salad for three."

"I like peanut butter and jelly." She took out the left-over bread and started smearing peanut butter on it.

"But that's only peanut butter."

"Ran out of jelly."

"I gotta take you shopping."

"I don't need you to buy jelly."

"You need me to buy some decent food."

She said nothing.

"I bet you don't exercise either."

"Nope."

"Geez—junk food, no exercise—you're hopeless."

"I'm busy. I want to live life, not just preserve it. I've got too much to do."

"Doing it all night, ey?"

"That's right. . . . I was *working* with Dr. Vandermann on his book."

"Your boyfriend?"

"Yes, Daddy," she said, mocking him as she scraped the last of the peanut butter out of the jar.

"A *romantic* novel?"

"No, it's about heart transplants."

Ben stopped chewing.

"It's part of Richard's plan to find new ways of getting vital organs to save lives."

"New ways like what?"

"Prisoners on death row should be donors . . . human organs should be put up for auction."

"For auction?"

"So the rich could buy them and free donated organs for the poor."

"That sounds dumb."

She shot a cold look in his direction as she inhaled her sandwich. The bread was stale and it tasted awful.

"Sorry—I don't want to insult your boyfriend. I'm sure he's very dedicated."

"He is."

"You must be, too—working all night."

"Back to that again?"

"When do you sleep?"

"It's none of your business." Her voice rose.

"You've got an Italian temper."

She started to leave the kitchen, anxious to end the conversation. "If you'll excuse me I gotta get up early tomorrow."

"Good night," he said, "sweet dreams."

She didn't answer as she closed her bedroom door.

Geez, how could she have been so wrong, Ellen thought, kicking off her shoes. He seemed like such a nice old guy at first, interested in Jello and the Bobs, protective, full of funny stories from his past. But tonight—so nosy. And drying lettuce yet? What a prissy thing to do. He might be a great companion walking through a dark alley, but in the light of day. . . . Richard was right; Goldie was right—this was a *big* mistake. Well, what could she do now? For at least two months she was stuck. But after that he had to go.

In the kitchen, Ben washed the salad bowl and utensils and put them away. What a girl, he thought. Lots of spunk. Doesn't take any crap from anybody. But he'd have to work on her—diplomatically, of course—to get her to change her eating habits. That would take a little time.

He turned off the kitchen lights, swaying to the beat of the tango music. Then he turned off the stereo. He liked this place. He knew he'd be happy here.

9

Ellen was finishing up for the day—she had worked late again—when Goldie passed by the library door. Ellen let out a long whistle; Goldie sure was a sight to behold. Her hair was done up in the style of an Ethiopian princess in extension braids, and she wore a black-and-gold Gypsy dress with lots of gold chains and bangles.

"Yo, Goldie—new nurse's uniform?"

"Listen, girlfriend—I just finished a twelve-hour shift. And I do not mean to live my whole life in this damned place. I'm going out on the town tonight."

"Abdul taking you out?"

"That fool? Nah, it's the Black Nurses' Association annual dinner. And believe me, nobody wears white." Enjoying her own joke, Goldie burst out in her typical raucous laugh.

"Well, have a good time. I better get out of here myself."

"By the way, how are things with your roommate?"

Once Goldie started talking, she often lingered. "It's been a month, hasn't it?"

"Yep, a month. But I don't call him my roommate—I call him my pen pal."

"Say what?"

"We hardly see each other—we communicate by the written word." She pulled out a crumpled note from her pocket and handed it to Goldie. It read:

Dear Ellen, I hate to bother you again, but I must bring to your attention that the toilet is leaking. (There was a goofy drawing of a toilet crying crocodile tears.) *Would you mind letting the management know? I appreciate your attention to this problem. Your grateful sub-lessee, Ben.*

Below that was Ellen's scrawled response: *Will do.*

And then a thank-you from Ben: *The toilet and I are grateful.* (This with a drawing of a hand sticking out of the toilet bowl holding a bunch of flowers.)

Goldie burst out in another raucous laugh.

"See? He's not so bad, Goldie. At first he was a pain in the neck, but he turned out all right. Pays his rent, stays out of my way. Of course, I haven't been home much, working with Richard finishing up his book."

"How's it going?"

"We rushed it off to the publisher and now we're waiting to hear if the final draft was accepted."

"When will you know?"

"Any day now—I hope."

"Well, good luck."

"Thanks. Hey, you should go or you'll be late for your dinner."

"Yeah—I better get a move on, might have to fight my

way out the door—the baboon lovers are protesting out there again."

"Oh God, poor Richard—they just won't leave him alone. Which reminds me . . ." Ellen looked pointedly at her watch. "I'm gonna try and catch him before he goes off to lecture at Columbia—maybe he'll take me out to eat afterwards."

When she finally managed to send Goldie on her way, Ellen hurried to Richard's office. It was six-thirty and the surgical floor was very quiet. The nurses had gone on their dinner break; the nine-to-five office staff had left long ago.

When Ellen reached the office, Richard's secretary was just on her way out. "Oh, Ellen, I'm so glad you're here. I have to leave now, but look . . ." She handed her a fax. "The book's been accepted!"

Ellen could feel her heartbeat quicken. "Terrific. Where's Richard?"

"Making rounds in CCU, but I didn't want him to miss this. Will you get it to him?"

"Sure will."

Ellen read the fax three times, each time smiling more broadly to herself: "Dear Dr. Vandermann," it said. "We are delighted to publish your book *Heartbeat*. We are so excited we plan to accelerate our schedule and set an early spring pub date as you requested. Congratulations on a job well done."

Ellen couldn't wait to see the happy look on Richard's face when he read this. She already imagined the cover, shiny white with a big red heart and his name in large black letters, and of course, a photo of his handsome face on the back. She could see it lying on the coffee table in her apartment—their apartment.

Quickly, she picked up the phone and dialed CCU, only to be told that Dr. Vandermann had finished a half hour ago and had gone. Maybe his lecture at Columbia was earlier tonight or maybe he just wanted to avoid the animal rights people. She could call his hotel, of course, leave a message on his answering machine, but this occasion deserved something more.

A twinkle came into her eyes as she conceived her plot. She checked his schedule on the secretary's calendar. Yes, he was operating tomorrow, OR No. 3. She would leave a note on his surgical cart, where all his instruments, packed in sterile wraps, lay waiting for use the next day. He'd get it first thing in the morning. She scribbled: *Good news— book accepted—let's celebrate!* It would kill her not to call him late tonight, but the surprise would be worth it.

Everything was very still and quiet in the operating theater, the only sound the muted rumble of the monorail system, which, traveling unseen inside the walls of the hospital, delivered medical supplies to all the units. As she expected, his surgical implements for the next day were there already, waiting on a cart outside the operating room where she had watched him, like a god, bringing someone back to life. At the last minute, she decided it would be better to pin the note to the heart monitor. No chance of missing it there.

Repressing a giggle, she walked into the dimly lit operating room and stopped.

She swallowed hard, blinking rapidly, not believing her eyes, as if her vision would clear and what was in front of her would change. But it didn't.

Richard was sitting at the end of the operating table,

legs spread apart, leaning back on his elbows, the mass of Gina's red hair bobbing up and down over his crotch.

In a state of shock, she backed out of the room, then stumbled down the corridor, choking back tears.

She started running. She ran aimlessly, just moving, moving, trying to lose the picture in her mind. She rounded a corner, not even sure where she was. She leaned against the wall and gave in to her sobs.

Suddenly, she felt an arm around her shoulder. "Just leave me alone, please," she pleaded through her tears. She couldn't deal with a concerned soul just now. "I'm all right, really I am."

"Let me help you, my dear." It was the soothing voice of Sister Clarita.

Ellen tried to pull herself together long enough for the nun to leave, but she couldn't stop sobbing. Sister Clarita waited patiently, her comforting arm gently, unobtrusively, around Ellen.

When Ellen had finally exhausted herself, Sister Clarita handed her a handkerchief. She took it gratefully and wiped her running nose.

"I think, my dear, it's time for you to have some chamomile tea. What do you say?"

Without waiting for a response, she took Ellen by the arm. Feeling totally helpless, Ellen allowed herself to be led along the corridor, then down some stairs. Where were they going? It didn't matter.

"Believe you me," Sister Clarita said, "with all the medications we hand out in this hospital, there is nothing more effective than a hot cup of chamomile tea."

Ellen didn't respond, but Sister Clarita chattered on

happily. "You've never seen my little flat, have you? It's really quite nice. Lavish compared to what I had at the cloister."

It seemed that they were in the basement of the hospital; large pipes were now running exposed in the ceiling. Clearly, patients never came here. Ellen had thought that all the nuns who worked in the hospital lived in the dormitory up the street, but then Sister Clarita was unusual in many ways.

As if reading Ellen's mind, Sister Clarita said, "The nuns used to live down here, but now they prefer to get away. I still like to be close to my place of duty, though."

She opened a narrow door, not needing a key, and guided Ellen gently inside. "You just rest here and Doctor Clarita will give you the medicine you need."

Ellen glanced about the sparsely furnished room, which had no windows. There was a long wooden chest, covered with a thin, black cushion, a kneeler in front of a crucifix on the wall, a small bookcase with a lamp hardly bigger than a candle on it. There was also a small sink and cabinet beneath.

From that cabinet Sister Clarita extracted a chipped cup, into which she inserted an electric coil to heat the water.

Mutely, Ellen waited—a lamb conceding its slaughter, no longer caring how and when they did it.

A few minutes later, Sister Clarita floated toward her as if on roller skates, her long habit giving no view of her feet, holding out the cup of chamomile tea.

Ellen took a long sip of the hot liquid. It tasted slightly bitter. She drank more. It sent a strange hot wave through her. Sister Clarita's magic potion.

"You're right, Sister—it is good medicine." It was the first time she had spoken since the nun had found her. "Thank you."

Sister Clarita beamed. "No thanks necessary. Now, would you like to tell me what troubles you—perhaps I can fix that as well."

Ellen almost broke out in hysterical laughter. How could she tell her? Listen, Sister, there he was—his cock hanging out of his pants while his nurse friend sucked him off? How would that sound in this place? She just shook her head no.

"All right, my dear, say nothing. The Lord knows it all. In him you will find consolation."

Ellen was grateful that there would be no more questions. Yet, even if Sister Clarita didn't know the facts, she seemed to connect in an inexplicable way to her anguish. What a sweet woman she was. As a nun, she had never known the touch of a man, yet she didn't feel she had been denied anything in life. She had found true happiness in helping others. Once she had told Ellen that she had spent twelve years in a contemplative monastery living under a vow of silence. Perhaps that's what made her such a good listener. Perhaps that's what made her understand another's pain without words.

Feeling an odd calmness, Ellen drained the last of the tea.

When she got home, Ben was watching the news.

"Hi, stranger!" he called out. He always seemed happy to see her whenever they ran into each other. "Look at this!" On the screen, a car was burning up in flames on the freeway. "When the hell do they ever report *good* news?"

He shook his head. "I suppose it's good news for hospitals. Another body for the operating table."

The words hit Ellen like a sledgehammer. She stood frozen for a moment, her chin wobbling, then burst into sobs.

Completely stunned, Ben walked over to her. "What's the matter?" He pointed to the television. "It can't be that bad."

He put his arms around her and squeezed her hard, as if trying to strangle her pain. "Now, now, now," he kept repeating.

He was so different from Sister Clarita, but he too brought to her that same strange calmness. Her sobs subsided.

"That's better." He sat her down on the couch. "Just wait a moment, okay? Don't go away."

She nodded weakly.

He went into the kitchen and came back with a shot glass in his hand. He handed it to Ellen, who downed it in one gulp.

Immediately, she started gagging and tried to spit it out, but it was too late. Most of it had gone down. It was the most awful thing she had ever tasted.

"What the hell—" she coughed. "What was *that*?"

"Onion juice."

"Onion juice? Onion juice?" She started to laugh.

"See that? Works like a charm—you're laughing. A minute ago you were crying."

"You bastard," she was still laughing. "Playing jokes on me?"

"Honestly, it's no practical joke. An old Russian remedy. And you should be grateful I left out the other ingredients."

Ellen shook her head. "An old Russian remedy for what?"

"The grippe."

"The grippe? Why give me a remedy for the grippe?"

"It was all I could think of on the spur of the moment." He was laughing too, now. "I never know what to do when women cry—it makes me feel totally helpless."

"Okay, I forgive you. Now have you got an old Russian remedy for removing the taste of onion out of my mouth?"

"Yes." Chuckling he walked into the kitchen and came back with a slice of lemon.

"Take the bitter with the bitter, ey?" Ellen sucked on it gratefully.

"Now—" His voice assumed an authoritarian tone. "Let's spill the beans. What happened that was so tragic? The hospital burned down?"

She shook her head.

"They fired your boyfriend?"

She closed her eyes, but didn't answer. Her chin started to wobble and she felt she was about to lose control again.

"I'm on the right track—something bad happened to your boyfriend?"

"No, but it's about to." Her anger brought back her composure.

"How's that?"

She jumped up. "I don't intend to see him or talk to him ever again."

"Oh, so it's like that, is it? I thought it was a major problem."

He took her hand and pulled her down on the couch next to him. "Come on, Ellen—what terrible thing could he have done to you?"

She didn't answer.

"My daughter—she's the psychologist—says it helps to talk about it."

Ellen stared off into space and took a deep breath: "I got a fax that his book was going to be published. I couldn't wait to surprise him with the good news—" She stopped.

"So?" he coaxed.

"So I went looking for him—that was a big mistake."

"You found him?"

"Yes, on the operating table . . . with his nurse's face buried in his crotch."

Ben let out a low whistle. "That's a terrible thing to see."

"I'll never speak to that bastard again."

"Well sure, that's how you feel now. I understand. You're mad and you have the right to be. But take my advice, don't be too hasty—"

"Hasty? After what he did?" She was on the verge of tears again. "He said he wanted to marry me. . . . I believed him . . . and here he was—"

"Ellen, I know, I know," he interrupted her, fearing she would break down if she continued. "He disappointed you. But everyone you know will disappoint you sooner or later. Even those you love. You can only hope that those you love will disappoint you less. But they will disappoint you."

"Disappoint me? He betrayed me!"

"Hey, one quickie in the operating room is no reason to break up a relationship."

"I could never have done that to him."

110

"Ellen, men are different. . . ."

"Oh don't give me that double-standard shit."

"Don't get mad, just hear me out, okay?"

She bit her lip, but didn't say anything.

"I don't mean that men are allowed to screw around. I just mean they do, because they are stupid. And I know 'cause I've been there."

"You?"

"Yeah—it happened back in nineteen fifty-eight, 'fifty-nine, something like that."

"The year I was born."

He smiled. "Yeah, a long time ago. Milt was in Hollywood then and he had a client, an actress who was doing a play in New York. He sent her to me for fitness training. Oh, I tell you Ellen, she was young, beautiful . . . lonely. She came on to me."

Ellen listened.

"I was in love with my wife. We had been happily married for thirteen or fourteen years. But I couldn't resist a movie star. She sent her limo to take me to her apartment in Manhattan. It was just that one time."

"And what happened?"

Ben sighed. "It almost broke up my marriage."

"It should have."

"You're wrong. Very wrong." Ben's voice rose. "We had another twenty wonderful years together. Overcoming that made our marriage stronger."

"Sounds like bullshit to me."

"Our marriage was not bullshit!"

"I didn't mean that, but Richard and I aren't married. We're not even living together. I asked him to move in with me, now I know why he didn't."

"Hey, Ellen, all I'm saying is a couple of hours ago you were in love with this guy, so don't throw that away so fast. There may be other reasons why it happened. He might have been feeling low, and he's probably thinking of this as jerking off. . . ."

Ellen rolled her eyes upwards—more male bullshit, the look said.

"Listen, I'll tell you a little secret few men will admit to . . . but when a man has an orgasm and the erection is gone, he feels frightened."

"Why?"

"He wonders if he'll ever be able to get it hard again. You see, men look at sex differently. For women, I think it's always an emotional involvement. But for men, it's ego."

"I have an ego too. And I'm not gonna let somebody make a fool of me twice. You know the saying, fool me once—"

The ringing of the phone broke in. Ellen didn't move to pick it up. The phone rang twice, three times. . . .

"Aren't you gonna get it?" Ben asked.

"No, I don't want to talk with anyone."

"But it could be for me."

"So, you answer."

He picked up the phone. "Hello." He listened for a moment. "Who's calling?"

He covered the mouthpiece with his hand. "It's your boyfriend."

"Fuck him."

"Please, Ellen, remember what I said. Talk to him."

She gave him a long look, hesitating.

"Please . . ."

She stood up and took the receiver.

112

"Hi, Ellen," Richard's voice seemed cheerful. Sure, she thought, the bastard got a good blow job, no wonder he's so cheery, but instead she said "Oh hi, Richard," as if nothing had happened.

Ben exhaled in relief—he got her to see the male side of it after all.

"I'm so glad you called, Richard, because I have good news for you—the publisher accepted your manuscript."

"That's terrific news. And we have to celebrate. How about dinner?"

"Dinner? Oh that's a *wonderful* idea."

"What do you say we meet at the Grill in . . . an hour?

"Perfect." She hung up the phone.

Ben was beaming. "See that? I bet you feel better now. Admit it. Don't you?"

"Yes, I do." There was a wry smile on her face.

"I'm proud of you for taking my advice."

She said nothing, just walked into the kitchen and pulled out a jar of peanut butter from the refrigerator and started spreading it on a piece of bread.

"What're you doing? You're gonna have dinner with Richard in an hour."

"Like hell! The bastard is gonna sit there, waiting. It makes me feel good just to imagine the look on his face when he realizes I stood him up."

Ben laughed. "You're tough."

"Not really," she said flatly, "I . . ." Her voice cracked and she shut her eyes. "I just try to learn by my mistakes."

Bent over her sandwich, butter knife trembling, she stood there trying to compose herself without success. To Ben she presented a poignant picture of total vulnerability—tears seeping down from under her tightly shut eyelids, rolling down her cheeks, and landing in the peanut butter.

He took the knife out of her hand. "Tonight you need more than peanut butter."

"What?"

"*I'm* taking you to dinner."

She started to shake her head no, but he gently pushed her in the direction of her room.

"Go and get changed, we're going to Gage and Tollner's."

"Isn't that very expensive?"

"Yep—put on something nice."

She did—a summer dress that set off her Mediterranean looks very prettily, blue silk with a lacy white collar.

"It doesn't clash with my red eyes, does it?" she asked. The words were playful, but the tone still edgy, tense.

"Nah, last week was the Fourth of July—red, white, and blue are just right."

She laughed. She appreciated his efforts to make her feel better.

From the vantage point of the passenger seat, she studied him as he concentrated on driving. He had put on a handsome olive green summer suit, set off by a white shirt and beige tie. He had good taste. His mustache was neatly trimmed, following the line of his firm mouth, his skin taut over his high cheekbones. His profile made her think of the prow of a Viking ship.

"You're very sweet," she said.

"Please don't say that."

"Why not?"

"You'll ruin my reputation as a tough guy."

"You're not so tough." Then she added softly, "Like I'm not so tough."

She leaned back in her seat, the ache was still there.

He swung around Brooklyn's Borough Hall, looking for a place to park on a side street approaching Fulton Mall, which was closed to traffic. Then he spotted one—perfect—in view of the restaurant.

"Hey, look at that!"

He drove past the spot and started to back into it, then suddenly slammed on the brakes. Ellen almost hit the windshield. A beat-up Buick behind him had cut in.

"You son of a bitch!" Ben yelled, loud enough for the whole block to hear.

With Ben's car blocking it, the Buick couldn't quite get all the way in, and its trunk was sticking out into the street. The driver, a swarthy dark-haired type with a ponytail, got out. "You calling me what?"

Ellen grabbed Ben's arm. "Please, let's find another spot."

Ben glared at the approaching menace.

"Ben . . . Ben . . . let's not have any trouble."

Ignoring her, he got out of the car.

The Buick driver was now facing him. "You gonna apologize?"

"For you stealing my spot? You're dreaming, buddy."

"That's *my* spot—get your heap outta here."

Ben's brain quickly listed his options: a knee to the groin, a karate chop to the Adam's apple, fingers straight in the eye. . . .

"Please Ben, leave it alone—for me." He heard the

pleading in her voice. With what had happened to her to-night, he didn't want to spoil her evening. "Okay," he conceded.

"Okay what?" the bully sneered.

For a moment longer, Ben savored the mental image of the palm of his hand shoving the guy's nose up into his brain, but he said, "It's your spot."

"Wheell now, that's a good boy." The man contemptuously sauntered back to the Buick.

"I'm proud of you," Ellen said as Ben got back in the car.

"For what? For being chicken?"

"For humoring me." She gave him a quick peck on the cheek.

The humiliation was worth making her this happy.

He pulled around the corner and found another place to park.

"You're lucky," said the maitre d' at the entrance. "I saw the whole thing, he could have hurt you."

"Yeah," Ben muttered, walking inside, "I guess this is my lucky day."

Gage & Tollner was an historic seafood house taking pride in its original decor, which dated back to the late 1800s. The tables, covered with gleaming white linen, were lined up like soldiers in the long narrow room, and smoky mirrors on the walls reflected the softly flickering gaslight.

"What a charming place—I've never been here," Ellen said.

"I hope you'll be coming here often," said the affable, white-gloved waiter who presented them with menus. "Can I get you anything to drink?"

"I'll have a vodka and tonic, and don't spare the vodka, I need it tonight." Ellen was keeping up a cheerful front.

"Water for me," Ben said.

"You don't drink?"

"Sometimes." He picked up the menu. "Let's start with some clam bellies."

"Coming right up." The waiter hurried off.

Still admiring the decor, Ellen caught the sight of the two of them in one of the mirrors. Ben was mashing his napkin. She chuckled. "Still obsessing about that lousy parking spot?"

"I let him get away with it."

"So what? Why do you always have to win?"

He looked up. "Because it's the only way to survive in Brooklyn."

"Have you always been like that?"

Ben rubbed his mustache. "When I was a kid, Brooklyn was divided into war zones—Jewish, Irish, Italian. . . . My grandfather had a dairy farm in Canarsie. To visit him I had a choice—cross over Irish terrain, or else go way out of my way."

"Of course you chose to cross through the Irish terrain."

"That's right."

"And?"

"They made you pay a 'toll' or they beat you up."

"You ever pay?"

Ben shook his head.

"You ever get beat up?"

Ben picked up his water glass and smiled arrogantly over the rim. "Does this look like a face that took too many punches?"

Laughing, Ellen touched her glass to his. "Here's to your modesty."

He had her laughing through the entire night. It was only when they came home and she went to bed—and the memory of the day's events returned—that Ellen didn't feel like laughing. But she was grateful to Ben for all that he had done to keep her mind off the pain that was gnawing on her insides. He even went off his diet, ordered all the food that he thought she'd like. When he asked for she-crab soup, she made a face: "She-crab? What happened to he-crab?"

"We only cook the girls."

"Yeah, I guess that's life"—she poked her spoon at the bowl—"men go out to play, women have to pay."

Ben roared.

She liked the boyish way he laughed. She could picture him as a young kid punching his way through Brooklyn, scaling the Thunderbolt with Milt. . . .

Now she listened to the steady gush of his shower water running, and it released the tears she had been holding back all night. Oh Richard, Richard, how could you?

She sobbed into her pillow, muffling the sound so Ben couldn't hear until she was too exhausted to cry, too exhausted to think, too exhausted for anything but sleep.

On the other side of the wall, lying in his bed, Ben replayed the evening in his mind. He'd had a wonderful time. Nothing like this for years. . . . He could see Ellen sitting across the table from him, her eyes shining in the gaslight. She was a wonderful girl—she cared about others, about the homeless—she didn't deserve to be hurt like this. . . .

Once during the evening as he jumped from one silly story to another, she interrupted him: "You know, Ben, I'm so hurt . . . and it's not just that he didn't love me, or that he betrayed me, the worst is that he . . . he . . . discarded me, abandoned me."

"He didn't abandon you, Ellen, he just cheated on you a little bit, that's all."

"That's all, huh?" She laughed hollowly and stared into space. "I guess I'm just screwed up. All these years of therapy haven't changed a thing."

"I don't understand."

"Well, like everything—it goes back to my childhood. Shortly after I was born, my father abandoned my mother—he was an alcoholic, he just couldn't cope with a family. And my mother . . . it was tough on her. She had me just to get him to marry her and now she was stuck. I think she wished I'd disappear or something. She never hit me or anything like that, but maybe she was more cruel. Her way of punishing me was to say: 'If you disobey me again, I'm gonna die and then you'll have a wicked stepmother who will beat you every day.' "

It was a painful story to hear, obviously a painful one to tell. Ben just listened.

"That scared me so bad. Night after night I wouldn't be able to sleep. I'd sneak into my mother's room to make sure she was still breathing." She picked up her drink and gulped it down. "I'm always afraid of being abandoned."

He wanted to hug her then, but she broke the mood and said, "Tell me another story about you and Milt."

And he obliged, getting her to laugh again.

When they came home, she gave him a gentle kiss on the cheek before going to her room. He could still feel the soft touch of her lips.

He turned over in bed and stared at the wall that separated their rooms. She couldn't be more than ten feet away. "Good night," he whispered. "Sweet dreams."

10

Richard was not smiling. Out of the corner of her eye, Ellen could see him pacing up and down the general reference aisle while she printed out a research report for the head of Oncology.

He had stormed into the library, obviously set for a confrontation, but whatever he wanted to say had to wait until the other doctor left.

"I'll be with you in just one moment, Dr. Vandermann," she cooed, pretending not to see that he was fuming. "Now, Dr. Reuben, will that be all?"

The oncologist nodded and turned to leave.

"Oh, wait—there's one more article I should check out. . . . It was in . . . let me see . . . yes, here it is . . . last month's issue of JAMA."

She took perverse pleasure in making Richard wait. It was a small, petty revenge, but it was all she had.

When the oncologist finally left, she beamed brightly in Richard's direction. "How are you?"

"You stood me up." He spit out the words.

"I did?" She feigned total and complete surprise. "When?"

"Last night."

"Oh no—I must have got it mixed up. I thought you said we would celebrate tonight?"

"How could you make such a mistake—you distinctly agreed to meet me in an hour!"

"But I couldn't have—last night I had a date with my roommate."

"Your roommate?" Richard's tone was incredulous.

"Yes, he's such a nice man. Took me to Gage and Toll-ner's."

"While I was waiting for you at the Grill?"

"Oh, I'm so sorry, Richard. Obviously I had no idea."

"I felt like a fool eating alone."

"Alone? That's too bad." A hint of malice was creeping into Ellen's voice. "You should have brought Gina."

"Now stop it!"

"You take her everywhere."

"Ellen, you listen to—"

"Shh, Richard, lower your voice. This is a library."

A young doctor, who had come in during their conversation and was reading quietly in the corner, was now casting overt glances at them.

Through clenched teeth, Richard hissed. "We will talk later. I must get to the operating room now."

"I bet you do." The heavy sarcasm in her voice stopped him.

The words came out of her lips slowly, deliberately: "I

was trying to find you yesterday evening to give you the good news about the book. I found you all right." She confronted him steely-eyed. "Both of you."

"You mean . . ." he faltered, catching on at last.

"Yes, that's exactly what I mean." She sat down at her computer and focused on the screen, dismissing him.

He stood deliberating for a moment, then moved closer to her. "Listen to me, Ellen. . . ."

She did not look up.

"Ellen, please—I'm sorry."

"You're *sorry*?" she scoffed.

"It was a stupid thing to do, I admit it. But you know it doesn't mean anything. You're the one I'm in love with."

"Oh, I get it—just fucking her, but making *love* to me, right?"

Richard did not reply.

The young doctor was staring at them, openly listening.

She went back to the keyboard, pretending to be concentrating on her task, pretending to be oblivious to him standing there. She could hear his heavy breathing, and, after a moment, his footsteps walking away. Suddenly she felt a sharp pang—he was walking out of her life. Should she stop him? She didn't move.

The glass of the computer screen reflected her face: wide-eyed, unspeakably sad, tears brimming over. She certainly wasn't tough, no matter how hard she tried. Beneath all the tough talk was a soft core that was so vulnerable, so easily hurt, but she couldn't let herself come unglued. Impatiently, she brushed away the tears.

When she came home that night, Ben was out. Sitting on top of a huge salad he made for her dinner was his note—

in the shape of the ace of spades—saying that he was out playing cards.

She had no appetite for any kind of food, but she nibbled on it, trying to force some down, just so he wouldn't feel his effort went to waste. Then the thought occurred to her that she could flush it down the toilet. She did and left a thank-you note, telling him it was the best salad she'd ever tasted. It probably was.

She went to bed, but couldn't sleep.

She felt better when she heard Ben come in—his steady footsteps, the water running in the shower. . . . Just knowing he was home made her feel secure.

But it was more than that. Underneath Ben's gruff exterior she felt the presence of a kindred soul. There was something deep inside him that sensed and understood her pain in a way no one else could. She knew she had no friend like him, not even Goldie, who, when told about Richard and Gina, simply derided Ellen for being too naive. Couldn't she see it coming? Didn't she realize that she was letting Richard get away with too much? Didn't she know those smooth-talking foreigners weren't to be trusted?. . . And on and on. Ben had taken her feelings seriously. He understood how ego-crushing Richard's betrayal had been, and he had gone out of his way to make her feel special to make up for it. She appreciated that more than anything else.

That experience had formed a strong bond between them that was comfortable, easy.

It seemed natural from then on that Ben would have dinner waiting when she came home from work, or that they would go out to grab a bite together. Of course, she had dinner with Goldie sometimes, and he with Milt and

Sarah, but they spent more and more of their spare time together. They had fun.

They went to the movies often, Ben scouring the listings for nostalgic reprisals of all the films ever made that had a tango in them. She teased him about his efforts to force her to appreciate the tango, insisting she never would. But she went with him always. Once as they were waiting in line at the Plaza to see *The Four Horsemen of the Apocalypse* with Rudolph Valentino and joking in their usual way, an old lady behind them remarked that it warmed her heart to see a father and daughter enjoy each other's company like that. Neither one had bothered to correct her; Ellen could tell Ben was flattered by the comment. It had made her sad. Could she have been friends with her father, if he had stuck around? She sure would have tried to be anything he wanted her to be. . . . But it was no use fantasizing over what might have been. She was lucky to have a good pal like Ben, even if he was twice her age.

It became part of their routine to go together on Sundays to deliver food to Jello and the Bobs. He shared her fascination with their ways and personalities.

Once as they were walking on the beach together, their habit now after a visit to the Thunderbolt, he told her: "You know, Ellen, I used to dismiss the homeless—to me they were mental cases, drug addicts, the refuse of society, but now I see them like you do."

"Jello is something else, isn't he?"

"Yeah. I'm amazed, he's profound—a social commentator."

"I know. He might be homeless, but he's not helpless."

"I still can't figure out . . . what do they do about hygiene?"

125

"Well, water they get from Johnny Pump—the fire hydrant. And they bag number two."

Ellen kicked off her sandals, scaring a seagull.

"Geez, watch your feet—there's all kinds of garbage here—you can get an infection."

"Oh, I love the feel of the sand." She wiggled her toes all around. "Come on, you go barefoot too."

"Not me, no way." He had on a pair of heavy cotton socks and sturdy running shoes.

She gave him a teasing look and yelled, "Last one home is a rotten egg!" as she sprinted down the beach. He passed her easily. She was huffing and puffing and holding her side. He was barely winded. "You sure are out of shape."

"Nah—I just got a stitch in my side. Otherwise you'd never catch me."

"Honest, Ellen, you ought to come into my gym a couple times a week. I won't charge you."

"Oh, phooey. Don't try to make me over all at once. I eat your rabbit food, don't I?"

"Okay, okay," he conceded. "But that reminds me. There's a nice supermarket in Brighton Beach—we should stock up while we're down here."

"Oh no, I hate shopping!"

"Come on—you need a little education about nutrition."

"I see I'm gonna get something I didn't bargain for."

"Maybe." He laughed.

He loved shopping. Betty had done it all for most of their married life, and he did not set foot in a supermarket until she got too sick, too incoherent to perform this chore herself. He was amazed when he first went in: the fine spray misting an array of exotic vegetables (what the hell were kumquats, anyway?), the bakery and deli counters like sep-

126

arate stores within the store (you could take home a whole cooked dinner), the selections—freezers with glass windows showing stacks of yogurt, milk, low-fat, enriched, milk without lactose, buttermilk. Of course, the prices appalled him. He remembered when milk was five cents a quart.

Now, pushing the cart behind Ellen, he gave instructions as she reached on tippy-toes to get what he ordered. It was the only way he could trick her into some back exercises. She arched and stretched to get a box of whole-wheat cornflakes.

"You *sure* we want this?" She grimaced.

"Yes."

"All right, but it's one for you and one for me." She tossed a large bag of potato chips into the cart."

"You sure you want this?" He mimicked her.

"Yes, I do—it's a staple of my diet—and you promised not to criticize what I buy."

"I know, I know, I'm just a beast of burden. Carry the bags, say yes ma'am . . ." He picked up the bag of chips, looked at the ingredients, and let out a low whistle. "Check the salt content! Don't you worry about your blood pressure?"

"Oh please, Ben." She sighed.

He wouldn't relent. "The human body only needs two hundred and twenty milligrams of sodium a day and look what's in that bag. Too much of it can also cause strokes, stomach cancer. . . . That's probably why you have those stomach pains all the time—the salt is eroding your gastric lining!"

"Jeezus!" She yanked the bag out of his hand and put it back. "Buy what you want!" She moved over to the magazine rack.

Ben shook his head. He knew her well enough now not to be offended by her sudden outbursts; besides, it gave him a free hand to buy all the things that would be good for her.

By the time he reached the checkout line, his cart was overflowing. Unfortunately, so was the line. Guess they were short-handed on Sunday.

Patiently, Ben held his place with the cart while Ellen leafed through the tabloids. The front page of the *Globe* boasted a photo of desolate Don Arnold, looking pleadingly at his triumphant wife under the oversized headline: DAWN DUMPS DON!

Ben picked up *Sports Illustrated* to help him pass the time and didn't notice that a tall rugged man wearing a ripped T-shirt and holding a six-pack had swaggered alongside him. Suddenly, he realized that the man was muscling ahead of him in line.

"Yo," Ben spoke up, "wait your turn like the rest of us."

"I was ahead of you," the beer buyer announced with a sarcastic smile.

"Wrong!"

Slowly, the man twisted his thick neck to face Ben. "You tryin' to make trouble, old man?"

"Just get behind me," Ben said firmly, "and there won't be any trouble."

"How's this, pops?" The bully moved behind him, but so close that Ben could feel hot beer-breath on his neck.

"That's fine." Ben gritted his teeth.

In the glass door of the ice machine at the front of the store, he could see a reflection of what was going on behind him. The man's clenched fist came up, but before it could connect, Ben deftly eased his weight to his left and sent his right elbow into the guy's gut. The man stumbled backward, lost his balance, and crashed right into a display of Gerber baby food, the six-pack flying out of his hand.

"Now what have you done?" Ellen came running over. "Do you have to get into a fight wherever we go?"

Ben looked at her, shaking his head sadly. "Some clumsy fellow stumbles and I get the blame. Is that fair, Ellen?"

The bully, with broken glass and baby food all over him, tried to stand up, howling that he had broken his neck.

The manager rushed over to see what was the matter.

In the commotion, Ben paid quickly and they escaped without notice.

He left Ellen watching the groceries while he went to get the car and pull it around. Only in New York did the supermarkets have barriers so you couldn't wheel the shopping cart to your car. He found Ellen still reading the *Globe* when he returned.

"Why do you read that trash?"

"I like gossip, don't you?"

"It's all lies—Martians landing in Seattle, fleas bigger than dogs, two-headed babies . . ."

"Oh, I don't pay attention to *that* stuff. But how about this?" She pointed to the cover photo of Dawn and Don.

She had a point. It was probably true.

"But it's so sleazy. They exploit people's heartache. How would you like a headline: 'Richard Screws Gina— Ellen Watches!'"

She looked at him thoughtfully. "You're right." She threw the tabloid into the trash can and got into his car.

11

The book cover was almost exactly as Ellen had imagined—a large red heart dominating the center with the title *Heartbeat: Frontiers in Transplant Medicine* above it and "by Richard Vandermann, M.D." only slightly smaller below. The hospital gift shop had ordered several dozen advance copies, expecting all the doctors and a fair number of patients to buy them. She reached up and pulled one down from the shelf. The back had his photo in a most distinguished pose, staring directly at the reader, attired in a crisp white doctor's coat, a stethoscope around his neck. He wouldn't have looked nearly as handsome in a bulky and wrinkled surgical outfit, the mask dangling around his chin, the funny cap obscuring his handsome locks.

"Sure looks smug, don't he?" Goldie peered over her shoulder.

"Yeah, he does." Ellen agreed.

"You're not gonna buy one, are you?"

"Well, I kind of want to see how it turned out."

"He ought to give you a bunch of them—with all the work you did for him."

"I don't want *anything* from him."

"Atta girl!" Goldie slapped her on the back. "I'm glad you're coming around."

"Goldie—give me credit. It's been almost five months since I even talked with him."

"I know, but I suspect you still want him to come crawling back."

"No way. It's over—for good." Ellen's voice was firm and steady. "You were right, Goldie, I was behaving like an insecure small-town girl—I just couldn't believe that this famous doctor would be attracted to me. But I'm taking charge of my life now. I'm tired of being spineless."

"And your back has miraculously improved?"

"No." Ellen smiled wryly. "But I stopped seeing the shrink. You were right about him, too."

"See that!" The expression on Goldie's face said she liked hearing she was right. "Let me give you some more good advice—you need to start going out again."

"I'm ready—as soon as I meet somebody I like."

"Funny you should say that. What are you doing Saturday night?"

"I'm not sure. Ben's going to Jersey to visit his daughter for the weekend, so I might go up to Amsterdam, check on Uncle Pete."

"Geez—I don't believe you. One old geezer's out of town, so you go visit another? Saturday night, you and I are double-dating."

"What?"

"I'm prying Abdul away from the tube, and I got his brother Ahmed lined up for you."

"But—"

"I know, I know, you've seen Abdul. But believe me, I got the runt of the litter. His brother is a real hunk."

"Goldie, I—"

"Six-foot five. Could have played for the Nicks, got his Ph.D. instead. Teaches English lit at NYU. Just started working on a book . . . you never know, might need an assistant . . ."

"That's how I got into this mess."

"At least you got good experience."

"I guess so."

"So what do you say?"

"Well, I don't know. . . ."

"I'll take that as a yes. We'll have a great time."

The sky was like a gray slab of steel, holding back the November rain. The wind was building, and Ben could feel a slight sway in the Verrazano Narrows Bridge.

He felt a little guilty that he wouldn't be there to help Ellen with her packages on Sunday, but he knew he would also feel guilty if he put off a visit to Marion's again. The typical choice of a Jewish male: to feel guilty or to feel more guilty. He decided that not going to Marion's would be worse. Besides, he hadn't seen her in a couple of months.

There was not much traffic on the New Jersey Turnpike on Saturday morning, and he got to Princeton in less than an hour. Marion's house, which she had insisted on keeping after the divorce, was a stone colonial decorated with "English" antiques. It seemed that things English were highly prized among the Princeton set, and Ben could swear that some of Marion's friends faked British accents.

He wasn't looking forward to the dinner party Marion was planning for tonight. More of her dull, intellectual book-worm types. Why couldn't these people be like Ellen? She too read books all the time, but she didn't put on airs about it.

He parked at the curb and walked up the long brick walkway framed on each side by a neatly trimmed boxwood hedge. He hated that hedge—so regimental, so severe, so controlled, unplantlike.

He took the key from beneath the doormat—Marion had told him to let himself in, she'd probably be out shop-ping for the dinner. He walked in and was surprised to find her home, intently listening to a tape of one of her patients, which she discreetly turned off when she saw him.

"Oh, Father!" She removed her glasses and came for-ward with a smile. She kissed him on the cheek, a dutiful daughter's kiss, and took his duffel bag. "Your room is wait-ing for you." He followed her upstairs. "While you're here, maybe you could help me rake the leaves in the garden. The wind has brought so many down."

"No problem," said Ben. "I'll get to it right away." He liked having something to do, and now was the time to do it, before the rain started. "While I'm at it, let me cut the hedge back a little."

"Oh please, not again."

"I feel like I'm running a gauntlet just coming to your front door."

"What would make you feel more welcome?"

"How about a nice row of white or pink impatiens edg-ing the lawn."

Marion put on her glasses and studied him a moment. "You miss the garden at the house, don't you, Dad?"

"Yeah, I do," Ben muttered, noticing she was calling him Dad all of a sudden.

"Fine then, why don't you come back next weekend? Rip out the *whole* hedge, I'll hire a college student to help you."

"Well, okay . . ." he hesitated. This was more than he'd bargained for. He sure didn't want to come back next weekend. "But let's first see what the weather is like. You know when it starts raining in November, it can rain for weeks."

As if on cue, several drops hit the windowpane; a soft patter followed. Marion walked over to the window. "Oh dear, it *is* going to rain, and I have a dozen people coming for dinner."

"You're not planning to eat outside at this time of the year, so what's the problem?"

"I just hate wet raincoats and umbrellas—that damp smell in the house."

"They won't come growing mold, Marion." He wished she'd loosen up sometimes; she had so many odd dislikes and eccentricities. "And besides, rain is so . . . English."

She threw him a puzzled look, but said nothing.

He ducked out into the drizzle to rake the leaves. Getting wet was infinitely preferable to a long conversation with Marion.

But he couldn't avoid it altogether. He'd come back in, declaring he wanted to take a nap before dinner, and had just managed to stretch out on the bed when she poked her head into the room. "Are you comfortable?"

"Perfect," he muttered, his eyes closed.

But she didn't go away. "Dad—"

Now what's coming? he thought.

"You've worked so hard all your life, and now that Mom is gone and you don't have the same expenses, you ought to take it easier."

"Yeah," he agreed sleepily.

"I know you could never stop working, but why not open the gym just three times a week?"

"And what would I do the rest of the time?"

"Believe me, once you got started on the garden there wouldn't be enough days in the week for you."

He opened his eyes. "What does that mean?" This conversation could not be avoided.

She sat down at the foot of the bed. "My house is so big . . . and you like this room. . . . Three times a week is not much of a commute over the bridge."

"Live here?" He couldn't believe she was inviting him to move in. They never got along. Was she that lonely?

"Why be a boarder in the house of a stranger?"

"Because I like it there."

"Better than your own daughter's house?"

Ah, so that was it—a touch of jealousy. "Marion, please don't start about my living arrangement again."

"You said it was going to be temporary."

"It is."

"It's been six months!"

"You're counting?"

"Yes, Dad."

"What's it to you?"

"I want to protect you from making a fool of yourself."

Ben sat up abruptly. "When you grew up, I let you live your own life—even helped you out with the rent so you could have your own place. . . ."

135

"But what—"

"Please don't interrupt, Marion. Back then, you showed me a psychology book which said that every adult needed to be independent?"

"Yes, but—"

"Pretend I'm an adult and let me live my own life."

"I'm sorry, Dad, I didn't mean to insult you." She leaned forward, resting her hand on his arm. "But do you have any idea how you've changed since Mom died?"

Her closeness and the question made him uncomfortable. He got up and walked toward the window. The rain was stronger now, pelting the glass. To Ben it seemed to be rapping out in Morse code, "Get outta here!"

"All your life you've been concerned with your body," Marion was plodding on. "You're strong, you're in good shape. But no one has yet discovered the fountain of youth."

"I don't need a lecture, Marion," he said wearily.

"But you're so stubborn!" Marion was losing her patience. "If Mom were alive—"

"But your mother is dead and I'm not. Shall I stop living?"

"Of course not. But live sensibly. You're getting older, Dad. Accept it."

"That's enough."

"Look, I'm a psychologist—I know a great deal about human conflicts. I'm just trying to spare you . . . give you some advice—"

He whipped around from the window. "Save it for your clients!" His voice was much too loud. "They pay for it!"

Marion squared her shoulders, but he could see her lip quivering. She readjusted her glasses. "All right, Father." Stiffly, she walked out of the room.

Ben slumped down on the window seat. Out in the pouring rain, the hedge mocked him with its artificial perfection. He sighed. It was the first time in many years that he had yelled at his daughter.

Suddenly he felt very lonely, not so sure of himself. Maybe Marion was right. Maybe he was an asshole, but of one thing he was certain—he'd be a bigger asshole if he moved in with her.

By evening, they had declared a truce. Ben did his best to ease his guilt by helping Marion in the kitchen. It also enabled him to avoid mingling with her guests. They were an even duller bunch than last time.

As he busied himself passing out the hors d'oeuvres, he listened to them pontificate. One tweedy type expounded on his solution to the trade-deficit ratio with Japan. Another discoursed on the greenhouse effect. A short, chubby woman professor with her white hair cut blunt around her head like a Chinese doll earnestly addressed a pipe smoker (ugh!): "But Charles, your hypothesis rests on statistically unproven ground. . . ."

Ben shoved the raw veggie tray under the gesticulating bony hand of a gangly man who was declaiming in exasperated tones: "The Israelis need to accelerate Palestinian autonomy—moving too slowly will simply serve to undermine the peace process." Ben was proud of himself for biting his tongue and saying nothing. This snooty group had the solutions to all the problems of the world. It was easy to mingle in a well-heated room, stuffing one's face and criticizing everybody else. He'd like to see them all spend one rainy night under the Thunderbolt—just for shock value.

"Dad . . . Dad . . ." Marion caught up to him as he was

returning to the kitchen for more food. "Put that tray down for a while. . . . Priscilla wants to talk to you about a weight-lifting program." Priscilla was standing behind Marion. She was a stubby, masculine-looking woman with the good looks of a bulldog; he had heard her earlier denouncing sexual harassment. She should be so lucky.

"Are you in an exercise program now?" he asked politely. She looked as strong as an ox.

"Oh yes, I run eight miles before breakfast, bicycle to work, and I swim at least twenty laps after work."

"You training for a triathlon?"

"Oh, no." She smiled, improving her looks somewhat. "I just enjoy being fit."

"Well, let me give you some advice then. Don't enjoy being fit so much—enjoy life more. The goal of exercise—and fifteen minutes a day is all you need—is not just to preserve your body, it's to help you get more out of your life."

Priscilla's face fell, but before she could say anything Marion interrupted, calling everyone to the buffet table for the main course.

Hanging back, Ben realized that he had quoted Ellen's words to Priscilla. Oh no, soon he'd be eating peanut butter too, he chuckled to himself.

Not hungry, he moved over to the window. In the streetlight outside, the hedge was glistening with beads of defiance. It was still raining, but the rain had found a slower rhythm, steadily soaking the ground. He wondered how the Bobs were keeping dry. They'll be a sorry sight tomorrow . . . Ellen will probably pack something hot to ward off the dampness. The box will be heavier. . . . She'll strain her back again. . . .

He knew he could never last the weekend here, shut in with Marion. He decided to cut out early the next morning.

Hugging the box of sandwiches to her chest and clutching an umbrella, which did little to protect her from the heavy rain, Ellen hurried down the deserted street. She hated to be late because she knew they were waiting, especially in weather like this. But the grilled cheese sandwiches had taken extra time to make—God, she hated to cook. Well, the effort would be worth it if she managed to keep them hot until she got to Coney Island. She had wrapped them in double-thick aluminum foil and packed them in Styrofoam—that *should* hold the heat.

As she rounded the corner, a truck roared by on Flatbush and splattered her with water and mud. "Bastard!" she yelled after him. This was not her day. Yesterday had not been her day, either—the double date with Goldie and Abdul proved strained and uncomfortable. Ahmed was a good-looking, intelligent, and perfectly nice guy, who was obviously there because Goldie had forced him to come. Ellen breathed a sigh of relief when it was over. She hoped Ben was having a better time in Princeton.

Going down into the subway well, she heard the train screeching toward the station and scrambled madly to close her umbrella and extract a subway token from her purse. Of course she dropped the token, and the subway doors closed just as she pushed through the turnstile. She was fuming. Now she'd have to wait fifteen minutes or more. It turned out to be more.

When she finally reached the end of the D line at Coney Island, she was at least glad to see that the rain had stopped. Running down the steps from the elevated platform, she didn't notice a man standing there blocking her way, and she crashed into him.

"Watch it, lady!"

"Oh, I'm sorr—Ben!" Her face lit up. "So glad you're here."

"Miss me?"

"Nah, just your car."

"Well, it stopped raining—I guess I can go back."

"Don't you dare!" She thrust the box of sandwiches into his arms.

"Thanks a lot." He feigned annoyance.

The wheels of his Camaro sent up jets of water on either side as they drove the two blocks through flooded streets to the Thunderbolt. At the turnstile, they spotted Knowledge, a plastic bag draped like a cape around his shoulders, leaning nonchalantly against a decaying chariot. "Good morning, Miss Ellen."

"I'm sorry I'm late."

"Your table is waiting." He bowed in an exaggerated manner as he swept his arm forward. "This way, please."

They trudged after him through sodden weeds, the bottoms of their jeans getting soaked.

"What's this?" Ellen pointed at a fresh mound of earth topped with a small wooden cross. "Looks like a grave."

"It is," Knowledge affirmed.

Ellen stopped in shock. "Whose?"

Knowledge pointed to the top of the roller coaster.

"You don't mean Sunny?" Ellen was aghast.

Knowledge nodded.

"What happened?" Ben interjected.

"Like Icarus, his wings got melted by the sun. Of course, a little too much crack didn't help."

"You mean he fell?" Ellen just couldn't believe it.

"Broke his neck on the spot—died instantly."

"Oh my God. Did you take him to the hospital?"

"What for—he was dead."

"Did you call the police?"

"And have them chase us out of this great spot?" His face said he couldn't believe she even asked the question. "We gave him a proper burial. You go when you gotta go. You do what you gotta do—" He waved them on. "Come on, we're all hungry."

Ben looked up at the spine of the roller coaster and remembered the image of Sunny's legs dangling happily. He glanced at Ellen's stricken face. "Knowledge is right—people die, but life goes on."

She said nothing.

As they advanced toward the trash heap that housed the regulars, the place seemed more deserted than usual. Ben never knew where they would crawl out from, but Ellen noticed something was amiss. "Where is everybody?"

"Choo-choo and Flyer went south for the winter." Knowledge threw a couple of twigs into a rusted-out metal drum where a fire was smoldering under a pot of coffee.

"Where is that?" Ben asked.

"Up three blocks, under the Belt Parkway." Knowledge hungrily bit into a cheese sandwich. "Hmm—nice and hot."

"Sounds like a sensible idea," Ben said. He couldn't imagine what it was like to weather the rain in a cardboard box. "Why didn't you go?"

"I can't take those commuters rushing back and forth over my head."

Ellen was looking around. "Where's Jello?"

Knowledge, his mouth full of food, motioned with his

head to the back of the roller coaster. Jello's refrigerator box had come apart and he sat huddled on the wet ground, looking into space with a glassy stare.

She ran over to him. "Jello, you're soaking wet. Are you okay?"

"Fine," he muttered. "I just need some cough syrup." He was shivering.

Knowledge shook his head. "He's been like this since Wednesday."

"Oh my God, four days?" She felt his forehead. "Ben, he's burning up with fever. We better take him to the hospital."

"I won't go," Jello protested, wrapping his scarf more tightly around his neck and tucking his little mouse in the folds.

"Better do what she says," Ben advised, offering his hand to help Jello up.

Jello waved him away weakly. "Can't leave Junior." His body shook with a violent cough.

"Jello, be reasonable—you need help. I'll take care of Junior," Ellen assured him.

He looked at her through bloodshot eyes. He seemed to be weighing the offer.

Seeing him hesitate, Ben urged, "You know you can trust her."

"I know." Jello looked from one to the other. Another coughing fit seized him. "Okay," he rasped out.

Ben pulled Jello to his feet, but the frail man couldn't stand on his own power. He crumpled to the ground again. Bracing for the load, Ben swept him up in his arms to carry him to the car. It took no effort at all—Jello weighed next to nothing.

12

It was dark by the time they got back to the apartment, and they were both exhausted.

"You know, Ben, it was such a shock to me when I filled out the admission papers—I didn't know his name."

"So what did you put down?"

"Jello, the Bob."

"A name as good as any." Ben's voice sounded sad, hollow.

Ellen looked over at him, but he seemed absorbed in his own thoughts. She went back to her task, rummaging through a closet, searching for something that might make a suitable home for Junior. A shoe box. Perfect. She punched holes in it, then lined it with a paper towel and put the mouse inside. "Don't worry, Junior—Jello will be fine. They'll fix him up as good as new." She set the box on the kitchen table and looked up.

Ben had pulled out a bottle of vodka from the cupboard

and poured himself a stiff drink. Ellen was amazed—she had *never* seen him drink before.

She started to ask what brought this on, but something in his mood—the masklike expression on his face—warned her to keep quiet. She crumbled a cracker and sliced off a few bits of cheese. The mouse munched happily. She closed the perforated lid.

Ben was pouring himself a second drink. Now Ellen couldn't hold back. "I've never seen you drink before."

"I hate hospitals."

"Yeah—I guessed as much."

"That's the first time I've been in a hospital since my wife died almost two years ago."

Ellen wished she had kept quiet. She didn't know what to do. She poured herself a drink too—misery loves company, right?

He had walked into the living room and sat down on the couch. She followed and sat in the armchair opposite him.

He downed his drink. She waited patiently. If he wanted to talk, she was there, if not, that was all right too. She'd just keep him company. Sometimes it was kinder just to sit with someone in silence.

But he wanted to talk. "Betty had Alzheimer's." He looked up at her, eyes so full of pain it stopped her breath. "Do you know what that's like?"

"I know it's a very sad disease," she said softly. "We have many articles about it in the library, though very little is known about it, really. . . ."

He nodded. "When it first started, nobody knew what it was. There was just this . . . this change in her personality. But Betty knew before the doctors did—she asked me to promise never to put her in a nursing home."

"And you promised?"

"Sure—and I had to keep my promise."

"That must have been hard."

"No kidding." He had a look of twisted anguish on his face.

"You took care of her yourself?"

He nodded. "Betty was always such a gay, optimistic person, full of jokes . . . to see her deteriorate like that . . . become confused, violent even . . ."

"Violent?"

"Yeah—she'd get so mad over little things. Beat me in the face with her fists." He let out a tortured sigh. "That was *not* my wife. I felt my wife had died."

He paused. The silence lay heavy. Ellen waited.

"I would sit by her bed. . . . She didn't recognize me. She would just stare . . . sip a soda . . . munch on gumdrops from a candy dish. . . . She would go into a rage when the candy dish was empty. I thought at first she had a passion for sweets, then I discovered that she just wanted the candy dish full—it didn't matter what was in it, nuts, raisins, popcorn. . . ." He stared at the floor.

"And then what happened?"

His answer rang out sharply. "She died for real."

Ellen didn't know what to say. She had a hard time holding back her tears.

He looked up at her, saw the silent solace that she offered, saw the kindred spirit shining through her brimming eyes. Softly, he asked, "You want to know what really happened?"

"Yes," she whispered.

"I never told this to anyone."

Another heavy silence. Then, seemingly resigned to the necessity of this confession, he started in a monotone: "I thought about it for a long time. Then I knew I had to do it—I had no other choice. Somebody had to have the guts to put this poor creature out of her misery. . . ." He stopped.

"Oh, Ben, you don't have to—"

"I want to." He put his head down and in a barely audible voice, went on, "I took a bottle of sleeping pills . . . poured them in the candy dish. . . ."

Ellen didn't dare breathe.

"I watched her sipping a soda and munching . . . until the dish was empty. I just sat there until she nodded off." He stopped again. To Ellen the silence was almost unbearable.

"Did I do wrong?" He seemed to be asking himself. "I've had nightmares about it—but I think I would do it again. I couldn't bear to see her like that. Yet I couldn't break my promise and put her in a nursing home."

"You must have loved her very much."

"I did."

Ben got up slowly and walked to the window. With the cold of the night, the rain had turned to snow. He pushed the curtain aside and stared out at big white snowflakes, illuminated by the streetlights, lazily falling down into the street, where a barely visible white veil was forming over the ground. He felt as light as the snowflakes. Eased of his burden. Clean. In the distance, the rhythmic hum of traffic was interrupted by the gong of the Williamsburg Bank clock. "Hmm—eleven," he said matter-of-factly. "I've got to get up early."

He looked over at Ellen, still sitting in the same position. "I didn't mean to depress you."

"It's all right," she said softly. "I owed you one."

He took the glasses into the kitchen, put them in the dishwasher. "Who does he bunk with—you or me?" He pointed to the shoe box.

Before Ellen could answer, he decided. "I'll take him. . . . Well, good night."

"Night," she mumbled as she watched him walk toward his room, gently carrying the shoe box. He didn't look back.

Sister Clarita said she was sorry, but she couldn't do anything about it. She looked very sad as she informed Ellen that she would be willing to speak to the mother superior on Jello's behalf, but really the mother superior couldn't do anything about it, either. All decisions involving money were made solely by Mr. Ted Grabowski, the hospital administrator. Yes, the nuns technically owned the hospital, but finances were so complicated . . . *et cetera, et cetera, et cetera.*

Ellen knew what that meant. Mr. Grabowski saw life in terms of debits and credits. A homeless man like Jello counted as a double debit. Of course, Jello would be treated free of charge as long as he was an emergency case. After that, if additional medical care was necessary he had to be transferred to the county facility.

Jello had made an amazing recovery from the pneumonia that brought him here. She could see an improvement each day. But he was far from stable, and he needed to be on a rigid schedule of antibiotics. Good food, proper sleep, and above all, no alcohol, would do the rest.

If they transferred him to county, Jello would probably

walk out—it had been hard enough getting him here. In a week's time he'd be just as sick as when she brought him in. And then what?

Jello's preferences were not likely to sway Mr. Grabowski's heart. What could she say to convince him? Logic wasn't going to do it. Maybe if she broke down and cried. . . .

"I'm sorry to keep you waiting." Mr. Grabowski trotted into his office—he was always in a hurry and talked twice as fast as he walked. He was a short, fat man who wore tight tailored suits from which his body always seemed to be trying to escape. Too much Polish sausage. She hadn't seen him for a while, not having any reason to, and he seemed to her plumper than usual. His stiff shirt collar cut into his thick neck, the overlapping flesh struggling for relief. He plopped himself down behind his desk.

"Ellen! It's always so good to see you. With all the complaints I get during the day, it's so gratifying to walk around this hospital and hear the nice things that doctors say about you." He twisted his neck, straining out of his collar. "Now, what can I do for you?"

But before she could answer, he went on. "It's about the homeless patient who came in a few days ago." He had a way of answering all of his own questions.

"Yes, that's—"

"Ellen, you're a good person. And I've heard about the wonderful work you do with the homeless."

"I'm trying to—"

"But you must understand that it is my job to run this hospital like a business. And there is a limit to how much free care we can extend."

"But can't we—"

148

"I'm sure that your friend—what is his name?—Yellow, is it? I had it written down somewhere. . . . Oh, here it is." He picked up a folder. "Mr. Bob Jello will be well taken care of at county."

"Isn't there a way—"

"I know you'd like to keep him here, but there is no way I can justify that unless some doctor would be willing to treat him without charge."

"Oh that would be—"

"You have many friends, see if you can arrange that. And then . . ." he leaned over the desk, the veins on his neck popping out painfully, and smiled, "we'll just have to write off the room."

He did give her enough time to say thank you.

What doctor could she get? She ran through a mental list as she rode the elevator to Jello's floor. There were several whom she had done special favors for recently.

She decided to ask Dr. Fineberg—he'd be her best bet.

"Where's Junior?" Jello greeted her when she walked into his room.

"Jello—be reasonable. I can't sneak your buddy in here every day. You've seen him a couple of times this week—he's being taken care of."

"Oh, I'm sorry, Miss Ellen," Jello said not too contritely.

"Now concentrate on your health."

"I know, I know—when I get outta here I gotta improve."

"You have to stop drinking—that's all."

"Oh, I doubt I'll improve that much." The smile coming through his newly trimmed beard was a happy one.

"Wrong attitude." Ellen shook her head.

A big, beefy nurse entered the room. "Mr. Bob Jello?" she inquired.

Ellen laughed.

"One and the same," Jello announced.

"Here's your medication."

"I don't want any."

"You have to—you heard Dr. Vandermann this morning."

"Yeah, yeah, yeah." Jello nodded and swallowed the pills.

"Dr. Vandermann?" Ellen asked in surprise.

"He's my new doc."

"Since when?"

"Since this morning. They said I was good enough to move to the charity ward, over at county, but he said he'd take care of me for free."

"For free? Richard?"

"He's a great guy, but you tell him, Miss Ellen, I want to go home as soon as possible."

"I'll go talk to him right now."

A new nurse, a middle-aged matronly type, was seated at Gina's desk. "May I help you?" she asked pleasantly.

"Ellen Riccio to see Dr. Vandermann."

The nurse pressed the buzzer and announced her.

"By the way," Ellen was too curious, "where's Gina?"

"Oh she left a month ago—moved to Chicago."

"Ellen!" Richard opened the door with a big smile. "Come in."

"You've taken over Jello's case?"

"Yes."

"Can I ask why?"

"I know how much he means to you."

The expression on her face must have communicated astonishment, because he went on. "And I . . ." He paused, searching for the right words. "I want to make up in some way for the hurt I have caused you."

She looked at him thoughtfully for a moment. He was being honest—he wanted to be nice.

"I appreciate the effort, Richard, I really do . . ." She wanted to put it delicately. "But nothing can change the past." It came out more coolly than she intended.

"I see." He stiffened.

"I am very grateful about Jello," she hastened to add. "I know he can be difficult."

"The pneumonia is responding well to treatment. Not a complicated case, if I could only stabilize that liver of his. His heart is strong, but his liver is cirrhotic."

"What can be done?"

"Nothing—if he doesn't stop drinking."

"Oh," she sighed. "I told him that so many times."

"So, why waste your time?"

Now this was the old Richard talking. She met his eyes. "Because he's my friend."

"Your *friend*—"

He needn't have stressed that word so cynically, she thought.

"—is committing slow suicide. You might help him more by letting him speed up the process."

"Thanks for your advice." She was angry now. She moved to the door.

"I'm sorry, Ellen." He caught her arm. "Please stay. Can't we talk about other things?"

She freed her arm, "I don't think we have other things to talk about," and walked out before he could stop her again.

Milt peeked under the cover of the shoe box and was met by two beady black eyes staring back. "Are you *meshugge*, Ben? Baby-sitting a . . . a rat?"

"A *mouse*," Ben corrected him, "and I'm giving him back today—Jello's getting out of the hospital."

"And you're on a first-name basis with the bum." Milt shook his head in disbelief.

In reply, Ben just handed him his weights.

With a shrug, Milt started his curls, keeping count out loud, "One, two, three. . . . What goes on with you and this girl, anyway?"

"Never mind me, just don't lose count," Ben prompted. "Eight, nine—"

"Are you shtupping her?"

Ben felt a flush coming to his face. "Come on, Milt, she's young enough to be my daughter."

"That would stop about half of one percent of all the men in the world."

"Well, I'm in that half percent, then."

Milt dropped the weights to the floor, which always made Ben wince, then walked over to the stair climber. His face wore a big smile. "If you're not shtupping her, I don't know what it is. But it agrees with you. You look the best I've seen you in years."

Not wanting to get any deeper into that one with Milt, Ben pretended to be busy putting some kernels of corn into Junior's box.

"If you can tear yourself away from your buddy, I've got another rat for you to take care of."

"Huh?"

"I need your help with Don Arnold."

"The crooner?"

"Please, Ben—they don't use that word anymore."

Ben rolled his eyes, "I'm sorry. Song-stylist."

"That's worse, but never mind. Listen—they finally found him—"

"I didn't know he was missing."

"Yeah, we tried to keep it quiet, but after Dawn dumped him he disappeared—went off on a drunken binge. We had to postpone his big concert tour in Japan—that's a lot of yen. Michaelson's going crazy."

"Stop right there, Milt. I'm not gonna sing in Japan."

"Just what I need—another comic. That's what started this whole fucking mess."

"All right, what do you want from me?"

"You gotta take him over—get him to lose weight, get him into shape."

"Will he do what I tell him?"

"I'll make sure he does."

"Okay," Ben agreed reluctantly. "Bring him in."

"I can't *bring* him in. He can't be seen in public in his condition. You have to go to him."

"Where is he?"

"We've got him holed up on Fire Island."

"Fire Island? In the middle of winter?"

"The perfect place. Nobody there to see him. Bars and liquor stores closed. And the best part, the ferry ain't running—he can't get off."

"How do I get there, then?"

"We fly you over—by helicopter from Bennett Field. It'll take less than a half hour. And the chopper will wait and bring you back."

Ben made a rapid calculation. "An hour round-trip, gotta allow for an hour there. . . . Okay, I'll do it. But it'll cost you."

"The agency will pay anything. How much?"

"A thousand bucks a pop."

Even Ellen was impressed when Ben told her about it that evening. "Are you that good?"

"Yes, I am."

"Well, you sure are picking up some impressive clients."

"But the one client I want, I can't get."

"Who?"

"You."

"Oh stop, you know I don't have the time. Besides, I run around the hospital all the day long, I get plenty of exercise."

"But you complain about your back all the time and you know what that comes from?"

"I guess you gonna tell me."

"Yes—sitting at that computer too much, hunched over." He demonstrated by slumping over the kitchen table.

"Oh, I hope I don't look like that."

"You need to strengthen your abdominal muscles."

"It's my back, not my stomach."

"The secret to strengthening any weak area is to work the opposing muscle group. You ever see those musclemen with bulging pectorals who walk around hunched over like gorillas?"

She laughed at his imitation.

"Yeah, exactly. They neglect the opposing muscle group."

"But I don't get how—"

"Here, sit down."

She obeyed.

"Now." He took her hand and placed it on her abdomen. "Feel that?"

"Yes."

"Okay, now tighten up."

She did, and her posture automatically straighened.

"You see what happens?"

"Yes, but it still hurts over here. . . ." She lifted up her sweater and pointed to the small of her back.

He placed his hand against her bare skin—it felt smooth and warm. "That pain should go away as you strengthen *this*." His other hand found itself on her belly.

"If you could hold me like this all day, I wouldn't have any problems."

She looked up at him and smiled, and suddenly an electrical current passed through his hands. He released her quickly. He was accustomed to touching many of his female clients. But this was different. Very different.

13

Ben had moved the coffee table out of the way, pushed the armchairs against the wall, rolled up the rug.

"Turning the place into a dance studio?" Ellen teased him, but she was excited. They had just come back from seeing *Scent of a Woman*. That did it—she had finally consented to let him teach her the tango. The movie made her see the tango in a new light—not as something stiff and old-fashioned, but as something exotic, sexy.

For a moment she had considered putting on a slinky black dress, like the girl in the movie wore, but she chickened out. On the other hand, jeans and a bulky sweater just didn't seem right.

While Ben fussed over choosing the right music, she dove into her closet and threw on a flowered lightweight knit that flared out prettily from the hips and put on flat pumps to match.

Kneeling by the stereo, Ben looked up, impressed. "I've got a serious student, I see."

She smiled expectantly.

"Now, the first thing you need to know about the tango," he lectured as he stood up, "is that your bodies never touch above the waist."

"Such a sexy dance and no touching?"

"I didn't say *no* touching, I said no touching above the waist."

"Ahh, big difference."

"See, the tango started in Argentina, a Catholic country where women were watched very carefully. This was the only way they had to get close to their partners."

"While pretending to keep this very proper?"

"You got it." He approached her, arms extended. "Enough history. Ready?"

She nodded, and he put his arms around her. His touch was soft, featherlike.

"First, we'll start with the promenade walk."

"Okay."

"We're gonna take two *slow* steps forward, not looking at each other, facing straight ahead . . ."

She nodded, remembering Al Pacino.

". . . and then you're gonna twirl around to look at me and we're gonna take two *quick* steps to the side."

"That's all there is to it?"

"No, there is one more step—*slow*—that's where you can take a dip if you want to."

Ellen giggled.

"No laughing. This is a very serious dance."

She tried hard to make a somber face.

"Let's go." With his foot, he hit the stereo power button

and a melancholy strain filled the room. "Now"—he arranged her body—"your hip should be pressing behind mine as you drive me forward."

"Drive?"

"Yeah—in this part the woman leads."

"The woman leads?" She was astonished.

"That's right."

"I like that."

"But don't rock, don't sway, and don't get on your tippytoes."

"Okay."

Ben kept time: "Slow, slow," and they took two coordinated steps forward. But as soon as he said, "Quick, quick," Ellen got flustered and stumbled in the middle of her twirl.

She felt embarrassed; she couldn't even take three good steps in a row. "I'm sorry. I'm such a klutz."

"No, you're not, it's your first time."

"You sure you wanna continue?"

He ignored the question. "Just pay attention to me for a moment." He stepped away from her and embraced an imaginary partner.

She watched him move around the room to the rhythm of the music, his movements fluid, elegant. His tango was different from what she had seen in the movie, smoother, almost delicate and yet filled with repressed energy. He reminded her of a graceful animal—a leopard stalking.

She pictured herself in his arms, and suddenly her embarrassment and apprehension left her. She knew she could do it.

"Now let's try again." His arms encircled her waist. "Walk heavy to the ground . . . like wading through water."

"Okay, I'm ready to get wet."

He chuckled.

"No laughing," she admonished. "This is a very serious dance."

"Nothing like a wise-ass student."

This time they executed the movement perfectly.

"Let's do it again."

"Slow, slow," she whispered, "quick, quick, slow."

"Very good," he congratulated her.

"That's all there is to it?"

"Not quite, but it all follows the same beat. Once you have that down, the rest is easy."

He was right. It was.

He led her around the room, showing her more and more intricate steps—they dipped, parted, whirled, then came together again.

For Ellen, there was something intoxicating about the tango. It was a totally new experience. The melancholy strains of the music hypnotized her, put her in a trance, and at the same time spun her into a delicious turmoil. She had never felt like this before when dancing.

Neither had Ben. He had danced many tangos, expertly, gracefully. He knew he was good. But Ellen, with all of her uncertainty and eagerness to learn, added a totally new dimension. When they had accomplished a sequence smoothly, he felt exuberant, a high he'd never experienced, even when winning first prize over hundreds of other dancers.

He had no idea how long they had been dancing—the tape was on continuous play and he didn't know how many times it had turned over. He just knew he didn't want it to stop.

They were good together now. He caught Ellen's eyes, they were glistening. She was loving it too.

They moved apart in the promenade walk, then came together on the third step, Ellen exaggerating the arc of her back, while her hips pressed against his. Suddenly, he was aware of the heat of her body and it sent a tingling wave down his spine. An erection was forming. He couldn't stop it; he didn't want to. It was pressing against her, but she did not move away and her face revealed nothing. "Slow, slow . . ." she whispered. The words were loaded now. She turned and her eyes locked on his. It was a split-second decision—kiss her or pull back.

He pulled back and bent down to shut off the music, his mind spinning. Thank God he had come to his senses in time. What the hell was he doing, getting turned on with this young girl? Sex was out of his life. He couldn't even remember the last time he had made love to Betty. And after she died, he had even lost the occasional urge to masturbate. He didn't mind—being impotent was just part of getting older. So where had this hard-on come from?

He knew—the heat of her body had set it off. Did she feel turned on, too? Nah, it was just the dance, but she must have felt him against her . . . yet she didn't move away. Leave it alone, he told himself firmly.

"It's late," he said gruffly.

"Yes, it's time for bed."

The words sent another electric wave through him.

Not looking at her, he stood up, letting his hand drop to his crotch to cover the bulge in his pants, and he walked toward the bathroom.

He heard her soft voice behind him. "Thanks for the lesson."

"Good night," was all he could manage.

Under the merciless cold water of the shower, the erection shriveled. Roughly, he rubbed himself dry as if to erase the jumble of thoughts in his mind. He gave his head a sharp shake, threw the towel aside, and went to bed.

He stretched out against the cool sheets. And there it was again. Another hard-on. This was ridiculous.

Then he heard his door opening slowly.

The hallway light sent a soft beam into the room outlining her naked form.

She stood there silent, waiting for him to speak, but he couldn't utter a word. He felt like he was on his first date—fear and anticipation churning within him. He pushed back the covers, inviting her in.

She moved quietly toward him, then lay on the bed, her body barely touching his.

His heart was pounding. He turned toward her and found her open mouth eagerly seeking his. They kissed hungrily, licking, sucking, exploring with lips and tongues.

In the dark, his hands, trembling with excitement, moved over her smooth skin, slowly following the curves of her body. Was this really being offered to him?

As if in answer to his question, she rolled over on top of him. She raised up on her elbows, rubbing her breasts gently back and forth across his chest. He could feel her nipples harden. He cupped one of her breasts in his hand, bringing it toward his lips. He sucked on it, feeling the nipple grow larger in his mouth.

She was on her knees above him now, and the sensation was intoxicating. What a delicious feeling to be the passive one. He who was used to giving orders all his life was now following the commands of her body.

Her hand found his cock, hard and firm, and guided it into her. She was hot and wet inside, ready for him. For *him*!

When it was over, she kissed him gently on the lips, on the eyelids, forehead, cheeks—featherlike kisses—and quietly left the room.

Not a word had been spoken, except at one moment he thought he heard a breathy whisper, "Slow, slow . . ."

The next morning, Ellen was still asleep when Ben left extra early, purposely avoiding her. He knew it would be uncomfortable for both of them. What could he say to her?

Thank her? "Ellen—you brought a dead cock back to life. I'm very grateful. . . ." Oh God, she'll think he'd want it all the time now.

Apologize? "Ellen—I'm sorry. This will never happen again. I don't know what got into me last night." But then, she had wanted it too. She had come into his room. . . .

One thing was certain—they couldn't go on as before, pretending this never happened. It was time for him to move out anyway. Their original arrangement was for two months—he had overstayed his welcome.

That evening, when he came back from the gym, she was in the kitchen, stirring a cup of instant coffee. "Hi, Ben," she greeted him cheerfully.

"How was your day?" he asked tentatively, waiting for her to say something about the night before.

But she didn't. She just chattered on about things at the hospital: the problems Goldie had with her husband . . . Sister Clarita's recent dream of dolphins ridden by angels. . . .

"The nun is nuts," Ben muttered, but he was perplexed.

She seemed happy, perfectly at ease, babbling on. He tried to catch a glimpse of some awareness in her eyes, but saw nothing. It was as if last night never happened. Had he dreamed it?

"Ahh, Ellen . . ." He'd tackle it head-on, get it over with.

"Yes, Ben?"

"I don't know what got into me last night." He decided that the humble approach was best. At least she couldn't get mad at him if he took all the blame. "I'm sorry."

"Sorry for what?"

"Well, aah . . . I had no right. . . ."

"No right?"

"I mean—it was my fault."

"What are you talking about? I came into your room, you didn't come into mine."

There was no denying that. "I know, but . . ."

"But what?"

"I understand what happened. . . ." Ben fumbled; he hadn't expected this reaction from her. "You thought I was coming on to you. You felt sorry for me . . . and . . ."

Ellen stared at him. "You think the whole thing was a mercy fuck?"

"No, no . . . I just . . ." Ben began to stammer.

"Well, thanks a lot!" she exploded. "Here, like a fool, I go around thinking something beautiful happened last night and now you tell me it was meaningless."

Ben was speechless. He watched her storm out of the kitchen. The bedroom door slammed behind her.

He didn't know what to do. He followed her down the hallway and stopped. He could hear muffled sounds through the door—something being thrown down, a faucet being turned on in her bathroom. . . .

He was a class A schmuck. Why did he have to spoil it? Why couldn't he admit that last night was one of the greatest evenings of his life? She called it "something beautiful." She didn't get all tangled up reading bad things into it.

He went into his own bathroom, stood in front of the sink, poured cold water over his face, and stared at himself in the mirror, letting the beads of water drip down into the basin. The face that was staring back was not bad looking at all—a few more wrinkles than he'd like, but full of vitality, curiosity, life. Last night, he learned he was alive in *every* way. It was something to celebrate.

He took a deep breath and walked out of his room. He found her in the kitchen munching a peanut butter and jelly sandwich—her way of thumbing her nose at him.

He sat down opposite her and started smearing some peanut butter on a leftover piece of bread.

He thought he saw the corners of her lips lift slightly in a hint of a smile, but she said nothing.

He took a bite. "You know, this isn't bad. I might be wrong about a lot of things."

"Yeah, be careful. You might enjoy yourself." She had finished her sandwich, and now she downed the rest of her coffee.

"I *did* enjoy myself last night. It . . . it was one of the best nights of my life."

She studied him for a moment, as if to make certain he was sincere. Then she nodded. "Okay." The word signaled both a truce and forgiveness.

He breathed a sigh of relief.

She picked up the coffee cup and rinsed it in the sink, her back to him.

"You have a beautiful ass," he said softly.

The cup clattered in the sink. She turned around. "You drunk?"

"I feel like I am. I feel," he looked at her, "like the first time I ever had sex. . . . It was with an older girl who lived upstairs from my cousin. She led me through it. . . . It was exciting, but strange, too—so many different, new sensations. . . ."

She moved to the table and sat down, listening.

"Ellen, you gave me something I never thought I'd have again. I couldn't believe that last night meant something to you, too. . . ."

"Oh, Ben . . ." Her hand reached across the table and touched his.

"And . . . I guess when I put my foot in my mouth a little while ago, I was really just trying to ask: What do we do now?"

"Well, I'd say more of the same."

He looked at her, astonished.

Her face broke out in a wide grin. "If you got it, flaunt it, use it, enjoy it, right?"

"Right." He nodded, grinning too.

He took hold of her hand and stood up, pulling her along. "It's my turn to lead."

14

The four-foot-high pile of dirty snow next to which Ron Michaelson stood did little to protect him from the biting wind whipping across the tarmac of the private sector of Newark Airport. Milt hated being there, but even he could muster up a little sympathy for poor shivering Ron. Didn't anybody tell Ron that his expensive Burberry coat was only good for stepping in and out of limousines?

Milt, on the other hand, had been dressed by Sarah, and for once he was grateful for her overprotectiveness. Fleece gloves, Russian-style hat to match, two pairs of wool socks in his winter boots, not to mention a sheepskin-lined suede overcoat, were just the ticket for waiting in open fields in subfreezing temperatures.

"Shit, it's cold," Ron said for the twelfth time, his teeth chattering as he stepped from foot to foot in his Gucci loafers.

"It's your thin California blood," Milt kidded.

"Damn right—I should be on a golf course in Palm Springs now."

"Instead of waiting for a Jap?"

Ron stopped twitching and looked at Milt with a glint in his eye. "This commission is worth a couple of frozen balls."

They both chuckled. It couldn't be much longer.

Just then the piercing wail of an ambulance siren got their attention. It was coming toward them, lights blinking furiously.

"What the hell?" Ron looked at Milt for an answer.

Milt shrugged his shoulders. "Beats me."

The ambulance had just come to a stop when they saw a sleek 707 come gliding down out of the sky. They watched the plane taxi toward them.

As soon as the boarding ramp was lowered, the paramedics ran toward it with a gurney. Milt and Ron followed.

An immaculately attired Japanese man appeared in the doorway of the plane and motioned the paramedics aboard. "That's Taro Hashikawa, the son of the boss," Ron informed Milt. "Mr. Hashikawa!" he called out, sending forth a cloud of steamy breath.

"Mr. Michaelson, how kind of you to meet us," the Japanese replied in impeccable English as he descended the steps and faced them with a stiff bow. Although he wore only a suit, he didn't seem to notice the cold.

"What's going on?" Michaelson asked, motioning to the ambulance.

"My father is . . ." Hashikawa paused as if searching for the correct English word, ". . . indisposed."

"Oh God!" Michaelson, who, unlike Milt, understood

the Japanese manner of understatement, was clearly aghast.

Milt shot him a quizzical look, but Michaelson seemed speechless.

"Perhaps we can be of help." Milt felt that somebody ought to say something. "We can arrange for the top specialists at Saint Joseph's Medical Center, the best hospital in New York."

"I appreciate your concern, but we have already made an arrangement with a private hospital in Manhattan. My father's ill health must be kept in the utmost confidence. Such news would have a drastic effect on the company stock values, as you might imagine."

Just then, the paramedics emerged from the plane, carefully carrying their gurney with a bundled-up, inert figure on it.

"Holy shit," Ron had found his tongue. "If he dies on us . . ."

Milt, mindful that the younger Japanese was close enough to overhear, jabbed Michaelson in the ribs. "Relax, Ron," he muttered, "he's still breathing."

His kid-gloved hands shaking—from the cold or from nerves, Milt couldn't tell anymore—Michaelson produced a new set of worry beads and started clicking away as they followed the gurney toward the ambulance.

"I can rely on you gentlemen to keep our secret." Hashikawa bowed to them again.

"Of course, of course." Ron nodded.

As the paramedics pushed the gurney into the ambulance, Milt caught a glimpse of the elder Hashikawa's face—a doll-like ivory mask with a small mustache drooping over the sides of his mouth.

Once his father was loaded inside, the son, with considerable agility, leaped up beside him.

"Mr. Hashikawa," Ron's voice had a near frantic quality to it, "we'll postpone the signing tomorrow."

The young Japanese gave him a disdainful look. "Yes, Mr. Michaelson, that would be wise."

The ambulance raced off, sirens screaming, leaving Ron looking after it helplessly as he continued to flip his beads.

"He hates me," Ron declared.

"Who?"

"The son—he hates me."

"Come on, you're exaggerating, how can he hate—"

"He's against the deal. He was going along only out of respect for papa-*san*."

"Yeah, I guess the Japanese are that way."

"Jesus, Milt, what are we gonna do?"

"Wait, I guess."

"Wait?"

"Till we find out something."

"And I had the legs cut off the boardroom table."

"Huh? What for?"

"For the signing ceremony."

Milt looked blankly at him.

"To make them feel at home. That high-priced consultant told us we had to kneel and drink tea."

"It'll happen, Ron."

"When?"

Milt had no answer.

"When?" Ron shouted, clutching the worry beads with both hands.

Milt shrugged. His boss was a bigger jerk than even he had imagined.

"Fuck! There goes ten million bucks."

Milt couldn't help being snide: "There goes your rosary."

Ron looked down. The string had broken apart in his hands and the worry beads were bouncing on the icy tarmac as if trying frantically to get away.

Ellen watched the helicopter take off from Bennett Field, carrying Ben toward Fire Island. Usually, Milt dropped him off on Sundays, but today he couldn't make it. Something to do with meeting a Japanese plane at Newark Airport.

Ellen had never met Milt. Was there a reason why Ben never introduced her to his best friend? But, on the other hand, she had never introduced him to Goldie. She knew why. It was just too hard to explain their relationship. People might not understand; they might condemn it. This wonderful thing between them was still so fragile. They both wanted to protect it.

She glanced at her watch—she'd better hurry if she was to come back in time to pick him up. She had less than two hours, just enough time to take care of her regulars and get back here.

The box of sandwiches beside her, she took off along Neptune Avenue, carefully guiding Ben's car along the icy streets piled with mounds of dirty snow. Ben's favorite tango tape was on the stereo—it filled her with such a feeling of exuberance. For her, the tango had become a symbol of so many things—of love and happiness, affection and sex, safety and security, and most of all of the man who had brought those things into her life.

She had never known anyone like him, and, she was

beginning to realize, she had never known herself. Through him, she was learning things about herself that had lain neglected and dormant and probably would have continued to if he hadn't come along.

Take sex, for example. She had always thought herself a well-functioning, average female who enjoyed a healthy amount of sex. But making love with Ben was breaking new ground. He could not always achieve enough of an erection to make intercourse possible, but that didn't diminish his desire for her, and together they searched out new ways of making up for the failings of nature. He explored every part of her with his fingers and tongue, taking the time to let her enjoy the new feelings, and she responded in kind. Each was absorbed in learning everything about the other's body, and new and astonishing things happened. Not driven to achieving orgasm by ordinary means, they achieved it none-theless, time after time, and the ecstasy far surpassed any-thing she had ever known in the past.

And yet she felt that what they did, or even how they did it, could not make miracles happen. The miracles came from what was behind it, under it, over it, and around it. The miracles came from the love.

Today, it seemed to her like the whole world was full of miracles, all ugliness transformed into sheer beauty. Driving along, she stole a glance over Sheepshead Bay. The water, with little white-capped waves rolling in, looked so inviting, but it was probably barely above freezing. Stopped at a red light, she watched warmly dressed boys and girls horsing around, throwing snowballs at each other, scream-ing with delight. She felt so good that if she had the time, she'd join them laughing and shouting and rolling around in the snow.

The driver behind her blasted his horn when the red light turned to green, and with an apologetic wave she continued onto Surf.

She pulled up next to the Thunderbolt, and just as she was reaching over to haul out her sandwich box, she heard a familiar voice: "You are late."

Richard, wearing a heavy fisherman's sweater she had given him for his birthday last year, opened the door for her.

She was astonished. "What are you doing here?"

"Unlike most doctors, I make house calls." He flashed his most captivating smile. "I thought I'd look in on my patient, Jello." He took the box from her hands.

"That's so thoughtful of you, Richard." She was impressed.

He followed her through the rusted turnstile caked with ice. "Bought a car?" he asked.

"Oh, no—it belongs to my roommate."

"That's nice. You know you can use my car"—he pointed to his Mercedes—"anytime you want."

That was the first time he'd made such an offer; even back when they were "in the heat of passion" the idea never seemed to occur to him.

"Thank you," she said, not knowing what to make of this. Maybe his recent successes and imminent appointment as chief of staff had made him extra generous.

While she distributed her sandwiches, Richard examined Jello, who protested that this was not necessary, since he was fine.

"You are not fine—I doubt you are taking your medicine," Richard scolded.

Ellen squatted down next to them. "Jello, do you want to go back to the hospital?"

Jello adamantly shook his head.

"So take your antibiotics."

"I am, I am—one with every meal, like you told me, doc."

"How many did you take yesterday?" Richard asked with disbelief.

"One."

"Only one?"

"I only had one meal."

Richard stood up with a sigh of resignation.

"Jello," Ellen pleaded, "you know you have to take three."

"Okay, I'll take one right now." He pulled out a crumpled piece of tissue from his pocket and extracted a pill. He squinted up at Richard. "You really think this will do the trick?"

"Yes, I do."

With a shrug he popped it in his mouth and followed it with a swig from a pint whiskey bottle.

Richard threw up his hands, saying nothing.

Ellen was very depressed when they walked back to the car. "Richard, I worry about Jello—I don't know what to do with him."

"And *I* don't know what to do with *you*."

She shot him a questioning glance. He wasn't going to start that again.

Yes he was. And he got right to it. "Ellen—I didn't come here to see Jello. I came here to see you."

She let out a deep breath and shook her head. "Please

. . . I really appreciate the help you've given me. But let it go at that."

"I won't, Ellen." His hands gripped her shoulders. "You mean too much to me. There is no one else in my life but you."

"I'm sorry, there's someone else in my life."

A wry smile appeared on his face and his eyes locked on hers. He shook his head slowly. "No, there isn't. I know you too well."

"I think that's been part of our problem—you think you do, but you don't. I am telling you the truth—I'm involved with someone who means a great deal to me."

"Who is it?"

The question was blunt, almost offensive, but she decided to answer. "My roommate."

He let out a short laugh, a snort of disdain. "Come on— the old guy?"

"His name is Ben."

His eyes hardened and his arms dropped from her shoulders. "You can't be serious."

"I am. I love him."

The words came out of her mouth so easily. And then she suddenly realized that she had never said them to Ben.

The helicopter flew low over the long deserted beach, where all the homes were boarded up against the wind and cold. Milt had certainly picked a secluded spot to hide out poor Don Arnold. When he said he had "put Don on ice" he wasn't kidding. Anybody walking this beach today would get frostbite.

On a sand spit where the chopper landed a lone dune buggy waited, flanked by two bulky figures holding their gloved hands over their ears to protect them from the roar of the rotors. These guys were Don's bodyguards. They drove Ben to the opulent Victorian home, complete with a lavishly appointed gym, which had become a prison for the singer.

At first, Ben had assumed that Don was nothing more than a spoiled brat. He whined about everything—about the food, about the exercises, about his wife, who wanted nothing to do with him. He was verbally abusive to his bodyguards, who, unfortunately, couldn't fight back. But Ben could and did.

"Yo, Mr. Crooner, you better put some effort in that exercise routine or none of that flab's gonna come off."

Don, who was moving on the treadmill about as fast as a snail, didn't answer, but he didn't speed up, either.

"I'm not gonna tell you again. I'm the boss when I'm here. If you want to work out with me, you follow my orders or I'm getting outta here right now."

"Good. Go. And fuck you." Don clearly had his fill of salads and barbells.

Instead of explaining or complaining, Ben came up behind him and gave him a swift kick in the ass.

Don stumbled off the machine. The bodyguards laughed.

Ben stared them down. "You boys excuse us for a minute. We have some private business to discuss."

When they'd left, Ben sat down beside the pouting Don. "Buddy, how come you act like such a jerk?"

He half expected Don to flare up again, but instead the singer's chin started to wobble. "Because I *am* a jerk."

And then his story came tumbling out.

Don was a poor boy from Louisiana, ignored by a father

who was always drunk. Never finished school. His childhood idol was Elvis Presley. He dreamed of becoming like Elvis, he imitated his voice, his gestures, eventually developing a style that was based on the King's but also uniquely his own. Then Elvis did him a favor and died. Suddenly Don—billed as "The Next King of Rock"—was hot. He couldn't believe that he had attained such stardom.

This guy, Ben thought, who is a superstar to millions, is a jerk to himself. He isn't bad, he's just trying to act like what he imagines stars act like.

"You know, Mr. Jacobs—"

"Call me Ben."

Don gave him a momentary look of gratitude. "Dawn's the first classy dame I ever met. I couldn't believe it when she agreed to marry me."

Ben listened patiently as he described his ex-wife in glowing terms, as if he completely forgot that she was the same tramp he'd caught fucking a comic.

"Where is she now?" Ben asked.

"Palm Beach. Her folks have an estate down there—just use it in the winter." Don looked up at Ben with mournful eyes. "I want her back."

"After what she did to you?"

"Yeah, ain't that stupid?"

"Well, I guess when you're in love you do strange things. You sort of lose yourself . . . or find yourself. It's confusing."

"Yeah, it's awful," Don agreed. "But I want her back."

"Okay Don, but the way to get her back is to get yourself back together."

"Yeah."

"Now come on—pick up those twenty-pound weights."

Don followed Ben's instructions obediently. He was

now putting a lot more heart into his routine. Ben was pleased.

When they stopped to cool down, Don, sweating profusely, looked at Ben. "You ever been in love?"

"Sure I've been in love. I mean, I'm in love now."

"You are?" There was a tone of incredulity in Don's voice.

"You sound surprised." Ben noted wryly.

"Well, it's just that you're a widower . . . older . . . aah . . . you just don't think of old guys being *in love*."

Ben didn't say anything. How could he explain to Don, or to anybody, that here was one old guy who was head over heels in love. Here was one old guy, pushing seventy no less, who felt like a kid again. Here was one old guy who had been sure you were supposed to be impotent at his age, but who found out once again what it feels like to hit a home run. Yes, sir! The sage who said, "You are young, you are young, you are young and then you're dead," didn't know shit. There was a magical zone in between if you only had the guts to step into it. In that zone love knew no time, no age, no handicaps, no limits. And thank God for that.

15

Ron Michaelson's pacing was getting on Milt's nerves. In his restlessness, Ron reminded him of a caged lion—nah, nothing so noble, maybe a hyena or a weasel. As he paced the length of the waiting room of this fancy Upper East Side hospital (disguised as a private residence to protect its wealthy patrons), Ron kept time with his ever-present worry beads. A new set. Milt wondered if they came in different colors—Ron only had brown ones. They matched his Armani outfits.

At last Taro Hashikawa entered. He bowed to them in his usual, deferential way. "Thank you for taking so much interest in my father, Mr. Michaelson, Mr. Schultz." He bowed again.

Awkwardly, Ron returned the bow. "Well . . . we are very concerned about him."

"As am I. But at this time, we can only await a report from the doctors."

Ron smiled, a bit too patronizingly. "Let's hope the news is good and we can complete our negotiations."

"Yes, I know that this is uppermost in your mind, Mr. Michaelson." Hashikawa lit up a cigarette.

It was some strange Japanese brand, very strong, and its acrid smell filled Milt's sinuses. What was it with these people—they smoked like chimneys and had the world's highest salt consumption. No wonder they led the pack in sky-high blood pressure. He had learned that from one of the articles on Ben's bulletin board.

"I would be less than honest with you," Hashikawa continued between puffs, "if I were to tell you that I share my father's enthusiasm for the film industry."

"Ahh . . . I am aware of that," Ron muttered.

"My father has always loved your American movies. With all his successes in the world of electronics, it has been his dream to own a Hollywood movie studio, long before others in our country had contemplated such an acquisition."

So, thought Milt, the Sonys and the Matsushitas beat the Hashikawas to the punch.

"My father wanted this to be his final achievement before he stepped down as—"

The door opened. They all turned expectantly. The doctor who walked in wore a somber expression on his face. Hashikawa put out his cigarette.

"How is he?" Ron blurted out.

The doctor shot him a surprised glance, not comprehending his role in the drama.

The young Japanese spoke up. "I fear, Dr. Howard, you bring no surprises. You may speak in front of these gentlemen."

The doctor nodded. "I am sorry to tell you, Mr. Hashikawa, that your father has advanced heart disease. . . ."

Ron sucked in his breath loudly.

The doctor shot him another glance, but continued. "I see from his medical record that previous bypass grafting has not remedied his condition. . . ."

"Yes," Hashikawa nodded, "he has had four heart attacks."

Ron's eyes were the size of golf balls. If they had not been discussing a life-and-death situation, Milt would have laughed.

"At this point, my evaluation shows mitral regurgitation and ejection fraction below acceptable levels—"

"Speak English, doc." Ron was on the verge of losing it. "What's the bottom line?"

There was a look of disdain on the doctor's face, but he answered bluntly. "His heart muscle is severely enlarged. Of course, we will immediately begin therapy with oral vasodilators, but I hold out little hope. The only appropriate course of action would be a heart transplant."

Hashikawa only nodded as if this was old news.

"You knew this?" Milt had to ask.

"Yes, Mr. Schultz. For some time."

"So, why didn't you take care of it in Japan?"

Hashikawa smiled weakly. "In my country it is against the law to transplant organs; more important, it is against the Shinto religion, and my father is a very religious man."

"But . . . but . . . but," Ron stuttered, "this is a matter of his life."

"Of course, Mr. Michaelson. And I will try again to convince him."

"Excuse me," the doctor broke in, "but although that is

the only option, I'm afraid that your father is not eligible for a heart transplant."

For the first time, Hashikawa's face registered surprise and a hint of alarm. "I do not understand, Dr. Howard."

"In America, all transplant organs are assigned through a computerized system called the United Network for Organ Sharing, and your father does not meet the network's criteria."

"What?" That was Ron.

"He is older than the cut-off age of sixty-five. But even if he were younger, the degree of pulmonary deterioration would render him ineligible."

"You are saying, Doctor—" Hashikawa's voice was icy cold, "that your American system would consider an available heart to be wasted on a man in my father's condition, even if it would prolong his life."

"I would not have chosen those words." The doctor sounded sad. "But you are correct. I am very sorry that there is nothing I can do."

"Wait just a fucking second!" Ron had finally lost all control. "Do you know who this man is? Do you know what will happen if he *dies*?"

"I wish there was something I could do. Perhaps in another country his options might be better—"

"Can he be moved?" Hashikawa interrupted.

The doctor sighed. "That is a difficult question to answer. Any disturbance *could* provoke another cardiac arrest."

"So that's it?" Ron was beside himself.

"There is one possibility—although it is highly experimental at this time. . . ."

They all stared at the doctor expectantly.

"A transplant from a baboon."

Hashikawa's face registered undisguised shock. "Baboon?"

"As I said, it is highly experimental, and still extremely risky. But there is nothing else I can suggest."

"It is out of the question." Hashikawa's voice had returned to its former eerie coldness.

"But you heard the doctor," Milt broke in. "If you do nothing, your father can't make it."

"Geez, man, let's try it!" Ron almost shouted. "What do you have to lose?"

"I would only be saving my father's life in order to force him to end it."

"What are you talking about?"

"He would consider his body desecrated."

The doctor moved to the door. "I am sorry, Mr. Hashikawa."

The Japanese followed him. "May I see my father now?"

"Of course, please come with me."

Helpless, Ron and Milt watched them leave.

When the door closed, Ron hissed, "If he dies the deal is dead."

Milt shrugged. What could he do about it? And he wasn't about to weep for the loss of Ron's commission.

"For Christ's sakes, Milt, think of something."

"Who do you think I am, God?"

"You're the medical expert."

"You just *heard* the medical expert. *Nada!*"

"These Japs have so much dough—there must be something, somewhere. . . ."

"Well, maybe we could slip him a baboon heart and not tell him."

Ron lit up. "You think we could?"

"Oh come on, Ron, I was only kidding."

"No, no, I'm serious, you know that head baboon guy at Saint Joseph's—let's talk to him."

When Ben woke up it was still dark. He didn't move, relishing the feel of Ellen's warm body pressed against his. It must be very early . . . five something . . . 5:14, he guessed. He turned his head to check himself against the clock and smiled. Right on the nose! It was going to be that kind of day—everything going perfectly. The magic of being in love erased all the difficulties and annoyances of everyday life. He had the feeling that today anything was possible.

This evening he was taking Ellen over to Milt and Sarah's for dinner. He couldn't put it off again. Sarah had been bugging him for months, and he had always made some excuse, sure that such an event would only bring disaster. But now all his apprehension was gone. Today was guaranteed to be a perfect day.

Stretched out on his back, staring up into the darkness, he held his breath and listened intently to Ellen's even breathing. He found the sound so comforting. She was really there, next to him. He reached over and stroked her hair ever so gently, not wanting to wake her up.

But Ellen wasn't asleep. She didn't dare stir, afraid that he might stop. She wanted this blissful feeling to last forever.

As his strong hand continued to stroke her hair with feather-light touches, fragments of a poem floated through her mind. . . . It said love was like a small, fragile bird . . . *"and you know it's there only by the faint whirr of its wings. . . ."* Who had written it? Oh, yes, Carl Sandburg, a tough-tender man like Ben. . . .

He leaned over and his lips touched her forehead, so softly and gently she felt she would melt completely. The indescribable tenderness of it broke down all her defenses. She couldn't help herself: "I love you, Ben," she whispered.

He had not expected her to be awake and he trembled in the darkness when she said it. Then he whispered back, "I love you, Ellen."

She buried her face in his chest, feeling his strong arms pulling her close, holding her tight.

. . . and the little white bird's hush song
telling you nothing can harm you,
the days to come can weave in and weave out
and spin their fabrics and designs for you
and nothing can harm you . . .

Sarah's forced smile was frozen on her face as she opened the door. Ben took a deep breath. "Good evening, Sarah." He kissed her on the cheek. "I want you to meet Ellen Riccio, my landlady."

Ellen extended her hand. Sarah took it limply. "You don't look like a landlady."

"Oh come on, Sarah." Milt approached. "How many landladies do you know?"

"My father had a block of apartments," she snapped.

"You're right." Milt grinned. "And he sure didn't look like this landlady."

Sarah shot him a scornful look, but Milt, focusing on Ellen, missed it. "So, after all this time, I finally get to meet Ben's slum lord." He beamed.

"I've been anxious to meet you, too." Ellen took to Milt on the spot. Like Ben, he had a boyish quality; his twinkling eyes were full of mischief.

"I hope you're soaking him plenty," Milt continued. "With what he charges at the gym, he's got to be one of the richest men in Brooklyn."

"Now you tell me." Ellen laughed.

"You go to his gym?"

"No, I don't."

"Of course not, you can't afford it. Who can? I came back from Hollywood to retire, then I became his client. . . . Now I gotta keep working just to—"

Ben cut in. "I should pay you not to come to my gym. You're no advertisement for my technique."

"You hear that, Ellen?" Milt feigned indignation. "He soaks you and he insults you."

"Now stop, you two." Sarah took on her mother-hen role. "And get Miss . . . Rich—what is your name again?"

"Riccio." Ellen offered.

"Get Miss *Richo* a drink." She mispronounced it, as if the name left some kind of aftertaste in her mouth. Then she spun on her heel, muttering something about her pot roast, and retreated into the kitchen.

Milt moved to the bar. "What's your pleasure?"

"I'll take a vodka and tonic."

"Nothing for me," said Ben.

Filling the order, Milt kept his eyes on Ellen. "Ben tells me you work at Saint Joseph's."

"Yes, I do."

"You don't look like a nun."

"I left my habit at home."

185

Milt chuckled. "You know, I do a lot of business with the little sisters over at your place."

"So I understand. Didn't we have one of your clients a few months back?"

"Sure did." Milt rolled his eyes. "And what a fiasco that was. . . . Oh, by the way," he turned to Ben, "Michaelson is very happy with what you're doing for Don. We'll be able to send him out on tour soon."

"Yeah, the guy's really making progress now that he's decided to get into it."

"Thank God that's turning out, because Michaelson, the poor bastard, has had a big setback lately."

"What?" Ben always found the shenanigans in Milt's office very interesting.

"Well, old Hashikawa's still squirreled away in that private hospital. It's been a month, and they can't make his heart tick again. I gotta go over to Saint Joseph's and talk to that baboon expert over there—"

Ellen raised her eyebrows but said nothing.

"I tell you, it's a contest," Milt continued, "his heart or my knees."

They both looked at him quizzically.

"They cut the legs off the conference table, so you gotta kneel. . . ."

"What for?" Ben was still puzzled.

"You know . . . it's very Japanese. . . ." He did a bad imitation, "Aah, so, aah, so . . ." and knelt on the rug. "For the signing ceremony . . ."

"You all are crazy over there." Ben shook his head.

"It's not me—" Milt started when the doorbell interrupted him. "Who could that be?" He struggled to get up.

"Rest your sore knees." Ben chuckled. "I'll get it."

But when he opened the door, he wished he hadn't.

"Hello, Father."

"Marion! What are you doing here?"

"The same thing you're doing, I presume, coming to dinner."

"Well that's a nice surprise."

"Oh, I forgot to tell you." Sarah came out of the kitchen, wiping her hands on her apron. "You don't mind, Ben?"

"Mind? I'm thrilled." A lie. He wasn't the least bit thrilled. He wasn't prepared to take on Sarah *and* Marion in one sitting. But obviously there was nothing he could do about it now. Marion's eyes were already appraising Ellen, who was sitting on the couch next to Milt.

"Oh, Marion, this is his landlady, Miss . . ." Sarah shot Marion a see-what-I-mean look.

"Please call me Ellen."

Marion took Ellen's extended hand as if it were an icicle.

Talk about body language. Ben looked to Milt for help.

"Something's burning in the kitchen!" Milt bellowed.

"Oh my God!" Sarah forgot all about the drama in the living room and ran to save her pot roast.

Marion followed. "Let me help you, Sarah."

"That was lucky." Ben breathed a sigh of temporary relief. "But I don't smell anything burning."

"Something is now." Milt chuckled. "The heat from those two."

They all burst out laughing. Ellen knew that she had two allies in this tense situation.

Soon enough Sarah—who had obviously used the false

alarm to have a heart-to-heart with Marion—came out of the kitchen carrying a steaming platter. "Have I got a pot roast for you people."

Out of her line of sight, Milt made a puking sign to Ben, which Ellen pretended not to see.

They sat down to eat.

For a while, they chewed their way through the pot roast silently.

"Isn't fiber good for you, Ben?" Milt asked.

"Very, very important," Ben nodded.

Milt coughed. Ben wasn't sure if he was choking on the food or trying to stifle a laugh.

"Do you have a family?" Marion directed the question to Ellen, having obviously decided to cut to the chase.

Ellen looked up, surprised. "No. Aah . . . I mean, my father and mother died some time ago, but I still keep in touch with my Uncle Pete."

"I see, I was just curious." Marion paused. "Your father died when you were very young?"

"No, my father died when I was in college."

Marion adjusted her glasses. She played with the remaining food on her plate, as if an air of nonchalance would make the questions seem casual, conversational. "So you have many fond memories of him?"

"I have no memories of him at all." The answer was sharp, direct.

Marion cleared her throat, but Ellen spared her the trouble of phrasing another question. "He left my mother just after I was born."

"*So,*" Marion's voice seemed to grow stronger, "you never had a father really?"

"I had Uncle Pete. . . ." Ellen had laid down her fork, calmly facing her interrogator. "But, yes, I missed having a real father."

"Hasn't this bothered you?"

"Very much so."

They had all fallen silent, absorbed by the duel in progress. You had to be a total dunce not to figure out what Marion was driving at. Here was a psychologist obviously accusing a young woman of a fixation on an older man, and the young woman was not faltering, not defending herself, just calmly taking her on. It was fascinating.

"It is common in such cases—I am a psychologist, you know—to go searching for a father figure."

"Yes—having been in therapy myself—I am well aware of that."

"And has that been a problem in your life?"

"Yes, but then I found the father figure I needed, and through him I've been able to understand my own father, and to . . . forgive him."

Marion, clearly not prepared for such a direct answer, managed only, "Oh?"

"I am very fortunate to have found this man." Ellen smiled, and looked at Ben triumphantly. "He is a homeless man named Jello."

Milt burst out in a violent fit of coughing, and hid his face behind his napkin. Ben smiled.

Marion covered up her surprise by refilling her water glass.

Ellen looked at her sincerely. "You see, my father was an alcoholic, he died on the street. Through Jello, I learned to understand how someone can come to that and not be a bad person. I learned that some people are simply weak, and since not one of us is strong in all things, well, we must forgive them."

Ben's eye grew misty. She was wonderful. Even Marion had to be impressed.

Sarah was not. She had missed the point. "You always take in men boarders?" She took over the interrogation with the subtlety of a jackhammer.

"No, Ben is the first." Ellen turned to Sarah, answering her with the same calm air she had addressed Marion.

"It doesn't bother you?"

"Bother me? On the contrary, I consider myself lucky."

"Sarah!" Ben cut in before Sarah could ask another stupid question. "What's a man gotta do to get a cup of coffee around here?" He had enough of this, felt ashamed he had not moved to protect Ellen sooner. But she certainly didn't seem to need it.

"Oh, oh . . ." Suddenly reminded of failing as a hostess, Sarah got up from the table hurriedly. "Coming right up."

"Well," said Milt, "let's get more comfortable in the living room."

"I hate to eat and run but I'm afraid I have to leave now," Ellen said. "I must still finish a report for the head of Pathology."

"I'll get our coats," Ben said, but she stopped him. "No, you stay, Ben." She winked at him discreetly. "I'm sure your family has plenty of things to discuss with you."

That's what Ben was afraid of.

"How about a little after-dinner drink for the road?" Milt offered.

"No, thank you." Ellen smiled. She really liked Milt, although she couldn't say the same for Sarah, who was now back from the kitchen. But she said politely, "I can't thank you enough for your hospitality, Mrs. Schultz, but I really must be going."

"So early!" Sarah said with a complete lack of enthusiasm.

"And I was hoping to have a chance to get to know you better," added Marion.

"To further zero in on my Oedipus complex?" Ellen's tone was openly cynical.

Marion faltered again, totally unprepared for such a direct confrontation.

Ellen continued, "Don't you think that Freudian theories are sometimes too simplistic?"

"I don't follow you, Miss Riccio."

Ellen looked over at Ben. "Young people are attracted to older people for other reasons than substitute parents. Maybe they want to come to terms with aging, with mortality . . . maybe it just can't be explained."

"Miss Riccio—"

Ellen didn't let her interrupt. "As for me, Dr. Jacobs, it's not so complicated. . . ." She looked Marion directly in the eye. "I just want a man with a slow hand."

It was an audacious statement and it hit the room like a hand grenade.

Sarah shot Marion an uncomprehending look. But Marion was just staring, jaw hanging open.

Ben smiled broadly as Ellen turned on her heel and headed for the door, followed by Milt, who put his arm around her and kissed her on the cheek. "You're something else, sweetheart. Ben is a lucky guy."

"I'll see you at home, Ben," Ellen called out as Milt closed the door behind her.

Milt came back in. "What a way to say fuck you."

"I told you before, Milt, no profanity in this house!"

"You sure have a handful, Father," Marion started off, having recovered at last.

"Quit while you're behind, okay?" Ben had had enough.

Milt tried to break the tension in the room. "Ease up, Marion, you're worse than Sarah. So the guy has some fun for a couple of months."

"It started out as a couple of months," Marion shot back. "It's now been *eight*."

"What's wrong with that?" Milt was playing Ben's defender now.

"Oh nothing, Miltie," Sarah broke in. "When I'm gone you have my permission to play roomies with any young chippie you care to pick up on the nearest street corner."

Ben got up abruptly. "I better leave."

"Oh yes, Father, maybe you could help her with that paper on pathology."

Ben ignored her, walked over to Sarah and kissed her on the cheek. "There is nothing you could say, Sarah, that could stop me from thinking what a great woman you are." Then he turned to Marion. "And please keep your disapproval of Ellen to yourself."

"I don't disapprove. I withhold judgment." Her face was flushed with anger. "My only concern is that no one take advantage of you."

"I'm glad that I have you to look after me."

Marion didn't answer.

Suddenly, Ben felt sorry for her. She had meant to expose Ellen . . . no, worse, she had meant to humiliate her, but instead had found herself the defeated one—a pathetic, lonely woman, jealous of her father's girlfriend.

There was a sympathetic look on Milt's face as they said good night. Milt understood.

Ben felt sad when he left. The dinner had been a disaster. He should have known better. Of course, he might have expected something like this from his daughter. But from Sarah? How devious of her to invite Marion. Women like Sarah sometimes were very strange—so sorry for you when your wife dies, but their nose goes out of joint as soon as they see you with another woman. They liked you better miserable.

Couldn't Sarah see what a wonderful person Ellen was? With her he had some laughs. He liked going to Coney Island to deliver sandwiches to the Bobs. He liked helping her with her problems. He liked *her*. This was the happiest he had ever been in his life. A real friend should be happy for his friend's happiness. Thank God for Milt.

He went down the steps and walked along the promenade. It was not very cold for February. A slight mist was falling, just a soothing dampness, a promise of the heavy rains that would soon be coming with spring. Then he got in his car and turned on the ignition—tango music continued from the cassette. He looked out across the East River; a tugboat was passing by, emitting a low moan as it pierced the thin veil that hung over the river. But the sound was not sad. It was nostalgic. Then, like the fog, it faded into the distance. He sat quietly in the car, keeping time to the tango with his fingers on the wheel, watching the soft silhouettes of the Manhattan towers covered with a thin, white-gray shroud. He never tired of this magical sight. The far-off lights were winking softly, radiating a feeling of optimism.

He drove off with a tingle of excitement—something wonderful was happening to his life. He felt younger, fresher, cleansed by the mist.

The nearer he got to the apartment, the happier he felt.

"Why don't you come with me—it's a short hop." Ben had such a strange sensation of missing Ellen that for the first time he asked her to come along with him to Fire Island.

"I don't like to see people sweating." She winked at him.

"But you don't have to watch—take a walk on the beach instead."

"It's too cold. You just hurry back. I'll pick you up in two hours. Does that give you enough time?"

"More than enough."

"Oh yes, how could I forget? You believe in moderation in exercise."

"I believe in moderation in all things."

"Even sex?"

He kissed her on the lips. "There is an exception to every rule."

Ellen watched him stride across the runway to the helicopter pad. He seemed so young; with a spring in his step he almost danced across the tarmac.

Before boarding, he turned to wave to her. She waved back.

The helicopter blades were turning faster and faster now, and the bitter cold wind rushed against her face, but she didn't leave. She always waited until the helicopter disappeared from view.

From the corner of her eye, she saw a plane landing.

The helicopter waited for the airspace to clear. A few minutes later, it started slowly rising above the tarmac.

Another plane, a small Piper Cub, was getting ready to lift off. Bennett Field sure was busy today.

The Piper Cub rose into the air, moving toward where Ellen stood on the edge of the runway. Instinctively, she stepped back. The small plane passed in front of her, for a brief moment obscuring the ascending helicopter.

A fraction of a second later, the helicopter wobbled in the sky, its blades gone, and fell to the ground with a loud crunch. She stared, disbelieving her eyes. The Piper Cub, still rising into the bright blue sky, suddenly exploded in a ball of flames.

She didn't know what happened after that. She never saw the burning debris fall to the ground all around her because she was racing across the runway toward the still shuddering form of crushed steel.

"Ben! Ben!" she was screaming—out loud or silently, she never knew.

16

She reached the helicopter within seconds. The front of the bubble was smashed to bits, the pilot lying amid the shards of plastic and steel, not moving. He looked like a broken doll. She barely glanced at him; her only thought was Ben—where was Ben? But she couldn't see anything in the passenger compartment past the high-backed front seats.

"Get away, it's gonna blow!" A man from a nearby hangar was screaming at her, but she didn't hear him. A dead calm had come over her. Her emotions were detached from all this, her body moving deliberately, as if in slow motion, to accomplish her purpose. She must help Ben out of this wreckage.

She came around to the side, what had been the top of the helicopter, except the blades were gone. There was just the stump. Steam, or was it smoke, was coming out of the vents around it, and some kind of oil was oozing out. She came closer. The only way to reach the door—now the roof—was to get on top of it.

"Get away from there!" Other men were running to the rescue now, but she was oblivious to it all.

She didn't feel the heat of the engine as she climbed onto the stump and reached the door handle. It was upside down. She pulled on it, it didn't give. She pulled harder, every muscle in her body joining in the effort. The lock popped.

She opened the door and looked in. Ben was curled in a fetal position on the bottom. He wasn't moving.

"Ben, Ben, it's me."

A deep, guttural moan answered her.

He was alive. A flood of euphoria washed over her. Everything would be all right. He was alive!

"Ben, Ben, it's Ellen."

He twisted his neck to look up. She could see his face now. His one eye opened, looking up vacantly; the other was covered with blood.

He had lost one eye. That's okay, that's okay. No problem living with one eye.

"Get away, it's gonna blow up!" The voice finally penetrated her head. She looked down at her feet, where the engine was still whirring, sending out hot steam. Panic gripped her. She should get away, save herself. . . . For a fraction of a second, she was paralyzed. Then, through the steam, a scruffy man appeared in a dirty white T-shirt. He had a thick head of blond curls and he held a tiny green fire extinguisher. Angel Gabriel come to put out the fire. There was nothing to fear.

She turned back to Ben. "Everything will be all right. I love you."

He opened the bloody eye. It was all there.

She reached down, trying to touch him. "Give me your hand."

"Oh God, my back hurts," he moaned.

Some cracked ribs, probably. Nothing to worry about at all.

There were lots of people around her now—firemen, policemen, rescue workers.

"Miss, miss . . ." Someone took her arm. "Let us."

She nodded gratefully.

Ben's eyelids flew open and he stared into the darkness. It must be the middle of the night, he thought, and guessed the time—3:40. He turned to the digital clock but it was black. That's funny—hadn't he put in new batteries just last week?

Suddenly, he realized that he was not alone. Someone was standing in the corner of the room. He strained to see, but all he could make out was the dark form of a woman.

"Who's there?" he asked hoarsely.

"It's me, Ben."

"Betty? What are you doing here?"

"I didn't mean to wake you up—I just came to change the batteries."

"That's nice of you. Thanks."

"No trouble. Go back to sleep."

"Okay," he agreed, and obediently closed his eyes.

When he opened them again, he realized he had been dreaming.

"You sure look good alive, Ben." Ellen's smiling face came into focus.

"What . . ." he mumbled. "Where am I?"

"Oh, our patient is awake at last!" The loud voice that overwhelmed Ellen's reply came from another direction. He turned his head toward the sound, and a sharp pain shot through his body. Every part of him ached. He felt like he had just come out of a rock crusher, churned and battered all over. He groaned.

"Oh, you poor thing." Ellen took his hand tenderly.

"Poor thing nothing!" The loud nurse now came into his field of vision. She was a big, beefy woman whose broad dimensions matched her voice decibel. "Just be grateful you can feel pain, otherwise you'd be paralyzed," she cackled.

There was a perverse logic to that, Ben had to admit.

It was coming back to him now. The accident, the trip to the hospital aboard a Coast Guard helicopter (what a nightmare, out of one helicopter and right into another), the excruciating procession of CAT scans and X rays.

After all that, they told him he was fine. Not one bone broken even, just a lot of internal bruises, nothing the hospital couldn't fix.

"How's my pilot?" he asked Ellen.

"In intensive care. But he'll make it."

"What about the Piper Cub?"

Ellen shook her head. "A young kid was flying it—barely twenty-one—he was killed instantly in the explosion."

Ben muttered something.

"What did you say, Ben?"

"Young enough to be my grandson." He closed his eyes.

"All right now!" The loud nurse lowered the bed rail. "We'll take your vital signs to make sure you're alive." She cackled again.

"You go to nursing school or comedy school?"

That only made her laugh all the harder.

As the nurse took his pulse and blood pressure, Ben lay breathing heavily. Every movement pulled on some bruised muscle. It seemed to be the worst around his abdomen. He tried to ignore a sudden urge to urinate.

The nurse scooped up her equipment. "Breakfast coming up. Choice of lumpy oatmeal or soggy french toast. Take your pick."

"Nothing," Ben muttered.

"Nothing means I get to choose."

"The food's not as bad as that," Ellen said when the nurse had left the room. "And you should eat something."

Ben grimaced. "Maybe later. I think I could sleep a little more." The last thing he wanted was food.

"Okay," she said, kissing him gently on the lips. "You rest up, and I'll go talk with the doctor."

He nodded. He was glad when she left. The urge to relieve himself was now becoming intolerable. He looked at the yellow plastic urinal on his overbed table. He'd be goddamned if he'd ever use a piss pot. With great effort, he turned on his side and pressed the lever that released the bed rail, then swung his legs over the edge. He didn't know which part of his body ached most. Gritting his teeth, he pushed his arms against the mattress and raised his upper torso, his ribs sending screams of pain to his head. He broke out into a sweat and had to brace himself on the overbed table as he planted his bare feet on the floor. He needed all his energy to reach the bathroom, which suddenly seemed miles away. He took one step, but a wave of dizziness overtook him and he crumpled to the floor, bringing the table down with a loud crash.

He lay there in a heap, panting, when the nurse rushed into the room.

"Mr. Jacobs! What are you doing out of bed?"

"I'm trying to take a piss," he mumbled through clenched teeth.

"Well, that's what this is for!" She picked up the urinal, which he had knocked to the floor.

"I don't want to use that."

"You must—we have to measure your output. Doctor's orders. Now let's get you back into bed."

He felt like a rag doll as the hefty nurse grabbed him under the armpits and heaved his battered body onto the bed.

She raised the bed rail. "This has to stay up, Mr. Jacobs. And you have to stay in."

She handed him the urinal. "When you're through ring the bell."

Like a chastised little boy, he meekly took the plastic object. He had no choice, his bladder was exploding.

Obediently, he rang the bell when through.

She was back immediately, obviously taking no chances with his cooperation.

"Ahh," she said, peering into the pot. "Nice clear amber color. And about two hundred cc's. Excellent work, Mr. Jacobs!"

Ben wondered which was worse—the pain he felt in every part of his body or the pain of such humiliation.

Ellen was in and out all day, checking on him. Then at dinnertime, she brought in his tray and a sandwich for herself.

Neither of them ate much.

The night nurse, unlike Miss Hefty Bag from the day shift, was polite and detached—she came in to give him a shot of Demerol and left them alone.

Exhausted by the pain, Ben drifted off to sleep quickly. This time he dreamed that he was in his car. He was driving on a dark road. A big, black limousine passed him— he could see the uniformed chauffeur, but not the passenger, who was obscured by black tinted glass. He felt very, very tired. Suddenly he heard his tires crunching over gravel—with a start he realized that he had dozed off behind the wheel and had veered onto the shoulder. He'd better pull over and stretch before he got into an accident. Up ahead he saw a small gas station. He stopped the car in front of it and got out. There seemed to be no one around. It must be closed. Suddenly the door opened and a horse came trotting out toward him. It was a big, black, shiny carriage horse. It wore a sleek black harness decorated with black plumes. The horse seemed to be coming right at him, and it terrified him. He jumped to the side just in time and awoke shaking.

"Ben, Ben, are you all right?" It was Ellen. She was sitting beside him, watching him sleep.

"Just a bad dream," he muttered.

"Shall I crawl in beside you—to make you feel safe?"

He looked up at her. Her face, full of concern and kindness, seemed especially beautiful—angelic.

"Ellen," he said softly. "I'm scared of dying."

"You don't have to worry. You won't die. You'll be fine."

"Maybe not now, but soon."

"Not too soon."

"I feel very old."

"That's 'cause you hurt. . . . As you get better you'll start feeling like yourself again."

"I *am* old, Ellen—almost seventy."

"You don't seem old to me."

"You know what that fat nurse said to me?"

"Oh God—the Queen of Tact—what?"

"I asked her if I could fill out papers to donate my organs, and she said they have no use for anything over forty-five years old."

"So, you get to keep all your parts."

"Don't you see? I was useless for a long time and I didn't know it. That made me feel old."

"Don't talk that way, Ben. You have plenty of living left to do."

"Ellen, we both know that I'm gonna die before you."

"I don't want to talk about it," she interrupted, rising.

"I do." He held on to her arm. "I haven't thought about it until now, but coming into your life was a selfish thing to do."

"Please, Ben—"

"I couldn't help it. I wanted you so much. Now it seems like a dream that will end soon."

She looked into his eyes. "Never." And she placed her open mouth against his. It was a good way to end a talk about death, to remind him they were both very much alive.

"Okay," he conceded, smiling. "We'll talk about it later. Now you better go and get some rest yourself."

He didn't hear her leave. The medication overtook his senses again, and he fell off to sleep.

When he awoke, he saw that she had never left, after all. She was asleep on the floor beside his bed.

17

"May I help you?" Ellen asked, barely looking up from her computer.

The woman standing beside her desk was tall, blonde, wore wire-rimmed glasses. Ellen had seen her before, but she couldn't remember the name.

"You most certainly can."

The cold voice was unmistakable. "Oh, Marion—how are you?"

"I've been better."

"You must be worried about your father, but the doctors assure me that there is nothing to prevent his full recovery."

"I see you've discussed him with his doctors." Marion's hostility was palpable now.

Ellen hesitated before answering. "I work here. . . . I know them all."

"I thought such discussions were to be reserved for the next of kin."

"You weren't here."

"I only heard what happened this morning—from Sarah."

"Your father didn't want to worry you."

"Is that right? My father didn't want to worry me? Or is it that you didn't want me around?"

This is stupid, Ellen thought, obviously Marion doesn't realize how childish she sounds. But Ellen refused to be made a scapegoat for the conflict between father and daughter. "He has a phone in his room," she said evenly. "He can call anyone, anytime he chooses."

Marion was not prepared for that one. Her face registered it.

"Look, Marion—this really doesn't involve me. You should talk this out with your father."

"You're not helping things."

"What would you have me do?"

Marion's expression softened. "May I sit down?"

Every instinct in Ellen's body warned her not to talk with Marion. This would lead to no good. But how could she refuse? She looked around the library—the magazine corner was empty and quiet. "Let's go over there."

Sitting opposite Ellen, leaning forward earnestly, Marion might have been talking to a troubled patient instead of a woman whom she'd just attacked. "Ellen, you have a great deal of influence on my father—he trusts you, but . . . you are very young, probably half his age, that means a *thirty-five-year* age difference. . . ."

Ellen listened, waiting for the ax to fall. She didn't have long to wait.

"Didn't it ever occur to you that your relationship might be unhealthy—for both of you?"

"No." Ellen's answer was flat, firm. She doubted that anything she could say would change Marion's opinion anyway.

"I've had a great deal of training as a psychologist," Marion continued, "and I must tell you that volumes exist on the subject of aging men trying to deny the inevitable and making fools of themselves over younger women."

"Volumes also exist on father-daughter conflicts."

Marion stiffened slightly, but didn't lose her composure. "Look, Ellen, I sense your hostility toward me . . . but I am only concerned for my father. Don't you see how selfish you are?"

"Selfish?"

"Things might seem very romantic to you now, but in a couple of years when his arthritis is bothering him, when he has trouble walking or is in a wheelchair, you'll find yourself a younger man and leave him—destroyed."

Ellen rose—it was time to bring this conversation to an end. "Let's get this straight: I have a commitment to Ben, and that means I will stick by him, no matter what. It isn't a chore, Marion, when you love somebody."

Marion got up also. She had no choice—she was being dismissed. "Your attitude is clear," she said at the door. "You leave me no alternative."

What did that mean? Watching her stride out of the library, Ellen shivered. Marion was clearly determined to break up her relationship with Ben. She couldn't succeed, but she sure could make things ugly.

Richard interlocked his well-manicured surgeon's fingers and leaned back in his chair. A hint of a smile curled around his lips as he listened politely to the three men sitting in front of him.

Taro Hashikawa was speaking. "Dr. Vandermann— while I agreed, at the behest of these gentlemen"—he nodded in the direction of Milt and Ron—"to meet with you, since you are the most highly regarded heart transplant specialist, I made it perfectly clear that a baboon transplant would not be acceptable to my father."

"I understand." Richard's voice was matter-of-fact. "However, I must tell you that your options are very limited since your father does not qualify under the rules of the United Network for Organ Sharing."

"So I have been told repeatedly." Hashikawa's voice registered a slight impatience. "But I am beginning to learn that such rules can be bent. Didn't your Governor Casey of Pennsylvania receive a heart *and* liver without the customary wait?"

"I am not privy to all the information regarding that case," Richard answered calmly. "However, Governor Casey was very lucky, because no matter what rules may have been bent—if indeed any were—compatible organs were available immediately. That is rarely the case."

"Look, doc." Ron, who had promised Milt he'd keep his cool, and who had been keeping to it even though he fidgeted through the entire meeting, couldn't contain himself. "Somebody here ought to tell you that money is no object."

Richard's eyebrows went up slightly. "If you mean that funds are available to purchase a heart in a country where such sales are legal—India or Egypt, for example—you still have to overcome one of two problems"—he raised one long finger—"finding a way to bring the heart into the United

States in less than five hours. Or"—he raised another finger—"transporting the patient to the site, a journey he is not likely to survive." He shook his head. "A baboon transplant is your best—indeed, your *only*—option."

Hashikawa's eyes never left Richard. "Dr. Vandermann," he said softly, "may I speak with you privately?"

"Of course." Richard nodded.

Milt jumped up, pulling on Ron's sleeve. "We'll be outside if you need us, Mr. Hashikawa."

The Japanese ignored them completely.

"What the hell's he up to?" Michaelson looked to Milt when the door closed behind them.

"Don't worry. You know how secretive Japs are. But leave it to Vandermann. He'll work it out. You just sit tight." Milt picked up a brown paper bag and moved to the door. "If you need me I'll be in room three-oh-seven."

"Where you going?"

"I gotta give this"—he held up the bag—"to a friend who was in an accident."

"But I need you here." Michaelson seemed alarmed.

"Ronnie baby . . . relax. Money can do anything."

"Huh?"

Milt gave his worried boss a big wink. "I have a feeling that the good doctor might just find a little heart beating around somewhere."

"I've brought you some chicken soup, Dad—the way Mom used to make," Marion greeted Ben in lilting tones.

"Thanks," he muttered without enthusiasm.

"No matter how advanced medicine becomes," she went on cheerfully, "there is still no antibiotic that beats this."

She patted the container. "I'll have it heated at the nurse's station and you can sip it slowly through a straw."

"I can use a spoon."

"Of course you can."

"And I'm already full of chicken soup."

"What do you mean?"

"Milt was just here and brought me a gallon of it from Sarah."

"Oh." She seemed disappointed, but she brightened quickly. "I've had a long talk with your doctor, and he's willing to discharge you soon. He says you're going to be just fine."

"I feel like shit."

"Of course there is bound to be pain for some time, after the internal bruising you suffered, but that will go away. We must be patient. I've fixed up a room behind the kitchen, so that—"

"No, I'm going back to Ellen's."

For a moment she looked at him, as if weighing what to say next. Then she moved closer to the bed. "Dad . . . why should a stranger take on the responsibility of getting you back on your feet? Do you think it's fair to put that burden on her?"

"Marion—" Ben started to answer, but she cut him off again.

"Please, Dad . . . don't be unfair to such a sweet young girl. This accident was *very* serious. It means a lot of changes for you. First, we must close up the gym—"

"No way." Ben shook his head so vigorously that he sent spasms of pain into his neck and shoulders.

"Be sensible. You can't go back to lifting those weights.

You're lucky to get out of this alive. And, don't forget, you're almost seventy years old."

"I know how old I am!" he snapped.

"Dad, you're angry with me because I am saying things that you don't want to hear. But if I don't say them, who will? And deep down inside you know I'm right."

"Marion, leave me alone." He had no strength to argue with her. He felt very very tired.

"You'll be more comfortable in Princeton. I'll get a new television set with a remote control—"

"I don't want it."

"Your spirits will perk up once you're out of this horrible hospital. Your self-esteem is down when you're in pain and looking like this." She approached him and brushed the back of her hand against his stubbly beard. "I'll give you a nice clean shave."

"Please! I won't even let Miss Hefty Bag shave me."

As if on cue, the big, beefy nurse came bouncing in. "Visiting hours are over. Time for medication."

Marion moved toward the door. "Think about what I said, Dad."

He didn't answer.

"I'm your daughter. I want to take care of you."

"Take care of yourself."

"All right, Dad. Just remember, I'm always there for you."

Ben closed his eyes.

"I see you had a nice talk with your daughter," the nurse bubbled. "What a sweet girl—looks just like you, too."

"Yeah," he muttered.

"Open up!" The nurse held out a plastic cup, which she was stirring with a spoon.

"What's that?"

"I told you, Mr. Jacobs, Demerol often brings on constipation. You haven't had a b.m. in two days. We can't send you home with an impaction. But this will take care of it." And she handed him the milky liquid.

She waited until he drank it all, then triumphantly took the cup out of the room.

When the door closed behind her, Ben forced back the tears that were seeping into the corners of his eyes. Marion had upset him. She said so many things he had thought himself. He never felt so old in his whole life.

Goldie was absorbed in a magazine article when Ellen caught up to her outside the nurses' locker room. "Ready for a coffee break?"

Goldie nodded, but continued reading.

"What's so absorbing?"

"This article on safe sex—did you know a woman can put a rubber on a guy without him knowing it?"

"You're kidding."

"No. See, you take the rubber—"

"What rubber?" Sister Clarita was standing behind them.

"Rubber gloves," Goldie covered without a blink of an eye. "Nowadays before I do anything I wear rubber gloves— don't you, Sister?"

"Always." The nun gave Goldie a surprised look. "It's mandated by universal precautions . . . but no matter how well you protect yourself, the Lord decides in the end."

"You said it, Sister—took the words right out of my mouth." Goldie smiled sweetly.

"Would you like to join us for a cup of coffee, Sister?" Ellen asked.

"Oh dear, thank you, but I just got a call from the emergency room—a public relations problem I must take care of."

They watched her disappear down the hall, her long dress covering her feet so that she seemed to be floating off like a Manzù sculpture.

"Is she a kook, or what?" Goldie rolled her eyes.

"Oh, no," Ellen disagreed vehemently. "She may seem goofy at times, but she's got it all together. And she's excellent at what she does. You can bet if the emergency room called her in, there's a special wrinkle."

There was. When they left the cafeteria after their coffee break, they saw her again. She stood in the hallway encircled by a group of Hasidic men dressed in long black coats and black hats, with locks of hair hanging down their bearded faces. They were all gesticulating wildly, obviously highly agitated. Sister Clarita, looking like one of them in her black habit, was trying to soothe them.

"How did they end up here?" Ellen was utterly astonished. The last place you'd find an ultra-Orthodox Jew was in a Catholic hospital.

A doctor emerged from the emergency room, and the men scurried to surround him.

"Hey, Sister." Goldie motioned to the momentarily abandoned nun. "What happened?"

"Oh dear, another racial war. Poor Moishe."

"Is Moishe the victim or the perpetrator?" Goldie wanted to know.

"He's the Hasidic student who was shot during a field trip to the Aquarium. These are all his . . ." She waved her hand, at a loss for words, ". . . fathers."

Goldie puffed out her cheeks and let out a stream of air. "Now don't tell me a black did it."

Sister Clarita frowned. "What difference does the color of the assailant make?"

"Ever since that goddamn rabbi's car hit that little girl, Brooklyn's been a war zone." Goldie was upset. "Fourth victim in six months!"

Ellen took Goldie by the arm. "Come on, let's get out of here."

But Goldie was still distraught. "That poor Jew boy. You know, I feel sorry for kids today—gang wars, drugs, trying to find a job that's not there, AIDS. . . . Shit, they don't have a chance."

"The Lord in his wisdom—" Sister Clarita started, but the Hasidic men surrounded her again, and her words were muffled by the folds of their coats.

"Brussel sprouts, spinach, cauliflower, mushrooms, carrots . . ." Ellen was enumerating on her fingers, "romaine lettuce, Bibb lettuce, arugula, bran flakes, brown sugar, whole-wheat bread . . ." She took a breath.

Ben smiled. "And you got all that for me?"

"It was easy. I just bought all the things I hate."

He laughed and immediately winced.

"What's the matter?"

"Oh nothing, nothing—just a slight cramp in my stomach."

It was more than a slight cramp. Miss Hefty Bag's mighty potion had outdone itself and was galloping to the finish line. He pressed the call button to summon the nurse.

"In honor of your homecoming," Ellen continued, unaware of the magnitude of his discomfort, "I am giving you both sides of the refrigerator."

Ben had stopped listening. The cramps were becoming even more urgent.

"Where the hell is the nurse?"

"What is it, Ben? Can I help you?"

"Just get the nurse—quick."

Ellen dove into the hallway, but came back immediately. "They have an emergency down the hall, someone will be here in just a few minutes."

Ben knew he didn't have a few minutes. The urge to eliminate was now unbearable.

He lowered the bed rail, threw his legs over the side, and with superhuman effort pushed his bruised body into a standing position.

"Ben, what is it?"

Silently, he motioned toward the bathroom, fearful that speaking would break the last remnants of his self-control.

"Lean on me," she offered.

He did and, with her help, managed to shuffle across the room.

At last they were in the bathroom. Reaching to grab the rail next to the sink, he stopped, arrested, even in this great discomfort, by the reflection in the mirror.

The image revolted him: A bent-over scruffy old man was hanging on to a beautiful young woman helping him to the toilet.

18

The air around Ellen felt electric; the sun shone brightly, not a cloud in a crystal blue sky. She took a deep breath— lilacs! Where was that intoxicating smell coming from at this time of year? She didn't care. But the whole world felt right, because today Ben was coming home.

She ran up the stairs of the hospital, two steps at a time. In the lobby, she pushed the elevator button repeatedly, impatient to get to his floor. She couldn't wait till she got him home. He'd be so surprised! There was a banner hanging up in the living room spelling out WELCOME HOME, all the things he loved to eat stocked in the refrigerator, and a new tango tape on the stereo. She had even gone to Gage & Tollner to pick up a quart of the she-crab soup he liked so much. And she got Milt to bring over some of Ben's gym equipment—just a couple of weights and a small bench press—to help him in his recovery.

She practically flew down the hospital corridor, nearly smashing into the nurse who was dispensing morning medication. She burst through the door of his room and—

She stopped, confused. The room was empty. She looked at the door again. Yes, this was room 307. But where was Ben?

Suddenly fear gripped her. Something had gone wrong during the night! He must have been transferred to ICU.

Breathless, she reached the nurses' station. "Where's Ben?"

"Oh, Ellen, hiaya doing?" The big, beefy nurse recognized her.

"What happened to Ben?"

"He checked out about a half hour ago."

"Checked out? He didn't wait for me?"

"His daughter picked him up."

"His daughter?"

"Yeah, Marion. Isn't that her name?"

"Where did they go?"

"Lemme see, I wrote it down." The nurse reached for the chart. "She wanted a copy of all his records forwarded there."

It was a Princeton address: 447 Queensbury Lane.

Streaking over the Verrazano Narrows Bridge in a Dollar Rent-a-Car, Ellen bit her lip till it bled. The bastard! The goddamn bastard! How could he just decide to go to his daughter's and not even tell her? Of course, she knew how forceful Marion could be. But goddamn it—why was he so weak? Why did he let his daughter manipulate him? Didn't he know how hurt she'd be?

She gripped the steering wheel more tightly to try and

control her trembling hands, but she couldn't control the sick, empty feeling that was rising in her stomach—a creeping panic that something else was wrong . . . that Ben hadn't just gone to Marion's house to recover . . . that Ben had abandoned her.

Marion smiled sweetly. "Now Dad, why don't you lie down, watch some TV or take a nap. I'll get lunch started."

"I'm not hungry," Ben answered in a hollow voice as he lowered his aching body into an armchair. He hurt all over, but his head hurt the worst.

Marion disappeared into the kitchen, and Ben closed his eyes. He didn't know how long he had sat there suffering when, through the excruciating throbbing in his head, he heard a ringing. It reverberated loudly through his skull, then stopped. He pressed his palms to his temples. The ringing repeated itself. He realized that it was coming from someplace outside his head. The doorbell.

"Who could that be?" Marion chirped, hurrying to open the door.

On the threshold, pale-faced and wide-eyed, stood Ellen, breathing heavily as if she had run several blocks to get there.

The two women confronted each other for a moment.

"I want to speak with Ben," Ellen said softly, her breathing quieting down.

"I'm sorry, he can't—" Marion started, but Ellen had already advanced into the living room and was staring at Ben sitting there.

He looked so vulnerable, so broken, that the anger she had been nursing all the way down the New Jersey Turnpike dissolved. "We have to talk, Ben," she said softly.

"Come on in." His voice sounded tired, defeated.

She wanted to put her arms around him, hold on to him tightly and tell him it didn't have to be this way, but she didn't dare.

"Father, I'll be in the kitchen, if you need me." Marion announced, then retreated as Ellen slowly came forward to face Ben.

He couldn't look at her. His head felt too heavy to lift. Instead, he looked down at the brown corduroy slippers Marion had put on his feet a few minutes ago.

"How could you?" she asked simply.

"Because I'm a coward."

"Ben, Ben." Her voice cracked. "You don't belong here." She sat down on the footstool by his feet. It was impossible for him not to look at her now.

"Where do I belong, Ellen?"

"How can you ask that? With me! You know that we belong together."

He shook his head. "It's wrong."

"I love you—how can that be wrong?"

The hurt mixed with love in her eyes was too much for him to bear; he focused on his slippers again. "I can't go on being selfish."

"Don't bring up that nonsense again, please."

"It's not nonsense. I can't go on living in make-believe."

"Make-believe? What we had together wasn't real?"

"Come on, Ellen. You know what I mean. I'm thirty-five years older than you."

"Yak, yak, yak," she retorted, "Polly wants a cracker."

The remark was so incongruous that he looked at her, startled.

"You sound like a parrot—repeating everything Marion says."

"It's not just Marion. I know now that we have no future together. I saw that in the mirror."

"What?"

"You leading an old man to the toilet."

"Wouldn't you do the same for me?"

"But I want you to have a good life, not end up being a nurse to an old man."

"I want to be a nurse to an old man."

"Aah, go see a shrink—you're nuts."

"And you're a bastard. But don't think you can drive me away by being cruel. It won't work. I love you too much."

His head sank onto his chest again. "I'm sorry, Ellen, I've made up my mind—I just can't ruin your life this way."

"Let me worry about ruining my life, okay?"

He didn't answer. The silence seemed to be stretching into eternity. Finally, she said very softly, "I think I understand, Ben. It's not me you're worried about. It's you. You can't accept that for the first time in your life you're dependent on somebody. Well, it happens to all of us—we get sick, we have accidents." Her hand touched his gently. "We help one another."

He shook his head slowly from side to side. "I'm sorry, Ellen, I *just can't* do it."

She jumped up to her feet, wounded, rejected. "You can't do it? What does that mean?" Her voice cracked as it rose. "You write off our whole relationship—everything we meant to each other—with 'I can't do it'!" She was shouting now.

"Miss Riccio!" Marion strode into the room like a drill

sergeant. "I will not have you upsetting my father like this. Please leave."

"Ben! Answer me!" Ellen's voice was the cry of someone drowning.

But Ben just sat there, his head lowered.

He did not look up until he heard the door close.

Then he rose slowly, bracing himself against the chair. Marion immediately grabbed his arm. He jerked it away, even though the movement hurt like hell.

"I'm not a cripple," he muttered through clenched teeth.

"Of course you're not. But you've got to be patient," Marion chirped. "A patient patient."

He tried to take a step, but fell back in the chair. Marion didn't say anything, though her look said in blazing neon lights, "See what I told you."

With great effort, determined not to let her get the best of him, he stood up again. Holding on to the wall, he made it slowly, step by excruciating step, to the room behind the kitchen she had fixed up for him so he wouldn't have to climb the stairs. He was covered with sweat by the time he lowered himself onto the bed. He closed his eyes.

"Take a sip." Marion was pressing a water glass to his lips.

He was thirsty, but he shook his head. Some of the water spilled on his chin.

Marion sighed in exasperation. "Please, Dad—don't be a child. The doctor said you must have plenty of liquids."

Ben clenched his teeth to prevent the words he was thinking from coming out.

Somewhere inside of him, a voice was crying out, "Ellen, come back!" But it was muffled, buried deep down, crushed under a blanket of depression too heavy to push aside.

Later, Ellen couldn't remember how she got home that day. She cried so hard driving back that at times she couldn't see the road in front of her. But she returned the rent-a-car and managed to take the subway back to the apartment somehow. Once home, she flung herself on the bed. She sobbed until she exhausted herself, slept fitfully, woke up, remembered ... and her heart broke all over again.

She understood for the first time why people are driven to commit suicide—the emptiness inside is just too much to endure. She had not felt this way when she discovered Richard with Gina. Then she had been hurt and angry, but not destroyed. Ben was the first man who had destroyed her, because she had given him the power to. Loving somebody, like she loved Ben, meant stripping yourself of even the smallest fragments of self-protection, trusting completely that the other won't damage the most vulnerable part of yourself. How could he betray so much trust? How could he?

Yet a small voice inside her said that he couldn't, that he wouldn't ... that he'd come back. Each time she heard footsteps, she thought maybe it was him, and each time the disappointment brought on a new flood of tears.

By morning, all the muscles in her body ached. She could barely get out of bed. When she stood up, she doubled over with pain. By the time she reached the bathroom, she vomited. She called the hospital to say she wouldn't be in—she was taking a sick day.

She was sicker the next day. She couldn't tell if she had the flu or if it was her suspected ulcer acting up, or if the whole thing was psychosomatic, but she was strangely grateful. The acuteness of the physical discomfort was welcome—it overwhelmed the unrelenting pain gnawing at her heart.

On the third day she called him. Marion, coolly polite, answered the phone.

"May I speak with Ben Jacobs, please."

"Who is it?" Marion's voice hardened.

"Ellen Riccio."

"Yes, I recognize your voice."

There was a pause.

"May I speak to him, please?" she repeated.

"Miss Riccio, my father is sleeping now, but I'll give him your message. If he wants to talk to you, I'm sure he'll call you."

The line went dead.

Ellen was sorry that she had called—she had hoped so much to hear his voice, had convinced herself he'd call back, that when he didn't, the disappointment brought back another flood of emotion. She resolved not to call again.

A week later, she made herself go back to work. She moved like a zombie, felt like death warmed over, and obviously looked it, too, because Goldie freaked when she saw her.

Ellen hated to tell her friend what happened, expecting a long, loud lecture. But Goldie said nothing. She just put her arms around Ellen, held her close, kissed her on both cheeks, and handed her a fistful of Valium. She was a true friend who knew when it was time to shut up.

A few days later, the gnawing pain eased, to be replaced

by something worse—an oppressive feeling that nothing she did mattered, that there was no point to it all. She did her job as before, but totally without enthusiasm. She was a machine, going through the motions by rote.

She called Uncle Pete, who, thrilled to hear from her, immediately insisted she come up to Amsterdam for a visit. She promised she would. She even mulled over moving back there. Why not? What was here to keep her in Brooklyn? She'd have to give up the apartment anyway—she couldn't afford it. She started putting some of her things into boxes. . . .

Should she clean out Ben's room? Yes! Get rid of all reminders of him—once and for all! With determination, she opened the door to his room. Instantly, she melted. Everything was there as he had left it. Oh God.

To recover her firmness of purpose, she tried to muster some anger, to recall all the hurtful things he had said to her. "I'm too old, you're too young, it's wrong. . . ." She believed none of it. He wasn't that noble. He loved her but for his goddamn ego. He just couldn't stand being weak and dependent on a woman who was his lover. Well, fuck him. She made herself remember his faults—that narcissistic way he had of looking at himself in the mirror, stroking his neatly trimmed mustache, running his hand through the mass of steel gray hair. Such conceit. Of course she used to think how cute it was whenever she caught him doing it. . . .

She walked into his bathroom. On the sink was a half-squeezed-out tube of toothpaste, no cap. It had been there since the morning of the accident. Probably all dried out. But she didn't throw it out. Carefully, she replaced the cap and put it on the shelf in the medicine cabinet next to his toothbrush and dental floss.

She remembered the night she'd got up from his bed, while he was sleeping so peacefully. She had walked quietly to the bathroom in the dark, not wanting to wake him by putting on the light. Damn! Her bare bottom had hit the cold porcelain. Naturally, the seat was up. She couldn't complain—after all, it was his bathroom and he was paying rent.

She bit her lip and put the toilet seat down again. She left his room and closed the door tightly. It would remain that way, a symbol of a part of her life that she had to block out.

A month later she told Goldie she was over Ben, but she still caught herself absentmindedly doodling his doodles: a weeping toilet, the ace of spades, a bunch of flowers. . . . She knew she had lied to Goldie—she was over nothing.

Day after day she'd come to work and rip off a page from the calendar and think that somehow she had survived another twenty-four hours.

When she ripped off April 6, she realized that Ben's birthday was three days away. It would be a hard day for him—he'd be seventy years old!

Maybe she should send him a card, or a letter, something that said she accepted his decision, forgave him, wished him well.

By the time she got home that night, she knew it was the right thing to do—the birthday wish would also underscore her resolve to get over him, to get on with her life. The decision made her feel better. The thought crossed her mind that people who were considering suicide also felt better once they made the decision to go through with it. She sat down to write.

19

Restless, Ben turned over in bed, adjusted his pillow, closed his eyes again. He didn't guess the time. He didn't care what time it was. He didn't care if he ever got up. Without Ellen, nothing mattered.

He took a deep breath and expelled it. Ahh, Ellen. . . . He knew he had to forget her. But he couldn't help himself—a thought about her was always around the corner. He didn't think much about sex, just how warm her body felt next to his, how comfortable, how comforting. He used to love it when she came quietly into his room during the night, her silhouette outlined by the light filtering in from the open door. Quietly, she'd crawl in beside him, pressing her body against his. They were like two figures in a Chagall painting, floating in time and space, communicating in their silence by just being, not doing.

He had tried without success to forget those peaceful

nights when they lay close like two spoons in a drawer, feeling her hand hanging on to his pajamas when he made a movement to roll over. She was always afraid he'd get up and not come back. . . . Oh God, that is what he had done to her.

"Happy birthday, Father!" Marion's high-pitched voice jolted him out of his thoughts.

"Happy birthday, my ass!" He turned away from her.

"Now, now, wake up, sleepyhead—I brought you breakfast."

"For God's sakes, Marion. I told you a million times. I'm not in the hospital. I don't want meals on a tray."

"But Dad." The voice was that of a long-suffering martyr. "I made it special for your birthday."

"I don't want to be reminded."

She said nothing as she placed the tray on his bed and strode out of the room, ramrod straight.

A wave of guilt engulfed him. Why was he so nasty to her all the time? She meant well. She had brought him an all-white omelette, toast, jelly, the *New York Times*, and even a bud vase holding a single red rose, against which was propped up a note: *Happy 70th!*

Enough to destroy his appetite, if he had any.

He sat up and opened the paper, flipping almost instinctively to the back of Section C, where the obituaries were listed. Today was a bad day. At least yesterday there was one guy at eighty-three, another at eighty-nine, and one geezer, bless his heart, went at ninety-five. But today everyone was under seventy.

He didn't get dressed and leave his room until he heard Marion driving off. He had wanted to apologize before she left, but he was afraid she'd only make him lose his temper again. They seemed to be pushing each other's buttons constantly now. It wasn't her—it was him. He was the shit.

He threw on a sweater and walked out of the house to do some work outdoors. Now that nearly all of his aches and pains were gone, he was determined to get her garden in shape. Spring was in the air, and it was the perfect time for seeding and planting.

But the hobby that he used to love so much no longer brought him any joy. He found it awkward and messy; he didn't understand why he ever enjoyed it. But he had taken on this responsibility—he'd grit his teeth and finish it.

He raked the area where the hedge used to be and where he planned to put in some impatiens and petunias. Marion had picked up four flats at the nursery yesterday and now he carried them out of the garage, along with a small trowel for digging. He started in, and eventually the old rhythm returned. He was only vaguely aware of the traffic up and down the street, young nannies pushing their strollers, joggers going past.

He got half the petunias in when he stood up to stretch. That's when his eye caught a new pair of passersby. A nurse was helping an old man trundle along with a walker.

The Ghost of Christmas Future. That would be him in a couple more years.

He dropped his trowel and went back into the house.

He turned on the TV, letting the boob tube hypnotize him. The afternoon programs were inane. On one show a mother-daughter duo related their experiences as partners in prostitution. On another, a group of grossly obese people calling themselves the "Cholesterol Chorus" espoused the "beauty" of overeating and, by implication, dying young. Ben hit the remote control impatiently. Now here was a nicely dressed man confessing to over 100 cases of adultery while his prison matron of a wife glowered. Ben shook his head in disbelief. As far as he was concerned, the guy hadn't screwed around enough. He hit the remote control again and got a young couple bemoaning the loss of sexual desire in their marriage of less than a year.

Who were these people? What made them spill their guts on national television? Who were the people watching this crap? Well, here he was, watching this crap. It was the same strange fascination that made you gawk at highway carnage.

The sound of letters falling through the mail chute brought him out of his thoughts. The mail didn't come till late—it must be after four. Marion would be home soon.

He turned off the TV, got up, and collected the stack of envelopes and magazines from the floor. Marion sure got a lot of junk mail. Several of the letters were addressed to him—obviously birthday cards—but the handwriting on the blue envelope was unmistakable. His heart started beating rapidly.

He put it in his pocket. Like a child with a secret prize, he climbed the stairs to his room (he had graduated to his regular bedroom upstairs last week), stretched out on the bed, and pulled it out again.

He remembered so well that round generous handwriting from the notes she used to leave him. He turned the letter over in his hand. On the back was an awkward drawing of a rabbit. He smiled, but he found his hands trembling as he ripped open the envelope. It wasn't a birthday card— it was a letter . . . several pages long, it looked like.

But before he could remove it from the envelope, he

heard Marion's voice calling from below. "Dad? Dad! Are you awake?"

Shit! "Yeah?"

"Please come down. I have something to show you."

"Oh no," he muttered, "what the hell is it now?" He opened the door and came out on the landing.

"Happy birthday to you . . . Happy birthday to you . . ." a loud chorus sang out.

Ben couldn't believe it. At the foot of the stairs stood Marion holding a cake with one big lighted candle in the center. She was flanked by Milt, Sarah, and a woman who looked somewhat familiar.

He tried to put on a pleasant expression as he came down, slipping the letter in his pocket.

"Boychik, you don't look a day over a hundred." Milt winked at him.

"Blow out the candle, Dad!" Marion thrust the cake in front of him while the strange woman clapped her hands in glee.

"No, no." Sarah broke in. "First he must make a wish."

Ben wished they'd all disappear, but not surprisingly his wish didn't come true.

They applauded as he obediently blew out the candle and led him to a table in the dining room loaded with all the things he preached against: chopped chicken liver, potato salad, herring heaped with sour cream.

"I wanted to make a pot roast," Sarah announced, "but something went wrong with my oven."

Milt leaned toward Ben. "My birthday present to you," he whispered.

Ben had to laugh despite his mood.

They all sat down at the table as Sarah heaped gobs of food on their plates. "Brenda made the potato latkes." She loaded more on Ben's plate than any human being could possibly consume in a week.

"Aah, Brenda." Now it clicked—she was the one with the roomy apartment and the newly deceased husband.

"Of course you remember Brenda, Ben. . . . We played cards together." Sarah was working on Milt's plate now.

"How could I forget."

"We'll play cards after we eat," Marion said. "We want this day to be filled with all your favorite things."

Milt choked on his gefilte fish, and Ben shot him a mournful look. It wasn't funny anymore.

"Brenda," Sarah's mind was still on the food. "I should have taken the pot roast to your place and put it in your oven. Oh I wish I'd thought of that. You're the only one I could trust with it."

"We can do it next week," Milt offered mischievously. "What do you say, Brenda?"

"Oh, yes," Brenda readily agreed.

"She has a lovely apartment," Sarah gushed, "and she is a terrific cook."

"I cook the Pritikin way," Brenda offered shyly.

"What's that?" Milt asked, his mouth full of food.

"Well, I learned to cook with low sodium and low cholesterol while my husband recuperated from his angioplasty. Unfortunately . . ." she hung her head down, "it was too late."

"You were a wonderful nurse to him, Brenda." Sarah comforted her, adding, to the others, "This woman is a saint."

"I'm sure," Ben muttered, a frozen half-smile on his face. It was the worst birthday of his life.

Ellen didn't listen to anything the speaker said during the entire one-hour lecture. It was an important subject—bioethics—but she couldn't make herself care. She sat next to Goldie in a daze. Did Ben get her birthday letter? She hoped so. But then Marion might have intercepted it, thrown it away. No, Marion was bad, but not that bad. She mustn't blame it all on Marion, who was just doing what she thought was best for her father. Ben was not his daughter's prisoner; he had a mind of his own. He could pick up the phone and call, he could write, he could even come see her. But he had made his decision. He was the one who closed all the doors.

The smattering of applause made her realize that the lecture had come to a close. Everyone was getting up now. She rose too and looked around. Her eye caught Richard's intense gaze. He smiled and nodded his head.

Goldie gave her a hard nudge. "Let's get a move on, girlfriend. I gotta get back to the OR."

"Coffee later?"

"Sure." And Goldie was gone.

As Ellen exited the auditorium, she heard the familiar accented voice behind her. "Heading back to the library?"

"Yes, Richard."

"Mind if I walk along?"

Ellen mumbled something that sounded like "not at all," hoping her tone of voice would discourage him, but he didn't seem to notice.

"I have good news to report," he continued cheerfully. "I just received a royalty statement from my publisher. My book"—he paused—"I should say *our* book, has done very well."

"I'm glad to hear that," she said flatly.

"The paperback edition is coming out in a month."

"Oh, good."

"This is an advance copy." He pulled it out of his pocket. It had the same cover design, except his picture on the back had been replaced by excerpts from the glowing reviews the hardback had received.

"Very nice." Ellen knew she sounded inane, but it was the best she could do.

"I'm glad it's coming out," he went on, "because it gives me an opportunity to correct a major omission I made the last time."

They were now in front of the library.

"What omission?"

"Look on page three." He smiled broadly and walked away.

She watched him striding away, so sure of himself, then she opened the book. Page three was blank except for a small inscription that read: *To Ellen Riccio, with gratitude and affection.*

Even Goldie was impressed—she let out a long, low whistle when she saw it. "This guy still has a hard-on for you."

"Oh, Goldie, please . . ."

"Don't 'Goldie please' me—you know it's true."

Ellen said nothing. There was no denying that Richard wanted to get back together. He had made that overtly clear on a number of occasions.

"And is that so bad?" Goldie persisted.

"After what happened with Gina, I never could—"

"Listen, girlfriend, the guy made one mistake. How long ago was it? Almost a year? He's done his penance, right?"

"Well, he has apologized several times."

"So, nobody's perfect. He's seen the error of his ways. What does Sister Clarita say all the time—'Forgiveness is divine,' or something like that."

"I'm just not ready to be seeing anyone."

"Ready, not ready—who cares? When a guy makes this much effort to get back into your pants you ought to let him."

"Honestly, Goldie, you're the last one I'd expect to be making *that* argument."

"I'm just talking reality. Every man can be a jerk sometime. Some guys are jerks all the time. But this guy is not as big a jerk as a lot of others. The kind of money he makes on those heart transplants"—she raised her eyes to the ceiling—"and let me tell you another thing: all the nurses agree, he is the best doctor in this whole damn hospital."

Ellen nodded. She knew that was true.

"And as far as I'm concerned—" Goldie was on a roll. "He is the *only* competent doctor in this hospital. You wanna hear what Fineberg did?" The expression on Goldie's face said it was a doozie.

"What?"

"Remember that Jew-boy that got shot?"

"The Hasidic?"

"Yeah, him. You know the poor bastard died, right?"

"Yeah, that was awful."

"The more awful thing is he could have lived. It seems that fumble-fingers was so busy removing the bullet in the front, he forgot to look in the back."

"What?"

"Yeah—the kid had been stabbed, too. He was leaking like a sieve, but the old myopic fool didn't see it."

"Oh, no."

"Oh, yes. I'd hate to see what the Hasidim will do when they find out."

"They'll sue."

"No kidding. Nobody will convince them that a Catholic hospital didn't kill a Jew on purpose."

"But Fineberg is Jewish."

"A small fact that can be easily overlooked in the heat of passion."

Ellen shook her head. She knew Goldie was right. This sure was a disaster for Saint Joseph's.

Ben breathed a sigh of relief when they all finally left. Marion, obviously very pleased with the success of the party, chattered on, but he wasn't listening. At the first opportunity he yawned, said he was dead tired, and locked himself in his room.

He took out the letter, but he was too excited to read it. Very deliberately, he placed it on his night table, got undressed, brushed his teeth, clipped a few protruding hairs from his mustache. Then he showered, dried himself thoroughly and then, finally, got into bed.

He had endured enough anticipation. He removed the letter from the envelope and started to read.

Dear Ben,

Once upon a time, at the University of Ohio, there lived many bunny rabbits.

These were special laboratory bunnies that were fed

*toxic doses of cholesterol to see how fast their arteries
would clog up.*

*And sure enough, like the researchers had expected,
all the bunnies developed clogged arteries right on a
predictable schedule . . . except for one bunch.*

*It was a huge mystery. How could this be? Why did
this one bunch of bunnies stay healthy while the others
got sick and died? They had all been fed exactly like the
others. So what had made the difference between life and
death?*

*The professors couldn't figure it out, until they found
out that the healthy bunch of bunnies was very much
loved by the lab assistant who took care of them. Each
time she came to feed them fatal doses of cholesterol, she
took each one out of its cage, held it, and stroked its head.*

*The professors were astonished, but not easily
convinced. So they repeated the experiment, this time
ordering the lab assistant to pet only certain bunnies. And
they found out it was true. The lucky bunnies who were
loved lived happily ever after.*

*So tell me, dear Ben, will anybody take you out of
your cage and stroke your head on your birthday?*

He put the letter down. Tears were rolling down his
cheeks.

20

Through the window of the Amtrak train speeding along to Amsterdam, Ellen's eyes followed a tugboat plying its way up the Hudson River until it disappeared from view, outdistanced by the train. Then she leaned back in her seat and listened to the rhythmic clippity-clop of the wheels against the tracks. She knew those tracks well, two lines of blue steel stretching out until they joined together in the distance. As a child she had never understood that optical illusion when she played on the tracks, pretending she was doing gymnastics on a balance beam.

She remembered so well the excitement mixed with fear when a train would appear in the distance, hurtling toward her soundlessly. She'd scream and jump away at the last minute and watch the train roar by almost in a blur.

The express trains never stopped in Amsterdam. She'd

catch glimpses of men and women seated at tables covered with white linen and wonder where they were rushing to. She envied them—she too wanted to be on a train going somewhere.

Finally, she did get on that train and it took her 170 miles south to the biggest city in the world—New York. It seemed to her that day—when, at age seventeen, she'd first boarded the train for her admittance interview to Columbia University—that it was much more romantic watching the train from the outside than sitting in a stained seat on the inside.

She had taken that train often since then. Even after her mother had died, she dutifully returned to Amsterdam to spend every Christmas with Uncle Pete and Aunt Marie. She didn't care about Aunt Marie, really—she was a perfectly sweet woman and Ellen had nothing against her— but it was Uncle Pete, her mother's older brother, who had always looked after her, who loved her as if she were his own daughter, who made her feel that she was not alone in the world. She owed him. After Aunt Marie passed on two years ago, she tried to visit more often.

But this time the homecoming would be different. It wouldn't be just another visit—she was here to decide if she would return for good. Uncle Pete had called her, all excited because the librarian at local Memorial Hospital was retiring. With his political clout as the former mayor and former member of the hospital's board, and with her qualifications, the job was hers if she wanted it.

Could one go back? She didn't know.

Another life choice that loomed also meant going back—going back with Richard. Goldie had convinced her that she had been too hard on him. What, after all, was she waiting for? How much more could she expect from a man? Wasn't it enough that he was brilliant, rich, and crazy about her?

She had finally agreed to have dinner with him, and it was a pleasant enough experience, Richard taking great pains to be a gentleman, letting her warm up to him gradually, not even hinting that they might spend the night together. She had kept the dinner short, complaining that back pain made it difficult for her to sit still very long, and that part was true, but also, she didn't want to lead him on.

It was obvious that he was more than eager to get back into her good graces—the right way, this time. He even offered to drive her and her sandwiches to the Thunderbolt on Sunday, and when he found out about the trip she was planning to Amsterdam, he insisted that she let him substitute for her. She had agreed to that, surprised and happy that he should really want to change his attitude about the homeless.

So let's suppose she did give him another chance. What would the future with Richard be like? Would they marry, have a house in the well-to-do suburbs, a couple of kids, maybe? Then, as his career advanced, would they move to some exciting or exotic place—Zurich, Vienna, Paris? Richard would be famous, she the dutiful wife at his side, helping with his research while raising the kids.

What a choice to have: she could return home where things were quiet and familiar and secure; or she could plunge forward with Richard into a life that promised the moon and the stars, but which also was likely to include a great deal of uncertainty and anxiety.

She wished she knew some rule that would guide her. And then again, perhaps, without knowing it, Goldie had given it to her. Right in the middle of one of her go-back-with-Richard monologues, Goldie stopped. After a long pause, so uncharacteristic of her, she said, "Something just kinda popped into my head right now."

"What is it?"

"Well, there is an old African proverb that was passed down in my family. . . ."

"Tell me."

"It goes: 'You can escape what is running after you, but not what is running inside you.' I don't know why I thought of it. It doesn't make much sense in your situation."

It made perfect sense to Ellen—she knew what was running inside of her. She knew that going back to Amsterdam or going back with Richard were just ways of escaping her feelings for Ben. But what else could she do, if he didn't want her?

Richard had insisted on driving her to Manhattan to catch the train. But once they arrived at Grand Central, there was absolutely no place to park in the vicinity, and they had to say their good-byes by the station door.

"Enjoy yourself and don't worry about anything." His hand touched her shoulder. "I'll be very good to your homeless friends. I've already ordered the sandwiches from a deli—"

"Oh, that's so thoughtful of you."

"Of course they won't compare to your homemade variety."

"A change of diet will be a treat for them. They'll be very pleased."

"More important, Ellen, I want *you* to be pleased." He lowered his voice, implying something more intimate.

It made her very uncomfortable. She didn't want him to kiss her good-bye.

"I better go or I'll miss my train." She moved away.

"Have a good trip!" he called out, waving.

She didn't wave back; she just ran as fast as she could.

She was the only passenger to get out at the Amsterdam stop. Uncle Pete, clearly thrilled to see her, picked her up at the tiny train station, a dilapidated brick structure that looked sad and forlorn.

As they drove through town, it seemed to her that it had shrunk even more since she was last here. The town was shriveling up, a skeleton of what she had known as a child. It made her think of the Thunderbolt—both were fossils of the past.

They passed over the Chuctanunda Creek—swelled this time of year with spring rains and rushing to join the Mohawk River—then turned the corner at Church and Grove. Here stood the town library, which used to be her home away from home. How many hours of fantasy and escape it had offered her. It looked like a toy replica of a Greek temple with four tired Doric columns trying to hold up a sagging overhang. It didn't seem to beckon like a place of refuge anymore—it just seemed like an old, somewhat neglected building. But maybe there was a little girl curled up in the corner right now for whom it was a palace with no equal. . . .

"I don't even have to ask if you're hungry." Uncle Pete chuckled, pulling up in front of DiCaprio's Diner. Ellen's voracious appetite was a joke between them, and DiCaprio's was their favorite dining spot.

Over spaghetti—what else?—she listened to the news of distant relatives she hardly remembered: Aunt Marie's brother was in the hospital with cancer, Cousin Henry got fired as manager of the *Gazette*, Cousin Angela had her fourth girl, to the chagrin of her husband who was hoping for a boy. They all would be so happy to see Ellen come back to Amsterdam.

As Uncle Pete talked, Ellen, only half listening, studied his kindly face. He still had the rosy cheeks and dark luminous eyes, which always seemed sad, but of course, the jet black hair that figured in her earliest memories of him was now all white.

"Uncle Pete—I want to ask you something."

He was twirling his spaghetti expertly without the aid of a spoon, something Ellen (a failure as an Italian) had never mastered. He looked up from his plate. "What is it? Don't hold back."

"Didn't you ever want to leave Amsterdam?"

He chewed for a while thoughtfully, then said with a faraway look in his eyes, "I thought I did, but I couldn't because I never passed the bar exam."

This was a subject that was rarely brought up, but it had long perplexed Ellen why someone as intelligent as Uncle Pete could graduate law school with honors and then fail the bar exam half a dozen times.

"I agonized over that for years," he continued, "until I realized that I didn't want to become a lawyer. I wanted to stay here."

"But you could have—"

"Not as a laywer. A lawyer is someone who makes his money off people's mistrust of each other. I wanted to help folks learn to get along better."

"And you did that all your life. You're the most popular man in Amsterdam."

"Well, I don't know how popular." He smiled. "But you know, Ellen, you're a lot like me."

"I'm glad you think so."

"Except you catch on quicker. You knew right away you couldn't be a doctor, so you became a medical librarian."

"Yes, I did."

"The question remains—is Amsterdam the place for you?"

"I'm not sure. . . ."

"You know I'm hoping you'll decide to come home again, 'cause I love seeing you. But the most important thing is finding out what's right for you. As long as you're true to this part of you"—he pointed to the middle of his chest—"in here, you'll be fine."

Leaving the diner, Ellen felt calmer and lighter than she had in days. She was glad she came to see Uncle Pete this weekend.

She didn't have to think about it anymore. At last, she knew what to do.

21

Before he opened his eyes, Ben played his usual guessing game. Right now, the time is . . . 6:44. Then he squinted at the digital clock—6:45. Not bad, not bad at all, almost there. A good omen on this Sunday morning.

With a surge of energy, he sprang out of bed, ignoring the few aches and pains that were still there. He moved over to the window and pulled open the shade. The sky was gray, but on the horizon the sun was already peeking out. Somewhere in the garden a bird was singing, a fluty tune that sounded like *"weela-weeo, chuck-chuck weeo."* He scanned the branches of the nearby oak tree. Sure enough, a large, brilliantly yellow bird was perched on one of the branches. A golden oriole already? Summer would come early. *"Weela-weeo,"* the bird sang out again, and Ben pursed his lips to answer it with a whistle. The bird cocked its head to listen.

Ben grinned. Everything said it was going to be a good day—he was going to Brooklyn.

By 8:30 A.M. Richard had already showered and was dressed. He had no time to waste. Ellen was coming home this morning. He flipped on the phone answering machine to replay the message she had left late last night. "Hi, Richard, this is Ellen. I've decided to take an early train back Sunday morning, so I'll be able to get down to the Thunderbolt by lunchtime. I appreciate your being such a willing substitute, but you won't have to go to all that trouble now. Thanks again."

With a tight smile on his face, he turned off the machine. He'd better leave now. But he was a careful man. With customary precision, his eyes scanned the room for anything he might have forgotten. Oh yes. He went over to his desk and picked up a fax lying there. It was a message from the Credit Suisse Bank: *As per instructions of Taro Hashikawa, we are pleased to confirm wire transfer of the first installment of three million U.S. dollars from Bank of Tokyo to our account number #764135.*

He ripped the message into little pieces, then quickly flushed them down the toilet.

Milt got out of bed quietly so as not to wake Sarah. She liked sleeping in on weekends and could be grouchy if deprived of this indulgence.

He threw on a robe, went into the kitchen, and made coffee. This was the best time of the day—when it was quiet, when you could read the *New York Times* cover to cover without interruption. But that would be denied him this morning.

To start with, he had to meet Michaelson for brunch, no pleasure under the best of circumstances, and the circumstances were far from that. Michaelson was a nervous wreck, worrying about his deal with the Japanese.

Milt suggested that he go home to the West Coast and fly back whenever something might be happening, but to Michaelson leaving was synonymous with giving up. So he stuck around driving everyone—mostly Milt, who was given the boss-sitting job—up the wall.

Fortunately, the meeting with Vandermann had proved fruitful. Whatever the doctor had said to young Hashikawa behind closed doors worked. The Japanese finally—after much deliberation—agreed to a baboon transplant on a long list of conditions, the first and foremost being that everything be kept in the utmost secrecy. Milt could only imagine what kind of dough the good doctor was gonna make on it.

You'd think that Michaelson would relax now that old Hashikawa stood a chance, but noooo . . . Michaelson was in a new fit of frenzy, obsessing about anything that might go wrong.

Lots of things could. And if something were to go wrong, it was most likely to happen during the operation—scheduled for later today at the private hospital to avoid moving the patient and to continue keeping everything hush-hush. Apparently no special equipment was required (just the same stuff they'd normally use in a bypass), as long as you had the two essentials—a fresh heart and a doctor who knew what he was doing with it.

Milt sighed, folded up the *Times*, and forced himself to get into gear. Sarah was still sleeping blissfully—oh, how he envied her peace of mind.

When he left his house the streets were still largely deserted. For a fleeting moment, he thought he saw Ben's car round the corner. But what would Ben be doing in Brooklyn on Sunday morning—and this early? Nah . . . ridiculous.

Ben's running shoes barely made a sound as he slowly walked up the three flights of well-worn stairs leading to his gym. He stepped into the dark waiting room and flipped on the lights. His bulletin board was just like he had left it, crammed with articles and inspirational messages for his clients. IF LIFE GIVES YOU LEMONS, MAKE LEMONADE, a prominent one read. It used to give him such delight to find clippings and cartoons to put up there. Here was one of his favorites: IF YOU HAVE ONE LEG IN YESTERDAY AND ONE LEG IN TOMORROW, YOU ARE PISSING ON TODAY. He sure had done a lot of that in the last couple of months. Well, it was high time he started practicing what he preached. Start making lemonade, stop pissing on today . . . and today was a good day to start.

He unlocked the door to the gym and walked in. It was very quiet. A strong shaft of sunlight poured through the window, illuminating little diamonds of dust and making them bounce off a chrome rack of weights. Everything seemed to be accusing him of neglect. He got a towel from the bathroom, wiped all the equipment, then removed his shirt.

He stood straight and tall, flexing his biceps. It felt good. He wouldn't leave here until he worked up a sweat and got his blood pumping. As he picked up a pair of barbells, he caught a reflection of his well-muscled chest in the mirror. Gone was that hunched-over old guy with the scruffy beard being led to the toilet. He looked good—damned good.

On the train back to New York, Ellen sat huddled in the corner of the dank, empty coach. It had been a good visit. She had made a decision, and she knew it was the right one.

She would definitely not be moving back to Amsterdam, and she would not be going back with Richard. She would go on as before, doing her job and then . . . she didn't know what then. When she looked into the future all she saw was a blank. But that was all right. The thought didn't depress her. Just the opposite—it made her feel calm and light.

Uncle Pete understood that coming back to Amsterdam wouldn't work for her. But he couldn't hide his disappointment when he learned she wasn't going to accompany him to Sunday Mass as she usually did, or stay for the big family meal after church.

It was hard to explain what propelled her to return so early this morning. Something about Richard's parting words had stuck in her mind, disturbed her. He had been too solicitous, too . . . what was the word? . . . unctuous. Thinking of it made her shiver slightly.

The train entered a tunnel and in the window she caught a reflection of her face wearing a cynical smile. A year ago Richard's attention would have delighted her. Now it seemed empty, cold, Teutonic in its efficiency to win her back. She didn't want him trying to get close to her by scoring points with Jello.

Richard left his Mercedes in the doctors' parking lot at the back of the hospital. He flashed his ID badge at the door, but the guard, immersed in the Sunday paper, barely looked up.

He took the elevator to his laboratory, encountering no one in this section of the hospital, and entered the baboon room. The medical student whose job it was to clean the cages and feed the animals was just leaving. She looked at him with surprise. "Good morning, Dr. Vandermann, I didn't expect you here today."

"Well, I am a bit behind on my paperwork and this seemed a good time to be able to concentrate in peace and quiet."

"Do you need me for anything?"

"Not at all—get out in the sunshine, enjoy the day." He flashed her his most seductive smile.

It was almost too seductive, because she hesitated. "Well, I hate to leave you toiling all alone. . . ."

"I'd rather you get well rested today, because I might need you to work through the night tomorrow."

"In that case . . ." she moved to the door, her eyes not leaving his, "I'll see you tomorrow."

As soon as she left, Richard opened up the supply room where the medication and surgical equipment he used for his experiments were stored. From the pharmacy cupboard he extracted an ampule of potassium chloride, which he deftly transferred into a syringe. Carefully, he wrapped the syringe in sterile cotton and stowed it in his doctor's bag. Moving over to the refrigerator, he pulled out an IV bag preloaded with Roe's solution, to which he added 250,000 units of streptokinase and 10 milliliters of dextrose. He did it swiftly, in a practiced way, like a bartender mixing a cocktail. Then, he took a small Igloo cooler, filled it with ice, and placed the IV bag inside. Ready.

He picked up the cooler, and on his way out the door

pulled an unopened cardio-pack off the shelf. It was heavy, containing all the instruments—sterilized and double sealed in plastic—for a full heart transplant. He carried both down the hall to where empty monorail carts waited. He placed the cooler and cardio-pack on a cart and checked the department-code list. Autoclave B03, Laundry B26, Maintenance B42 . . . yes, here it was: Morgue B53.

As soon as he punched in the number, the cart started to move, rolling smoothly away into the bowels of the hospital, propelled by an unseen mechanism to its predetermined destination.

On her way from Grand Central to Brooklyn, Ellen had stopped at a deli and bought fresh bread, bacon, lettuce, and tomatoes, everything she needed to make BLTs for Jello and the Bobs. Now she stood in the kitchen frying the bacon and toasting the bread, two slices at a time.

Ben would be annoyed if he were here. He'd recite the caloric value of bacon, gripe about the fat. She'd of course counter that maybe people who didn't eat regularly could use it. He'd think about it, then concede she might be right. . . . She could hear his voice in her head so clearly.

How many imaginary conversations did she have with him since he left? She couldn't count. How many times had she looked out the window, thinking that if she'd only wish hard enough Ben would appear, hurrying home, taking two steps at a time, unlocking the door. . . .

Inadvertently, she drifted over to the window and looked down. She blinked twice, not believing her eyes. There was Ben's car—or what looked like Ben's car—pulling up in front of the curb. A man got out—it was Ben. He walked up the steps.

She rushed away from the window and ran down the stairs. Her feet couldn't move fast enough, and she had to hold on to the railing so as not to trip and tumble down.

She expected to see him as she started down the last flight, but he wasn't there. He probably didn't have his key. Breathless, she flung open the door. No one. She looked outside. The spot where he had parked was empty.

She had imagined it. She had wished so hard for him to come home that she was finally seeing things that weren't there. The feeling of being let down was too much. The lump in her throat was so tight she could barely breathe. She swallowed hard. If she didn't get ahold of herself, she'd cry. And she could not let herself cry. Not anymore.

Slowly, she started up the stairs again. Up on the second-floor landing she could smell the bacon burning. Oh, hell—how stupid could she be!

Ben stepped on the accelerator. His Camaro responded with a jerk. The car was definitely in need of a tune-up. It had sat idle for too long. His brain had sat idle for too long, also. He had almost made the biggest fool of himself just now.

What was he gonna do? Ring the doorbell, say, "Hello, honey, I'm home"? He had to be crazy to think he could hop back into her life just like that. There was that word *hop*— he was thinking like a bunny. His mind sure was getting warped.

Her letter never suggested that she wanted him back. It was just a cute way of wishing him a happy birthday. It probably was her way of saying good-bye, and here he took it as an invitation to come home.

He drove along Prospect Park. This was where they had walked that first night after the movie. He knew he had impressed her with the way he handled the punks. And then they sat and talked for a long time at the Café La Fontana.

He stopped at the traffic light. To get back to the expressway, he should make a right here. Instead, he just continued around the park. What the hell—he was in no hurry to get back to Jersey.

Of course, there was another way of looking at the letter. First, she took the time to write it—she didn't just send a card. And it wasn't a short letter, either. In fact it was a very long letter for somebody who was usually so very brief with her notes. She put a lot of effort into it. Goddamn—he was right the first time—she *was* trying to tell him something. He was just scared to find out that it wasn't what he hoped for.

He had come around the park for the second time—where to now?

Michaelson ignored his eggs Benedict, but did drink two glasses of Chardonnay. Milt didn't stop him. Anything to calm Ron down. His own appetite wasn't affected one way or the other.

He had just finished his western omelette and was considering a slice of fudge cheesecake when Michaelson stood up and demanded the check.

"What's your hurry, Ronnie? We got plenty of time."

"I can't stand it. Let's go."

"When the boss says let's go . . ." Milt got up reluctantly. As they were going out the door, he cast one last mournful look at the pastry tray.

Of course, they got to the hospital much too early. When they asked for Mr. Hashikawa, they were told he was with his father; Dr. Howard was scrubbing up.

"I told you we should have come earlier," Michaelson immediately started in. "That way we'd have been here when they—"

"Ron, we're not performing the operation. I don't even know why we're here at all."

"Don't be flip. We have to make sure everything's on schedule."

"Vandermann doesn't need us to tell him when to bring the heart."

Michaelson's look said he could kill, and the only available victim was Milt, who immediately realized he better change his tack and humor the boss.

"Ronnie, Ronnie, relax. I hear that once they put in the new heart, the guy's gonna be fit as a fiddle. He'll jog out of here in a few days' time."

"Honest? Recovery is that fast?"

"Absolutely. Before the week is out, we'll all be kneeling around that table with the legs chopped off drinking tea and counting the dough."

Michaelson brightened up momentarily.

Milt couldn't help but wonder what Ron would say if he knew that lately, when the agents had meetings, they brought in chairs and put their feet on the conference table like it was a giant footstool.

Ben's car seemed to have a mind of its own. Like a creature of habit, it was following its old Sunday morning route, driving down to Coney Island. Ben sat mutely at the wheel. But the closer he got to the ocean the better he felt.

He imagined the happy, surprised look on her face when she would come down the stairs at the BMT stop and bump into him, just the way she had the day it rained.

"Gee, it wasn't my fault," he'd say. "I was heading for the Verrazano—on my way to Jersey—but this goddamn car hasn't been used much, and the next thing I know it takes me to Coney Island. Ellen, I gotta take it in for a tune-up."

She would laugh then, let him take the box with the sandwiches, and it would be like he had never left.

He was a block away from Nathan's Hot Dogs. He could smell them. He looked at his watch. Not quite nine-thirty. Too early—Ellen didn't usually get here until around eleven. But what the hell, he'd talk with Jello for a while, and then greet her at the turnstile.

He could see the scene so vividly in his mind.

He'd strike a Bugs Bunny pose and say, "What's up, doc?"

She would, of course, be very surprised.

And he'd say, "Haven't you seen a bunny rabbit before?"

He stopped at the red light at Surf—he was practically there.

He imagined the big grin on her face. She'd drop the box of sandwiches and open up her arms. She'd—

Suddenly, he stopped breathing.

Striding across the street in front of him was a tall, handsome figure he had seen before—Dr. Richard Vandermann. He was carrying his doctor's bag and heading for the Thunderbolt.

Ben sagged in his seat like a deflated balloon.

He didn't see the light change. He didn't hear the pickup truck honking behind him. He just sat there as the driver, obviously losing his patience, swerved around him and yelled, "You dumb old fart!"

22

Richard pushed his way through the turnstile, impatiently brushing off some rust that got onto his windbreaker. An eerie silence pervaded the weedy domain of the homeless. No one seemed to be awake as yet, except for Choo-choo, who sat over a Sterno can heating a pot of coffee.

"Where is Jello?" Richard asked.

Choo-choo wordlessly motioned with his chin in the direction of a heap of humanity curled up in the fetal position and snoring loudly.

Richard squatted down beside him and tapped him on the shoulder. "Wake up." Jello stirred and little Junior's beady eyes peered out of his coat pocket. Richard tapped him again. "Your guardian angel sent me to look after you."

"Huh?"

"Miss Ellen."

"Oh, that was nice of her."

"How are you doing?"

"I'll feel fine in a minute," Jello mumbled and reached for a nearly empty bottle of cheap whiskey lying nearby. He propped himself up on his elbow and took a long swig. He started coughing almost immediately. "For all the cough syrup I've drunk in my life, why can't I shake this?"

Richard placed his manicured hand on Jello's filthy forehead.

"Don't pamper him, doc," Choo-choo broke in, coming near. "He's just got a hangover."

"I doubt it." Richard's face was stern. "His temperature is elevated—I think he may be gravely ill."

Choo-choo seemed skeptical. "He don't look no different to me."

Richard took out his stethoscope and checked Jello's heartbeat. "I don't like it," he declared more loudly than was necessary. "We must start a course of antibiotics immediately." He pulled out his cellular phone and started dialing. "This man belongs in the hospital."

"No I don't," Jello objected weakly.

"What's he got, doc?" Choo-choo wanted to know, but Richard was already speaking into the phone. "Need an ambulance stat. Pulmonary arrest. Under the Thunderbolt . . . that is correct . . . Three minutes? I will meet the paramedics at the entrance."

The word *paramedics* alarmed Jello. "Hold it, doc. Nothing wrong with me. All I need is some coffee."

"I'll get it," Choo-choo called out, heading back to the pot.

"I'll get it myself." Jello started getting up.

Richard restrained him. "You are very ill."

"I ain't going back to that hospital."

"Let me first give you a shot, then we'll see." Quickly, Richard extracted a prefilled syringe.

"No way."

"If the shot makes you feel better, you won't have to go."

With bleary eyes Jello looked up at him. "You promise, doc?"

"Yes."

"Okay, one shot of that crap. No more."

Richard pushed up Jello's sleeve and deftly injected the needle directly into his vein. "This will make you feel much better."

Jello didn't answer.

When Choo-choo returned with a steaming cup of coffee, Jello was sitting on the ground, his head slumped on his shoulder. "Geez, doc, he don't look so good."

"I told you—he is seriously ill."

"Jesus, he ain't movin'!"

"Help me!" Richard commanded, grabbing Jello under the armpit. "Let's get him to the entrance."

In the distance, the siren of the ambulance could be heard coming closer.

A sudden gust hit Ben's car as he entered the top level of the Verrazano Narrows Bridge suspended high above New York Bay. Moving across it, he could feel the bridge swaying under him in the wind.

He was one big schmuck! Here he was, planning all this cute bullshit to tell his girl that he just decided, on the spur of the moment, to move back in. In his arrogance he expected her to forget how miserably he had treated her and open up her arms with a grin. Only a *real* big schmuck would dream up anything like that.

Of course she went back with her old boyfriend. And why not? Didn't he himself tell her to do it? He had to be delirious to think that she would be sitting at home, pining away for an old man who told her he didn't want her.

He was not just a schmuck—he was an asshole.

The paramedics, stretcher in hand, ran toward where Richard and Choo-choo stood beside the inert body of Jello, which was lying in a tattered chariot at the entrance to the Thunderbolt.

"Get him loaded," Richard ordered.

"But, doc, shouldn't we first—"

"Do it! I'm coming with you."

They quickly obeyed. As they shoved the gurney with Jello's body into the ambulance, the mouse fell out of his coat.

The paramedics gave each other a disbelieving look. "Now I've seen everything," the driver muttered.

Richard jumped aboard, followed by a paramedic.

"Can I come too?" Choo-choo asked.

The driver nodded. "You can sit up front with me."

"No!" It was almost a shout and it came from Richard. In a softer voice, he added, "Ellen will be here shortly. You must stay and explain what happened. Tell her I will do everything possible."

"Okay, doc," Choo-choo conceded.

The door slammed shut and the ambulance took off, siren screaming.

Bewildered, little Junior scurried down the gutter.

* * *

When she finally got on the subway with her sandwich box, Ellen was still berating herself about the burned bacon. A whole pound of it ruined, charred to a crisp. The apartment full of smoke, smelling like an incinerator. Thank God the kitchen hadn't caught fire.

She aired the place out and scrubbed the scorched griddle clean. She considered just slapping a couple of slices of cheese on each sandwich and forgetting about BLTs. But they so rarely got something nutritious. They really needed the protein.

She walked the three blocks to the nearest deli, bought some more bacon, and fried it up fresh. Jello was worth the extra time and effort it took.

The ambulance had barely pulled into Saint Joseph's emergency entrance when Richard jumped out, followed by the paramedics.

"You did your best," he assured them.

They nodded.

"You're some guy, Dr. Vandermann," the driver spoke up.

"You bet," his partner agreed. "Not many doctors would try that hard to save the life of some bum."

"Anyone who has taken the Hippocratic oath would be obliged to do the same."

"On a Sunday morning? You're one in a million, doc."

"I appreciate the compliment, fellows. Thank you."

They were still shaking their heads in admiration when he walked inside.

He approached the emergency-room clerk.

"What you got?" she asked in a bored voice.

"DOA. Have the body taken to the morgue. I will take care of the death certificate."

She handed him the form without looking up.

Before Ben could put the key in the lock, the door was flung open. "Where have you been?" Marion was frantic.

"I took a drive."

"A drive?"

"Yeah, I went to the gym."

"To Brooklyn?" She followed him to his bedroom. "Are you suicidal?"

Ben shot her a glance that said "leave me alone." But she didn't catch it.

"You might have killed yourself."

"Calm down, Marion." He was far too depressed to deal with one of her outbursts.

"You're in no condition to take a trip like that."

"Come on, Marion, I'm not an invalid. The doctor said I've got to be more active."

"Be more active around here. Finish planting those impatiens."

"I'll do it tomorrow."

Marion looked at him more closely. "Father, you don't look well. I'll run you a hot bath. And then—"

"I can run my own bath." His voice was cold and firm.

She eyed him for a moment, then smiled indulgently. "You've done too much today and you're tired. I'll leave you alone so you can rest." She moved toward the door. "I'll bring you some soup in a little while."

Fuck the soup, Ben thought. He hated being mothered, but this was more oppressive than that—he felt downright smothered. Worst of all, there was no way out.

* * *

Gomez, the morgue technician, had his feet up on his desk. He was on break and nothing was about to disturb the consumption of his corned beef on rye. He barely turned to look when Jello's body was wheeled in through the doorway. The orderly shoved it in and left hurriedly. The live ones always wanted to get away. The dead ones would have to wait. There was no hurry in Gomez's dominion—after all, his customers weren't about to complain.

"Good morning, Gomez." Richard entered smiling.

Gomez raised an eyebrow—a doctor on a Sunday morning was not a common occurrence, but not enough to interrupt his meal. "Hiya, Dr. Vandermann," he mumbled, his mouth full.

"Prepare this one for me, please."

Gomez was surprised. "You doin' an autopsy?"

"No, I just need some tissue samples for medical research. . . ."

"On Sunday morning? What kinda union you belong to?"

"Not every day do you get a warm John Doe without family to object."

Gomez laughed. "Know what you mean, doc." He finished the last of his sandwich, wiped his mouth with his sleeve, and looked longingly at the slab of cherry pie that was to be his dessert.

"Get the body prepped," Richard said. "If I don't harvest the heart in twenty minutes, it won't do me any good."

"Okay, doc." Gomez wasn't exactly thrilled to be rushing around on a Sunday—a day he expected to be slow—but what could he do? Heck, it was a job with a steady paycheck.

Richard left the morgue and walked down the hall to where the monorail cart waited. He passed Sister Clarita coming out of her room, greeted her with a quick nod, and hurried on before she had a chance to engage him in lengthy pleasantries. When he returned a little while later wearing his surgical outfit, carrying the Igloo box and his equipment, Gomez was standing in the hallway outside.

"Haven't I told you to get started?" Richard's annoyance showed.

"I can't. The sister's praying over the body."

Through the partially opened door, Richard could see Sister Clarita anointing the body as her lips moved wordlessly. He looked at his watch. He had eleven minutes left. With a sharp intake of breath, he pushed the door open.

"Sister! There'll be plenty of time for that at the funeral."

"Oh dear, Dr. Vandermann. I fear not. The sacrament of Extreme Unction should have been given this unfortunate man before he died. And I dare say, his soul may need all the help it can get."

Momentarily, Richard was at a loss for words. He put down his cardio-pack and turned away from her, busying himself with unwrapping his implements.

"Well, Doctor, I shall go make my morning rounds, and leave you to your work."

"Have a good day, Sister."

Breathing a small sigh of relief, he checked his watch. He had nine minutes left. "Gomez!"

The morgue technician stirred into action and began removing Jello's tattered clothing. "What you wanna do with his tuxedo?"

"It's a gift for you." Richard chuckled.

"Oh, thanks a lot." Gomez tossed the pile of rags into a refuse can.

"Please get me more ice—sterile," Richard directed, approaching the body.

"Sterile? I gotta go down the hall for that. We don't get much call for sterile here."

But Richard wasn't listening to the technician jabber. He picked up a scalpel with his gloved hand, pulled back the skin on Jello's bony chest, and cut a deep gash down the center.

23

"Taxi! Taxi!" Ellen was screaming frantically. A young couple headed for the beach threw her a strange look, but she was oblivious to everybody and everything.

She spotted a cab rounding the corner at Surf and raced across the street to cut it off, narrowly missing being hit by a station wagon. "Watch it!" the driver yelled, but she didn't hear.

Breathless, she jumped into the cab. "Saint Joseph's Hospital," she gasped.

What could have happened to Jello? Why did he get this sick so suddenly? Last week, when she saw him, he had been coughing, but he was always coughing.

Thank God Richard didn't get her message and came here after all. She fervently hoped he had rescued Jello in time. The picture that Choo-choo painted had alarmed her terribly. But Richard was the best doctor she knew.

Jello had lucked out—Richard would do everything possible.

That thought calmed her down a little bit. Yes, Richard would do everything possible.

Richard dumped his gloves into the refuse can, removed his gown and put it in the laundry hamper, deposited his bloody instruments in the sterilization box. No matter his hurry, he always took care to follow procedure.

Gomez was busy sewing up the body.

"Thank you." Richard was always polite to the help. "And have a nice day."

"Will do, doc." Gomez's mind was already on the pie he never got to finish.

Igloo box in hand, Richard took the elevator to the street floor and exited into the parking lot through a fire door. No one saw him leave.

Before starting his Mercedes, he took his cellular phone out of his pocket. He dialed quickly. "Dr. Vandermann here. You can start now. I'm on my way."

He drove across the empty parking lot to the gate, pulled out, and stopped. He could advance no farther. The street was completely blocked by a crowd of Hasidic Jews, all dressed in their black coats and hats. Some carried signs proclaiming THIS HOSPITAL KILLS JEWS. They were obviously protesting the botched treatment of Moishe.

They marched around, stomping their feet, shaking their fists, yelling. Police barricades protected access to the emergency entrance but that didn't help Richard any.

Furious, he leaned out of the window. "Officer!"

The cop watching the crowd looked in his direction but did not move.

"Officer!"

Slowly, the cop ambled over. "What's your problem?"

"I'm trying to get out!"

"What do you want me to do about it? They have a permit."

"I'm a doctor and I have to get to an important appointment."

"The hospital said this parking lot wouldn't be used on Sunday."

"The hospital made a mistake."

"Nothing I can do about it now."

"It's a matter of life and death."

"Yeah, that's what you doctors always say." The cop started to move away.

"But I must get to Manhattan!"

"Take the subway like the rest of us."

Not about to waste any more of his time arguing with this snooty foreigner, the cop turned around and returned to his post.

"Those damn Jews are at it again!" the cab driver muttered.

"What?" Ellen had been absorbed in thought. She looked around. A mob of black-clad men was carrying on up the street.

The cabbie made a U-turn. "I gotta swing around. This way is blocked off." He pulled up at the emergency entrance.

She gave the driver a five-dollar bill for a two-dollar fare, but didn't wait for change. She practically ran inside.

"Where's Dr. Vandermann?"

The unfamiliar clerk stopped punching the keys of her

computer and handed her a form. "Fill this out and wait your turn."

"No, no, no," Ellen said impatiently. "I'm not sick. I'm here about a patient."

"What's wrong with him?"

"I don't know—that's why I have to see Dr. Vandermann."

"Where is he?"

"That's what I asked you!"

"Miss—calm down—just tell me where the patient is."

Ellen took a deep breath. She knew that in her agitated state she was not communicating clearly. "He was admitted this morning—Dr. Vandermann brought him in. That's why I have to see him."

"Okay, now we're getting somewhere. What's the patient's name?"

"Jello, Bob."

The clerk punched some keys on her computer. She frowned. "I don't have an admission by that name."

"But I know that an ambulance brought him here, no more than an hour ago."

"An ambulance? Hour ago? Wait a minute." She flipped through some papers on the counter. "Oh, here it is." She looked up at Ellen and without a word handed her the form.

It read: "State of New York, Certificate of Death."

Ellen leaned against the counter. A strange tingling sensation was racing through every part of her body, all blood drained from her face.

"You okay?"

Ellen didn't answer.

"A relative of yours?" There was real sympathy in the girl's voice.

Tears formed in Ellen's eyes as she bit her lip. She shook her head no.

"A friend, huh?"

Ellen nodded. In a barely audible voice she asked, "Where is the . . . ?" Her lips formed the word but she couldn't say it.

"In the morgue."

She stumbled away from the desk.

The sharp ring of the phone outside the operating room startled both of them. Ron looked at Milt. The phone rang again, but there were no medical personnel around to answer it. "Pick it up, Milt," Ron whispered nervously.

Milt shrugged. "Hello?"

He listened for a moment.

"It's Milt Schultz, Dr. Vandermann. . . . They're all inside."

"Where is he?" Ron demanded.

Milt waved him away. "Subway?" he was saying. "Well, you can take the BMT right by the hospital, the D line . . . to Broadway and Lafayette, then you gotta switch to the Lex . . . yeah, the Lexington, number six. . . . But doc, they don't run much on Sunday."

When Milt hung up, Ron hissed through clenched teeth. "What the fuck is he doing?"

"I didn't get what happened. But he's taking the subway."

Feeling like she was moving in slow motion, Ellen made her way through the hospital's subterranean maze. It all looked strangely familiar. She had the sensation that she had been here before, but she couldn't remember when. Everything seemed hazy, blurry.

She turned a corner, and the sign screamed out at her—MORGUE!

The door was open. Near the entrance sat a technician devouring a slab of cherry pie. He looked up, his mouth full.

"I'm here about Jello," she said almost inaudibly.

"What?"

"Jello."

"Hate Jell-O. Cherry pie"—he held up a forkful—"that's my favorite."

Ellen was on the brink of bursting out in hysterical laughter. Every conversation since she'd entered the hospital felt like "Who's on first?"

"A man was brought in this morning. . . ."

"Yeah."

"Can I see him?"

Gomez, his mouth full, looked up at her. "You wanna see the John Doe?"

"He is . . . was . . ." Her voice cracked. "Someone very dear to me. I have to make sure."

He shrugged, put down his fork—Sunday was definitely not going according to plan—and lumbered toward the stainless-steel wall that resembled a giant filing cabinet. He pulled open a drawer. The rumbling of the rack sliding out echoed in the room and a blast of cold air hit Ellen in the face. She could see the outlines of a body covered with a dingy white sheet.

"He's all yours." Gomez moved back to his pie.

Slowly Ellen approached the rack. Cold air was rushing

out of the vault. Gently, she pulled back the top corner of the sheet.

The gray pallor of his face matched the gray of his stubbly beard. His eyes were closed, but his lips were slightly parted as if he was trying to speak.

"Oh, Jello," she whispered. "I'm so sorry."

Tears were running down her face freely, dropping onto his eyelids and forehead. With the edge of the sheet she dabbed them away tenderly.

Michaelson was sitting with his face buried in his hands, the picture of despair.

Milt shook his head in disgust. "For God's sakes, Ron, his own son is taking it better than you."

"Sure! He just inherited a fortune, I lost ten million bucks."

"We knew it was a long shot."

"But we came so close." Ron's voice was dripping with woe-is-me. "It was all arranged. Your baboon guy, the heart . . ."

"It didn't work out—who knew the old Jap would have another heart attack right on the operating table, while Vandermann is looking for the Upper East Side in Harlem?"

"You gave him the directions."

"Look, it's not my fault he told them to cut the Jap open and then got lost on the subway. I told him to change from the D to the Lex. Can I help it that he missed the stop?"

"You should have arranged the transportation."

"Oh, fuck!" Milt had reached the limit of putting up with Michaelson's hysteria. "What did you want me to do— carry him?"

"Whatever it took!" Ron's voice was rising. "That's your job!"

"No, Ron, that's not my job. My job is representing actors—or it used to be."

"Fuck the actors—they're just the bait."

"Yeah, right—so you can buy studios and peddle soda pop?" Milt was aware that he sounded like poor young Bill who had been fired a year back, but he didn't care anymore.

"You dumb shithead!" Ron spat out. "How many actors' hands do you have to hold to make that kind of money?"

"That's conflict of interest, Ron."

"Conflict of interest?"

"Yeah, that means it's *wrong*."

"Wrong!" Ron shouted. "You've made plenty of money for a lot of years, and now you start telling me it's wrong?"

Something snapped in Milt. "Yeah, now I've got the guts."

"You're an ass."

"And you're an ass*hole*."

"You can't talk to me like that. You're fired!"

"You can't fire me."

"Like hell, I can't."

"No, you can't—I quit!"

24

Marion answered the doorbell on the first ring. "Oh, Milt, what a surprise! Come on in."

"What's cooking?"

"Good chicken soup. You're just in time for lunch."

"Oh no, I can't stay that long—heading down to Atlantic City—"

"You, Milt? Gambling?"

"Just rescuing a former client, that's all."

"I'm relieved to know that."

"How's the boychik?"

"Well, he *thinks* he is back to normal." She shook her head in exasperation. "I have my hands full making sure he doesn't strain himself lifting bags of peat moss—"

"That's great news. Maybe he can come back to Brooklyn soon."

"Oh no, no, no. He has suffered a major trauma. Recovery from something like that can take a very long time. And there are psychological considerations to keep in mind. This is my field, you know."

"I thought your field was child psychology."

"With children and old men the same rules apply." She chuckled at her own joke.

Milt didn't join in. "Where is the little tot?"

"In his room," Marion answered, as if unaware of his sarcasm.

"I'll find him." Milt headed up the stairs.

"There's plenty of soup if you change your mind," she called after him.

Ben was lying on the bed, fully clothed, reading the paper when Milt walked in.

"Come on, Ben, up and at 'em. You're gonna get fat. Remember—spare tires are only good for rafting."

"My words coming back to haunt me."

"And don't I love rubbing it in." Milt slumped into a chair.

"I see your Japanese friend got a front-page obit." Ben pointed to the paper. "Quite a write-up."

"Yeah, sent the Hashikawa stock into a tailspin, too."

"Lot of trouble for you?"

"Don't even ask. Nothing but one big disaster."

"That guy Michaelson getting under your skin?"

"I don't give a shit about him. I told him to kiss my ass and I quit."

"You quit?"

"Yeah, and that's the problem. Now I've got Sarah to deal with twenty-four hours a day."

Ben nodded, knowingly. "I can imagine what that must be like."

"No, you can't. Sarah's the only person who could make me miss Michaelson."

His friend's wry humor and poker-face delivery should have made Ben laugh, but instead he just nodded sadly.

It didn't escape Milt's attention. "Boychik—how come you look so happy?"

"Oh, I'm such an idiot. . . ."

"This have something to do with Ellen?"

Ben nodded.

"I don't understand you. Why the hell did you ever leave her?"

Ben didn't answer. Sitting on the bed, his shoulders slumped, he kept his hands busy twisting the newspaper into a tight log.

"Ben, you were happy with her." Milt glanced in the direction of the doorway and lowered his voice. "Go back . . . before Marion sticks you into a baby buggy and starts wheeling you around."

Ben sighed. "It's too late now."

"It can't be—the girl loves you."

"No, Milt. Sunday morning, I went down to the Thunderbolt. . . . I thought I'd surprise her, help her feed her buddies. . . ."

"So? What did she say?"

"I didn't see her, but I saw her boyfriend."

"Who?"

"You know, the heart doctor, Vandermann. They're back together again."

"Wait a minute, Ben—you saw Vandermann?"

"That's right."

"This past Sunday morning at the Thunderbolt?"

"Yeah."

274

"It couldn't be. He had a heart transplant scheduled."

"But I'm sure I saw him there."

"Ben, let's face it—your eyesight ain't what it used to be."

"He passed right in front of me."

"Couldn't have. I saw him in Manhattan, in person, Sunday morning."

"You did?" Ben looked up at him.

"Yeah—it's a big secret, but he was the one who was supposed to put a new heart into the dead Jap."

"Could I have been wrong?"

"You sure were—in more ways than one." Milt threw another look at the door. "My advice—get the hell out of here, go back with Ellen."

For the first time since their conversation began, Ben smiled. "You're a good friend, Milt."

"And you owe me—I expect you for cards and pot roast this weekend."

"Our favorite things."

"I refuse to suffer alone."

"Okay, you got a date."

"Great." Milt glanced at his watch. "I better get going. Don Arnold's waiting for me in Atlantic City. He's doing a show tonight and he's jittery."

"I thought you quit working."

"Well, this is just a favor to Don."

"Send him my regards."

"Will do—he asks about you all the time."

No sooner had the door closed behind Milt than Marion's shrill voice could be heard calling from downstairs. "Ready for lunch?"

"In a few minutes!" he called back. "Just want to finish the paper!" Anything to delay that daily ritual when Marion fussed over him like he was an idiot child.

He turned back to the obituary page. Today was a better day than usual. Three of the four prominent personages had died over age eighty-five.

His eye wandered to the small print of the death notices. It always amazed him how many people died in one day.

What? He brought the paper closer to his face and adjusted his glasses. A tiny item in the *J*s read:

"JELLO, BOB will be sorely missed by all whose lives he touched. Friends may call at the Carlucci Funeral Home, 1722 Bensonhurst Ave. 5:30 tonight."

"Soup's getting cold!" It was Marion again.

"Fuck the soup," Ben muttered as he glanced at his watch.

His hand rubbed across the stubble on his chin. He kicked off his bedroom slippers and headed for the bathroom.

It was obvious to Ellen that Mr. Carlo Carlucci wasn't at all thrilled to "direct," as he put it, the funeral arrangements for Jello. Clearly, this was not a big-bucks affair. Ellen was going with the "economy package," having passed on the casket he'd recommended—"solid cherry with brass inlays, pure satin lining and a Sealy Posturepedic mattress"—in favor of a plain maple one. Furthermore, there would be no "entombment" since Ellen couldn't afford to buy a cemetery plot and grave marker. Jello would have to be cremated following the service.

"Of course, Miss Riccio, we do no cremations here," Mr. Carlucci informed her somewhat coolly, "since we are a Catholic funeral home."

"Oh, I should have known." Ellen remembered from her elementary school catechism classes that the Catholic Church used to excommunicate those who ordered crema- tion for themselves or others, and only recently had relaxed the ban somewhat. "Shall I find another funeral home then, Mr. Carlucci?"

"That will not be necessary," he added quickly. "We have an arrangement with the Neptune Society for those of our clients who wish that service."

"Oh, thank you." Ellen was relieved—she didn't have the energy to go through this rigmarole someplace else. But it was important to her that Jello's death be marked with a solemn service. He was not a nameless body to be buried in potter's field. He deserved a decent farewell.

She knew nothing of the ceremonies associated with death, except for the ones she had been a part of: her mother's and Aunt Marie's. She had chosen Carlucci's in Bensonhurst because it reminded her of Rizzo's Funeral Home in Amsterdam. At least she'd know what to expect.

She had no idea what Jello might have wished, what religion he was—indeed, if any—she never even learned his real name. So, she'd give him the best Italian-Catholic send-off she could reasonably expect to pay off in a year's time. That was all the sentiment she could afford.

She arrived a half hour early to make certain that Mr. Carlucci's assistants wouldn't mistakenly bar the way of any of the Bobs who might show up.

The bulletin board at the entrance informed arrivals that the "Jello Service" was listed for Chapel D. She made her way down the narrow corridor, which smelled heavily of incense, and found the correct room. Chapel D was decorated, as were all the funeral home chapels, with large portraits of saints in the midst of martyrdom, El Greco style. Whether this was gruesome or inspirational clearly depended on the eye of the beholder. The room was in semi-darkness anyway, so you had to take a perverse interest to make out the details.

Up toward the front, under an oversized cross, stood the open casket surrounded by white lilies and gladioli. She was surprised that her money had covered that quantity of flowers—how nice. She approached the casket slowly, and now she could see him. She had warned the funeral director about shaving the face or using too much makeup (Aunt Marie had looked like a hooker at her funeral), and she was pleased her requests had been honored. The only incongruity was the starched white shirt, black suit, and black patent-leather shoes. She had never seen Jello in such spiffy garb.

He looked quite comfortable and peaceful lying there. She would miss him terribly, but maybe he himself was glad to have life over. How else to interpret his excessive drinking after all the warnings he had received? Richard had told him in no uncertain terms that he was killing himself just a couple of months ago.

She was grateful that at least Richard had been there at the end. He did what he could to save Jello, but it was too late. He seemed so crestfallen telling her that he had failed to save a life so dear to her. She felt a little ashamed for the thoughts she had about him on the train.

"Excuse me, Miss Riccio."

Ellen turned around. "Oh, Mrs. Carlucci."

"May I begin?" The red-cheeked gray-haired matron, whose figure looked like she had consumed ten times the recommended daily allowance of pasta for years, motioned toward the organ. "Most mourners find the music soothing."

"Please, please do."

Mrs. Carlucci sat down and started pumping away on the foot pedals. It was an old-fashioned organ that required the organist to keep the pipes supplied with air or no sound came out. Soon the soft strains of "Ave Maria" filled the room. Ellen hoped Mrs. Carlucci wouldn't sing—she had forgotten to discuss that with Mr. Carlucci—but apparently singing was not part of the "economy package" because the woman pedaled mutely.

Ellen sighed. It was such a sad hymn. Well, she'd better go stand by the entryway to greet the arrivals. She had invited all her friends from the hospital and the Bobs, of course. She hoped there would be a good turnout—Jello always liked an audience.

Sister Clarita, bless her soul, was the first to show up.

"My dear, grieve not. He is the lucky one—he is with God."

"Thank you, Sister," Ellen said a bit coolly. She hated such platitudes, even from a nun.

"Did the flowers come?"

"What?"

"I sent some extra flowers from the hospital's chapel. We always have much too much, don't you think?"

No wonder she had thought Mr. Carlucci extra generous with the lilies. "Oh, Sister, you're a sweetheart." Ellen felt immediately guilty for being cool to her.

"I would have provided the casket too if I'd known you were making the arrangements with the funeral home."

"Sister, I couldn't impose."

"Oh, it wouldn't be any imposition. I am just so grateful I had the opportunity to give him the last rites before Dr. Vandermann performed the autopsy."

"Oh no, Dr. Vandermann didn't do an autopsy."

"But I saw him unpacking his instruments in the morgue."

"Oh no, it couldn't be. I'm sure he—"

Ellen was interrupted by the arrival of Choo-choo and Knowledge. They both had shaved and washed for the occasion, though their clothes still looked as dirty and tattered as ever. They seemed very uncomfortable in this setting.

"Thanks for coming," she said, hugging them both.

Ben poked his head through the doorway of Chapel D just as a young, pimply-faced priest had risen to address the small group of about a dozen people gathered near the front.

He recognized a number of them: Goldie, seated next to two other women in nurse's uniforms; Sister Clarita; Choo-choo and Knowledge; and, of course, Richard. The latter was seated next to Ellen, whose pale face seemed to match the white blouse she was wearing. She looked as fragile as a china doll. . . .

Seeing her after all this time sent a wave of such tenderness through him that he choked up for an instant. Then he took a deep breath, advanced into the room, and sat down in the back row. He tried to concentrate on what the priest was saying:

"This man who has died was a mystery to all of us gathered here. Did he leave behind a wife, a son, a daughter? We don't know. He chose not to share these things with us, perhaps hiding a great deal of pain.

"But what we know about the man who called himself Jello, the Bob, is that, in a small way, he wanted to make an imprint on humankind. He may have left behind no material possessions, but he left behind memories that we will always cherish.

"Please open your missals now and join me in reciting a passage from Saint Luke, Chapter Six, Verse Twenty. . . ."

The priest paused to allow everyone to find the correct page, and Ben found himself fumbling through the leatherette-covered book.

"Blessed are you poor, for yours is the kingdom of God," the priest began, the others muttering along. Ben located the spot and joined in the chorus, his rich voice rising above the others: "Blessed are you who hunger now, for you shall be satisfied. . . ."

Ellen turned around. Her eyes caught his and she smiled weakly. Ben smiled back. He could tell that she was happy to see him and his spirit soared. His voice rang out in the little chapel as he recited: "Blessed are you who weep now, for you shall laugh. . . ."

Following more prayers, and some truly god-awful organ playing, the priest invited the gathered to file past the casket for final good-byes.

As they rose to form a procession, a sharp beeping noise broke through the music. A doctor's beeper. Sure enough, Richard approached Ellen and whispered something in her ear. She nodded. Ben bristled as Richard kissed her on the cheek, but he was glad to see him leave.

Soon they all started to leave, most taking the time to

say a few words to Ellen before heading out. Nobody wanted to stay longer than absolutely necessary. And who could blame them?

Ben made sure he was the last in line. He rehearsed in his mind what he would say: "I'm very sorry, Ellen—I know you feel this loss deeply." Nah, too pompous. "I'm very sorry, Ellen—I know how much he meant to you." Better, but not quite right. "I'm very sorry, Ellen. . . ."

And there he was facing her. "I'm very sorry—" he started, but got nothing more out. She took one step forward and wrapped her arms around his neck.

They stood like that for a long time, holding on to each other for dear life.

Finally, they moved apart. It was necessary to let go to breathe.

"I'm glad you came," she said softly.

"I was just stunned when I read the obituary. When did it happen?"

"Sunday morning."

"I hope he didn't suffer."

"No, he had a quiet death. That's what Richard told me. . . . He was with Jello when—"

"Oh, then he *was* there." Milt was wrong.

"He tried to save him, but it was too late."

"That was very decent of Richard to go to Coney Island just before an important operation."

"What operation?"

"On that Japanese tycoon."

"No, no—it couldn't be."

"Yeah, Milt told me—he said Richard was to do a heart transplant on the guy."

"Heart transplant?" She seemed to be having a hard time comprehending his words.

"Yes, I'm sure of it. Milt was with him."

She stared blankly.

"Ellen—what's the matter?"

She didn't answer. She couldn't believe what he had just told her. It couldn't be true.

She turned away from him and slowly, deliberately, moved toward the casket. With trembling hands she pushed aside Jello's tie and unbuttoned his shirt.

She bent over the body and suddenly the pain in her back became excruciating. It traveled through her stomach toward her chest, closing her throat.

"Oh my God," she whispered hoarsely, staring at the long, gray-blue scar down the center of his chest. "Look what he's done."

"Ellen—what's wrong?" Ben was shocked by the expression of pain and horror on her face.

"He . . . he . . ." she started, but couldn't continue. She reached for Ben, but he had disappeared. All she saw in front of her was blackness.

He caught her as she crumpled to the ground.

25

Ben sat at the edge of a plastic chair in the waiting area of Saint Joseph's emergency room, next to a kid with a bloody nose, opposite a mother with a feverish baby and a man with a swollen arm in a sling. He barely noticed them. He was thinking about only one thing: Would Ellen be all right?

As they were wheeling her in, she regained consciousness and grabbed his hand, but the paramedics asked him to wait outside.

He had been waiting nervously ever since. How long had it been? He checked the wall clock: thirty-eight minutes. He inhaled and exhaled deeply a few times to calm himself down.

Two months ago he had left this hospital after his helicopter crash, vowing never to return. And here he was again. If there was a hell on earth, he knew what it was— a hospital.

Finally, a young woman doctor in a white lab coat, the

requisite stethoscope hanging from her neck, came out: "Is someone here for Ellen Riccio?"

"I am!" he shouted, jumping up. "How is she?"

"She's fine, but I decided to admit her overnight for observation and blood tests." She turned to leave.

Ben hurried after her. "What's wrong?"

She sighed in slight exasperation; she clearly did not want to get engaged in a long discussion. "Well, when I examined her I noticed that the whites of her eyes were yellow and when I palpitated her liver, it was enlarged. I'll be frank with you—I suspect hepatitis."

"Is that bad?"

"Probably not. With luck it's hepatitis A and we've caught it early. But we'll know more tomorrow when all the lab results come in. Then we can administer the appropriate medication and send her home."

"When can I see her?"

"You can talk to her now, but very briefly. I've sedated her, and we'll be taking her upstairs for the night."

An orderly was already pushing Ellen's gurney toward the elevator when Ben reached her.

"How are you feeling?"

"I'm fine, Ben, I'm fine," she said, but her voice sounded very weak.

"The doctor said you'll just be here overnight, and you can go home tomorrow."

"Okay."

He put his lips next to her ear and whispered. "I'll keep the bed warm for you."

Her eyes widened. "You will?"

"I saved my key." He held it up for her to see as the orderly pushed the gurney into the elevator.

She flashed him a wide grin as the door closed.

Going up in the elevator, the Demerol beginning to take effect, Ellen drifted off to sleep happily, only vaguely remembering that yesterday she had had a terrible nightmare in which Jello had died and Richard had stolen his heart.

Ben had a strange feeling as he slipped the key in the lock, opened the door to the apartment, and flicked on the lights.

In front of him was the living room he knew so well, but their dancing space was now littered with cardboard boxes. The books were gone from the shelves, china from the cabinets. She was moving out?

He walked into the kitchen. On the counter was a half-empty jar of peanut butter. He smiled. Goddamn it, he thought, when the general's not around, the troops get out of line. He'd take care of that.

His client list, which he used to use to confirm the next day's appointments, was still hanging by the kitchen phone. She had never taken it down. Maybe she always knew he'd come back. He sat down and started dialing the numbers, just as if two months hadn't passed and everything was in the same happy tranquil state before the helicopter accident had shattered it.

Everybody was happy to hear he was back. It was so easy to return to normal. But when he got through and put the phone down, he remembered that there was one more call—a not so easy one—that he still had to make.

He dialed the number.

"Hello," she answered right away.

"Marion—"

"My God, Father, you had me worried to death. Don't ever do that again. When are you coming home?"

"I am home, Marion."

"What?"

"I'm in Brooklyn."

There was silence. "With that woman?"

"Yes, Marion, with that woman."

She took a deep breath, then started in a very restrained voice. "Now, Father, we've been through this before—"

"Yes we have, Marion, and I don't want to go through it again."

"You have to listen to me," she went on nevertheless. "You had a traumatic experience—"

"Marion—"

"You need to be taken care of—"

"Marion, *please*—"

"No one can look after you the way I can."

"Marion!" he shouted. "If you want a child— get pregnant!"

He was ashamed of himself as soon as he hung up. He wanted to call her back. That was a cruel thing to say to his daughter, even if it was true. She had her problems, she was lonely, unhappy, but she had showered him with attention and affection. Too much, of course. His hand rested on the phone—the hell with it. He'd call her back tomorrow.

A new day was dawning for him; he felt like a young man about to embrace new adventures in life. Nothing could stop him. If it was hepatitis, he'd help her get over it, that's all.

He took off his jacket, loosened his tie, and walked into

his bedroom. Nothing had changed. Everything was the same in the bathroom, too. On the shelf in the medicine cabinet, next to his toothbrush and dental floss, he found a crushed tube of toothpaste—just as he had left it, except that she had put the cap back on.

He knew he was home.

Ellen opened her eyes and looked around. She was lying in a hospital room. She looked at the sheet covering her— it was stamped SAINT JOSEPH'S MEDICAL CENTER. She was a patient here. She shook her head to clear her drug-dulled senses. It was all coming back now. The sweet dream of seeing Ben again . . . holding his hand . . . his smile . . . the key to the apartment. . . .

She sat up with a jolt. All that was suddenly washed away by the image of Jello in his casket with a deep gray scar on his chest.

She reached over the bed rail and grabbed the phone. Mr. Carlucci answered himself.

"This is Ellen Riccio."

"Yes, Miss Riccio—I hope last night's arrangements for Mr. Jello were satisfactory."

"Yes, yes. But this is *very* important, Mr. Carlucci— please don't cremate the body."

"But Miss Riccio—it's too late."

"Too late?"

"We sent the body to the crematorium right after last night's service."

"Oh, I see. Thank you, Mr. Carlucci."

"You can pick up the ashes at your convenience."

Her mind was racing now. She threw off the sheet,

released the bed rail, and stepped onto the linoleum floor in her bare feet. Damn, it was cold. She was wearing only the flimsy hospital gown. She opened the little closet next to her bed. Empty. Where the hell did they put her clothes?

She poked her head out into the corridor. Not far from her door stood a cart loaded with fresh supplies, which an orderly was distributing on the floor. She pulled off a surgical gown pack and retreated into her room.

She put on a full scrub outfit—pants, top, and gown— and tied the shoe covers around her bare feet.

She couldn't waste any time. She had to know, and she had to know *now*. She caught the elevator as the door was closing and wedged her hand in. It snapped open. She jumped on and pushed the last button—B for basement.

Carrying a bouquet of flowers, Ben walked so quickly down the corridor to Ellen's room that he almost knocked over a nurse. "I'm so sorry."

"I know you!"

Oh no, it was Miss Hefty Bag who had taken care of him when he was here.

"Liked the hospital so much, you're back for a return visit?" She cackled.

"No, I'm here to see Ellen Riccio."

"Oh, sure—I remember—you're Ellen's friend."

"They said downstairs she's in room three-twelve."

"Yeah, but I just came from there and she's flown the coop."

"What?"

"Just kidding. They must have taken her down for the MRI already."

"MRI? Is that a test for hepatitis?"

"Oh no, she doesn't have hepatitis. And boy, are we glad of that. She's just anemic."

Ben shook his head. "I could have told you that. She doesn't eat right. She hasn't been taking care of herself." No sooner had the words left his mouth than Ben felt guilty. So much of this was his fault. Ellen had gotten stressed out by his accident and his leaving. Then Jello's death hit her double hard. And he wasn't there to look after her.

The nurse started to move on, but he stopped her. "But if she's anemic, why does she need an MRI?"

"Well, you know how doctors are—they just want to cover all bases."

Ben sighed with relief. "How long will it take?"

"Not long. An hour at most."

"Okay, I guess I'll go down to the cafeteria and kill some time there."

Only a few days ago Ellen had walked down the same corridor. She found the right door much more quickly this time.

Gomez was there hosing off a sickening glop of red and yellow fluids from the perforated autopsy table. The whole place stank. Breathe through the mouth, she told herself, and walked in.

"Hi." He looked at her. "I remember you. Looking for another corpse?"

"No, I just wanted to ask you a question."

"Shoot. Gomez at your service."

"Last Sunday—was an autopsy performed on that body?"

"Nah."

"Are you sure?"

"Sure I'm sure. I'd remember an autopsy, all right. It's a *lot* of work."

"But he had been cut open—he had a scar."

"Oh, that wasn't an autopsy, that was medical research." He shut off the water.

"Medical research?"

"Yeah—you know, like they take samples."

"Organ samples?"

"Yeah."

"What organ was taken out?"

"Just the heart."

"You did it?"

"No. Dr. Vandermann did it himself." Gomez finished his job and stashed his hose.

"When Jello got here, was he dead?"

"You gotta be kidding, this is the morgue."

"I meant—could he have been just *brain*-dead but still—"

"Look, lady—when they get here they're *dead* dead."

Ben sat at a cafeteria table sipping his second cup of decaf, his bouquet wilting slowly beside him. Poor Ellen. Anemia! Well, at least it wasn't hepatitis, but still. . . .

He vowed to himself to make up for everything. First he'd take her on a long vacation—someplace really nice. Was there anywhere she always wanted to go? California, maybe. California was fresh, sunny, famous for healthy foods. San Francisco. It would be romantic, too. Then he'd start her on a regular excercise program.

"Well, look what the cat dragged in." It was Goldie's cheerfully sarcastic voice. She plopped down beside him. "Saw you at the funeral home last night."

"Yeah," he muttered, embarrassed.

"So you back for good? Or just jerking her around again?"

He clenched his jaw. "I deserve that, Goldie, but I swear I'll make it up to her."

"You better."

"I will, honest."

"Okay." She smiled at him. "So you meeting Ellen for breakfast?"

"No—I'm waiting for her to get over with her tests."

"What tests?"

"Didn't you know? I guess maybe you wouldn't—it happened after you left. . . . She fainted."

"No wonder—she was too stressed out."

"They admitted her last night. They say it's anemia."

"Thank God it's nothing worse."

"Yeah."

"So where is she?"

"I told you—they sent her for tests, an MRI."

"MRI?" Goldie stood up, the alarm plain on her face. "What is it? What's wrong?"

"Oh nothing, nothing." She was making an effort to cover up, but Ben wasn't fooled.

"You gotta tell me, Goldie—what the hell made you jump?"

"Well, I was just surprised, that's all. It's a very expensive test and they don't give it just like that. But they probably want her to have the works—seeing as how she's one of our own."

Ben was appeased, somewhat.

"You sit tight, Ben. I'm gonna go to the MRI lab right now, and I'll come straight back to tell you what this is all about."

"Okay." He nodded. But a dark cloud had descended over him.

26

On the way up from the morgue, Ellen heard herself being paged. They must have noticed that she was gone from her room. Well, they'd just have to wait—she couldn't get diverted now.

The elevator seemed to be moving at a snail's pace. She chewed on her lip impatiently. Finally she got off and practically ran to the library.

"Good morning!" Penny, a new volunteer who came in a couple times a week to reshelve books, greeted her cheerfully.

"Hi, Penny."

"They were paging you over the loudspeaker," the volunteer said, eyeing Ellen's surgical garb. She'd never seen her dressed like that.

"I heard it—I'll take care of it in a minute." Ellen went directly to the stacks, but the book she was looking for wasn't there. "Penny—did somebody take out *Heartbeat*?"

"Well, I . . . here it is—it was just returned."

Ellen practically yanked the book from Penny's hands. Quickly, she flipped to the index. Here it was: "Re-animation, p. 274."

She could hear his voice dictating this section to her, but she needed to see it—in black and white—to make certain that this was how he had done it. She read:

If the experiments being conducted at Loma Linda University Medical Center in California prove as successful with human beings as they have been with sheep, a new pool of heart donors may open up. Surgeons there have shown that with the use of the correct mix of drugs it is possible to re-animate a heart in a sheep that has been dead for a half hour. . . .

The footnote cited the May 1992 issue of the *Annals of Thoracic Surgery*.

She sat down at her computer and entered the commands for a data search. It came up within seconds. Her eyes scanned the report, full of complicated medical language. Finally, she came to the list of drugs used in the re-animation:

250 ml Roe's solution
200,000 units streptokinase
10 ml of 50% dextrose

Again, the loudspeaker announced, "Ellen Riccio, please call extension 125."

Penny looked at her strangely. "Anything I can do?"

"No, no." Ellen picked up the phone and dialed extension 974.

"Pharmacy," a male voice came over the line.

"This is Ellen Riccio in the library calling. I'm compiling data on Dr. Vandermann's baboon experiments, and I can't quite make out his handwriting on the drugs list."

"Maybe I can help."

"That's what I was hoping."

"Let me pull up his file. . . ."

Ellen could hear the keys clicking on his computer. "Okay, I got it. What're you after?"

"Could you just read me the last order, if it's not too much."

"No problem."

Her pen poised, Ellen listened.

"Let's see . . . potassium chloride . . ."

Shit. That was not one of them.

"What else?"

"Roe's solution . . ."

Here it was!

". . . dextrose and streptokinase . . . that's spelled S-T-R-E-P-T-O-K-I-N-A-S-E."

"That's it. Thanks so much."

"Anytime."

"Hey, listen . . ." She stopped him before he hung up. "Just one more thing—can you tell me what potassium chloride is used for?"

"Well, it's normally used to replace potassium levels, but I think he uses it in his baboon transplants—twenty milliequivalents will stop a heart dead."

"Thanks. You have no idea how you've helped me."

Ellen was flushed when she hung up the phone. She had the bastard now.

Goldie's voice jolted her: "What the hell is going on?"

"Oh, Goldie . . . I don't know where to begin. . . ."

"I'll tell you—get your ass down to MRI."

With a soft whoosh, the pallet she was lying on slid into the MRI cylinder. It was a tight fit, the roof of the capsule only about ten inches from her face. She felt like she was stuffed into a soup can. The image struck her as funny. She had to be near hysteria to find any of this even mildly amusing, but the more she thought about it, the funnier it seemed. She giggled.

"Are you okay?" the operator asked. Patients didn't usually find this fun.

"Don't mind me—if I don't laugh, I'll cry."

"If you're feeling claustrophobic," he sounded worried, "just look in the mirror above you. It helps some people."

She looked up, but the mirror was skewed so it focused on her crumpled hospital gown. It made her look like an item inside a clothes dryer ready to tumble. She giggled again.

"Don't move now," the operator instructed from outside. "A liver section doesn't take long, but you have to keep still."

A steady knock-knock started, like Indian tom-toms, though not quite so hollow, more like coffee percolating in a pot, then grew more rapid.

"Okay, one more time."

More knocking and tapping. She was in a moon rocket, and a giant clock ticked off the countdown. She knew she couldn't laugh now. She tightened all her muscles, trying to keep still, and slowly, very slowly, tears seeped out of her eyes.

As soon as she was wheeled back to her room (over her objection that she could walk, but those were the hospital rules), she demanded her clothes.

"Don't worry, they're probably still down in emergency," the male nurse, a young guy she'd never seen before, assured her. "We'll send somebody for them."

"Could you do it now?"

"What's your hurry? You're not going anywhere."

"Yes, I am. I've had enough of this."

"Look, be sensible," his voice softened, became more cajoling. "If you want to leave against medical advice, no one will stop you, but what could it hurt to be a little patient? Huh? Dr. O'Brien thinks you should rest until he has a chance to interpret the MRI results."

She suddenly felt very tired. "Okay," she conceded. Meekly, she got into bed. She could use the time to clear her head, go over everything, plan carefully what to do next.

The nurse turned to leave.

"Wait—could you do me one favor?"

"What is it?"

"Mr. Ben Jacobs is in the cafeteria. Would you get word to him to come up."

A few minutes later there was a knock on the door. Ellen sat up quickly. "Ben! Come in, come in."

The door opened. But it was Richard, still in his scrubs.

"Ellen, I just found out you were here. . . ." His voice was full of concern. "What happened?"

So many angry emotions collided in her that her jaws locked and she was momentarily rendered speechless. She turned her head away. She did not want to look at him.

Worried, he came closer. "You have been through too much. I've been concerned about you for some time. . . ."

Listening to him, Ellen felt the color rising in her face. She was breathing rapidly.

"I know how much Jello meant to you," he continued. "I tried everything, but it was too late. Do you know how badly I feel that I couldn't save him?"

"You bastard!" she spat out through clenched teeth.

The force of her fury made Richard take a step back.

"You killed him!"

"Ellen . . . you must be delirious." His hand reached to touch her forehead, but her look stopped him.

"I know you killed him."

"Now listen to me." Richard's voice was calm and controlled. "Your emotions are not letting you think clearly. I told you months ago he had to stop drinking or he would die. Jello killed *himself*."

She raised herself on her elbow, her eyes burrowing into his. "I saw the scar. I talked to Sister Clarita and to Gomez. You took his heart."

Richard's mouth twitched slightly, but his measured tone did not waver. "Yes, I did—for medical research. It was good for no other purpose."

"Stop it! I researched your goddamn book, remember? I can tell you exactly how you did it—potassium chloride, streptokinase, dextrose. . . ."

Richard blanched momentarily, then a smirk crossed his face. "You have an excellent memory. But why would I want to do such a thing?"

"For your patient in Manhattan. That's where you went right after you stole Jello's heart."

Richard narrowed his eyes then turned on his heel and walked toward the window. With his back to her, he started tonelessly. "We have discussed this so often, you and I. How many people are in need of a new heart . . . how few hearts are available. You know people don't want to be donors." He spun around and pointed a long, accusing finger at her; he was speaking more rapidly now. "You Americans want many things, but no one is willing to pay the price. I experiment with baboons to save lives and what happens? Weeping animal lovers block the entrance to the hospital yelling, 'Cruelty!'" His voice was rising with emotion. "This country's values are insane. Tell me: Why should a drunken bum live and a giant of industry die?"

"So you admit it!"

"I admit nothing! Yes, I took Jello's heart—for medical research; it is upstairs in my laboratory. And yes, I had an operation scheduled in Manhattan with a baboon heart, but the patient died. Jello happened to die on the same day."

"I don't believe you."

"Oh, grow up! As much as you loved him, it couldn't have escaped your notice that he was killing himself with alcohol. No matter what I did, his life wasn't worth saving."

"How dare you decide whose life is worth saving? You are not God." Ellen's voice was shaking. "Only Nazis think like that. And you are—"

"I will not take this abuse from a delirious woman." Richard's voice was controlled and cold again. "And before you babble this nonsense around the hospital, think twice. I will not let you ruin my reputation. All I have said can be verified. Your weak suspicions rest on a mere coincidence."

"Maybe. But let's compare the blood types of your Japanese tycoon and Jello. Would it be another coincidence if we find a perfect match?"

Richard just glared at her.

"That, dear doctor, is called circumstantial *evidence*, and it has sent many a killer to prison."

The look on his face was frightening. He whipped around and stomped out of the room.

27

Ben found Ellen pacing the room in her bare feet and shivering in her flimsy hospital gown.

"Shouldn't you be in bed?"

She just ran over and threw her arms around him. "I'm so glad you're here."

"Did everything go all right with the MRI?"

"Oh, I'm fine, I'm fine. I'm just anemic."

He sighed with relief. Goldie's reaction had him more worried than he cared to admit. He had been so preoccupied with it that he'd left the bouquet of flowers in the cafeteria.

"There's something I've got to talk to you about," she went on, her voice sounding urgent, feverish.

"Okay, tell me. But get back in bed first—you'll catch pneumonia."

She did as he asked while he pulled up a chair. She

took a deep breath and began the story. When she finished, Ben said nothing for a long time.

"Ellen, do you realize that you're accusing him of murder?"

"That's what he's guilty of."

"Take it easy. What if he has Jello's heart up in his lab? After all, he never performed the operation on Milt's client. The poor sucker died before he got there."

"But I know that he—"

"Listen to me, Ellen. He is a very smart man. For sure he covered all his bases. I bet he has a record of a baboon heart being removed."

"It doesn't matter if—"

"Ellen, I hate to say it, but he's right—all you've got is a bunch of coincidences."

"You get enough coincidences and the courts call it circumstantial evidence."

"Maybe, but I doubt you got enough."

"I only need one more piece before I go to the district attorney. And you gotta help me get it."

"What?"

"I have to have a copy of the medical records on that Japanese tycoon."

"Why would you want that? He's dead."

"I'm positive that his blood and Jello's match perfectly."

"Ellen, I don't like this."

"He killed Jello! I can't let him get away with it."

Ben shook his head. "I don't know. . . ."

"Ben, please . . ."

"What can I do? I'm not a detective."

"Ask Milt to get the records."

"I don't—"

"Please, Ben—he'll do it for you." Her eyes were pleading.

Instinct told him to force her to end it—nothing good could come of it. But he couldn't refuse her. "Okay, Ellen, I'll talk to him, but you have to promise to keep quiet about this. Don't go telling Goldie—"

"Now you sound like Richard."

"Use your head—he is a very important doctor in this hospital. The heavy artillery is on his side. And right now, it's only your word against his."

Ellen became exasperated. "But if you help me it won't be *just* my word. I'll have real proof."

He could see how agitated she was. He took her hand in his. "Okay, I'll do what I can."

"Thanks." She smiled weakly at him. "Will you go see Milt now?"

"Later—I want to spend some time with you."

"We'll have all the time in the world to spend together, now that you're back." She kissed him on the lips. "As soon as they bring me my clothes I'm coming home."

"But does the doctor say you can go?"

"Oh, doctors! They'll keep doing tests until they find something wrong with you or kill you, whichever comes first. I just fainted—that's all."

She did look a whole lot better and some of the color had returned to her face. "Are you sure?"

"Absolutely. I feel fine. The only thing wrong with me is this." She spread her arms apart to show her oversized wrinkled hospital gown.

Ben smiled. "You look great in anything to me."

"Stop with the false compliments. Just get what you can out of Milt."

When Ben got to Milt's house, his friend wasn't home, but Sarah was glad for someone to lecture. "Come in, Ben—sit down," she pulled him inside.

"I can't stay, Sarah, I was just looking for Miltie—"

"I hear you're back in Brooklyn." News traveled fast.

"Yes, I am, Sarah. When will Milt be back?"

"Who can tell with him—when he gets wrapped up in his work, he loses all sense of time."

"Work? I thought he quit."

"For the umpteenth time, and for the umpteenth time he went back. You know Milt, he can never retire."

Ben shook his head. That was Milt, all right. "So I can probably catch him down at the office."

"Probably, but what's your hurry, have a cup of coffee with me."

"So you can abuse me some more, Sarah? No thanks."

A wounded expression appeared on her face. "That's very unfair of you, Ben. I only have your best interests at heart."

"So you always tell me."

"You men are all alike. You think younger is better. Well, I'll tell you something, Ben Jacobs. A mature woman has a great deal to offer."

"I don't doubt it, Sarah, but—"

"Brenda would have made you a good wife. She would have looked after you—"

"I don't need looking after."

Sarah didn't hear him, she was on a roll. "A shame it's too late, now that she's joined AA."

"She's an alcoholic?" He'd never have suspected it.

"Don't be ridiculous." Sarah's exasperated look said, "How dumb can you be?"

"I don't get it."

"She went there to find a man, and after her first meeting she had a date."

"What?"

"That's right. Another man recognized her value immediately."

"But why would she want to date a drunk?"

Sarah shot him a glance of disdain. "Not a *drunk*, Ben. A recovering alcoholic. Every man has a problem of some sort, and it might take a woman three years of marriage to find out what it is, but Brenda knows from the first date."

Well, there was a perverse logic to it, Ben had to admit.

"Not only that—*he* is dealing with it. And she will help him."

"Maybe I should join AA, Sarah."

She didn't appreciate the joke. "Don't make fun of me. . . . But now that you mention it, that's not a bad idea. Brenda attends the evening group over at the First Presbyterian on Henry."

Ben shook his head. Sarah was incorrigible. No wonder Milt went back to work so quickly.

The door opened a crack, and a hand slipped in, holding the white blouse and navy suit Ellen had worn last night—all neatly pressed and hanging on a hanger—followed by the smiling face of Sister Clarita.

"Sister! Thank you so much!"

"I found these lying in a heap in the emergency room and thought you might appreciate—"

"You're too good." Ellen walked over and embraced her. "How are you feeling?"

"Oh, great!"

The nun gave her a disbelieving look, but Ellen didn't notice. She immediately started to get dressed.

"I was worried about you, my dear. . . ."

"Nothing to worry about."

"I know this homeless gentleman—Jello—meant so much to you. And I know you haven't been feeling well for some time. Often the combination of shock and grief on an already weakened system—"

"Sister, please. I still have some fight left in me."

"I know you do. That's what concerns me."

Ellen was dressed, but she was missing one essential item. "What happened to my shoes?"

"Oh dear—they're downstairs in my room, I forgot them. I'll be right back."

"I'll go with you."

"But you're barefoot!"

"I don't care."

The hospital personnel, used to strange sights, didn't give much notice to the curious pair—old nun and barefoot librarian making their way to the basement.

"Shall I make a cup of tea?" Sister Clarita asked when they got there and the shoes were located.

"No, no—" Ellen started, then realized that it would be rude to refuse after Sister Clarita had been so kind. Also, the nun might have seen something more down in the morgue. "Why not."

Sister Clarita motioned for Ellen to sit on the large trunk against the wall while she busied herself with her chipped cup and electric coil.

"I can't get out of my mind how Jello died. . . ." Ellen ventured, trying to draw the nun out.

Sister Clarita nodded. "It is a very natural reaction— to ask ourselves what we could have done to prevent the death of a loved one."

"Oh, I don't blame myself, I just wonder if Dr. Vandermann did all he could." She knew she was going out on a limb but she didn't know how else to go about it.

Sister Clarita sat down next to her wearily. Ellen waited, but the nun didn't say anything. She seemed to be studying the crucifix on the wall, then she sighed. "Jesus said, 'Judge not,' and it is not our place to mete out punishment for the wrongs of others."

"Sister—" Ellen couldn't believe her ears. Was Sister Clarita validating her suspicions?

But the nun put her finger to her lips. "It is very easy in the quest for revenge to do a lot of harm. If the feelings of hate replace the feelings of love in your heart, the evil continues to win."

"But Sister, what—"

The nun stood up abruptly. "Our tea is ready!" she announced cheerily as if they'd just been talking about the weather. It was clear that she intended to answer no more questions.

She was back in an instant with a cup of chamomile tea. "Drink up—it will help settle you."

"Yes," Ellen muttered, lost in thought, remembering vaguely the calming effect the tea had had on her the last time.

"I was very sorry . . ." the nun sat next to Ellen again,

"that I could make no other contribution to the funeral. But I found out too late."

"Oh, but Sister, you gave all those beautiful flowers."

"Well, since he was your friend, I had hoped to offer something more personal." She patted the trunk they were sitting on. "This coffin."

"What?" Startled, Ellen looked down. The wooden trunk resembled a hope chest except it was somewhat wider and considerably longer. Big enough for . . . "Jesus!" she exclaimed.

"Yes, it's a coffin. Plain but quite usable. I made it myself. Believe me, it was no easy task. Feel it—took weeks to sand it smooth." She rubbed it affectionately.

Despite herself, Ellen did the same—the wood was like satin, so smooth it felt almost moist.

"I use it as my bed, this cushioned top is quite comfortable. Do you like it?"

Ellen didn't know what to say. How do you compliment someone's coffin? "It's nice," she managed. "It looks like a hope chest."

"It is a hope chest—preparing me for the time when I hope to meet God."

"Oh, Sister, that's so depressing."

"Not at all, my dear." Her eyes shone. "It is a joyful feeling not to be afraid of death. It should not be a time of sorrow—it should be a time of celebration. We go home, where we belong. This"—she patted the trunk again—"reminds me of that day."

Ellen gulped the rest of the tea. She couldn't wait to get out of there. It was too much—Jello's death, Richard's treachery, sitting on a coffin, and a lecture about how death is good for you.

This was plain crazy and she'd had enough madness in the last twenty-four hours.

The taxi moved slowly across the Brooklyn Bridge in the midday traffic. Ben was glad he had decided not to drive—this kind of tie-up would make him crazy if he was behind the wheel right now. Where the hell was everyone going? Why weren't they all at work, or at lunch, at this hour?

He looked out of the window at the twin towers of the World Trade Center, two giants that had almost come crumbling down into a pile of rubble. Their massive size would have done nothing to protect them if the bombers had been smarter, put the dynamite in a more vulnerable spot.

Ben had never liked the two buildings. To him, they unbalanced the beautiful skyline that he so often watched from Milt's balcony. It was funny that all the best postcards of New York City—those showing the famous skyline in silhouette against the setting sun or sparkling like a bejeweled necklace at night—were always taken from Brooklyn. The people who paid a fortune to live in Manhattan got only unobstructed views of obstructions.

He glanced at his watch—almost noon. He hoped that Milt would have the records by the time he got there. When Ben called him from the house, Milt promised he'd do his best, pull every string he had. Ben knew that if anyone could do it, Milt could.

Yet another part of him wanted nothing to do with all this—he didn't like Ellen running around to district attorneys, waiting for indictments, hoping to see Jello's killer behind bars. He didn't care if Richard did it. He just wanted life to get back to normal, to the blissful way it had been before the helicopter crash. He wanted to recapture the precious time he had lost—just to sit at home and love her. She might be back there right now and here he was, crawling in traffic to Manhattan. . . . Shit!

"What's the address again?" the taxi driver asked.

"Corner of Forty-third and Lex."

They were ten blocks away and traffic was moving even slower.

"Stop—I'll walk the rest of the way."

"Suit yourself." The driver didn't seem pleased.

Ben gave him an extra buck and jumped out.

God, how he hated Manhattan. Pedestrians were scurrying back and forth with the desperation of rats in a maze, pushing past street vendors selling purses and watches from cardboard boxes. Everyone trying to make a living any way they could.

At last—Milt's building. The elevator doors opened on the fortieth floor onto a futuristic reception area—if the Martians ever landed, they'd be right at home—and he approached the attractive woman seated under a large Famous Artists logo: FA. In Los Angeles, Milt had jokingly told him, the agency was known as FA-LA-LA.

"I'd like to see Milt Schultz, please."

"Your name?" she asked with a practiced smile.

"Ben Jacobs!" a voice boomed behind him.

Ben turned to see the outstretched arms of Don Arnold approaching him. He had gained some weight.

"I know what you're thinking, Ben—I haven't been exercising, but I'll get with it now that you're up and around."

"That's right, I'll start you on a program this week," Ben threatened, his finger wagging.

311

"Oh, you never met my wife." Don turned to present a beautiful blonde behind him. Ben recognized her immediately from her pictures. So this was the infamous Dawn.

"Mr. Jacobs, I want to thank you for helping Don so much." She extended a well-manicured hand, which was sagging from the weight of a large diamond ring.

"See the rock, Ben?" Don winked. "I got it for our engagement."

They both laughed.

Ben didn't get the joke—the last he had heard they were getting divorced.

"I know what you're thinking, Ben." Don seemed to be reading his mind. "But I got news for you. Yesterday, our divorce papers were finally signed. So we went out to celebrate. . . ."

Ben nodded mutely, still not comprehending.

"So guess what happened?" Don continued. "We had a few drinks—only a couple, Ben, I'm still on the wagon." He guffawed. "Anyway, we resolved our differences and we drove down to Elkton, Maryland, and got married all over again."

"Isn't that romantic?" Dawn chirped, looking up adoringly at Don, who squeezed her tightly. "The tabloids will have a field day when it leaks out."

One of the bodyguards, who had been holding the elevator open while the conversation was going on, called out, "Mr. Arnold, Mrs. Arnold, you're going to be late!"

"Come with us, Ben," Don urged. "Join me and my team for lunch."

"Thanks a lot, but I can't."

"Too bad, but see you soon, huh? I'll have my manager call you to arrange a workout schedule."

"Good." Ben agreed. "And Don—"

"What?" The elevator was in danger of closing on the singer's nose.

"When you order lunch, think about the punishment I'll put you through for every calorie you eat."

"I hear you!" Don bellowed out from behind the closed doors just as Milt came out.

"Poor sucker." Milt shook his head. "That broad got her ring through his nose for the second time."

Ben nodded. "I feel sorry for him, too, but he's gotta grow up."

"Well, he's one of those that learns the hard way."

"Yeah, like me. I just grew up myself."

Milt chuckled, leading the way to his office.

"Listen, Miltie—I don't wanna keep you from lunch. I just came to pick up what you got."

Milt sighed and slumped down in the chair behind his desk. "I got bad news, boychik. Your girl may be on to something. I had this feeling myself when Vandermann—"

"You couldn't get the records?" Ben interrupted him impatiently.

"Every piece of paper was taken back to Japan."

"I can't believe it."

"It's their legal right."

"Didn't the hospital keep a copy?"

"The son insisted on taking it all."

"Then maybe, Milt, you could call him in Japan."

"And tell him what, exactly? That I need his father's medical records to prove a conspiracy to commit a murder?"

"No, of course not, but you know the guy, make up something."

"Listen, that young Hashikawa hates Americans and I'm the number two American on his hate list."

"Well at least you're not number one."

"Oh no, that's Michaelson. And I can't say that I blame him."

Ben smiled. He had heard so much about the boss from Milt. "So how come you came back?"

"Well—what could I do?" Milt grinned sheepishly. "He needs me for the new deal he's trying to work out with Credit Lyonnais."

"Are *they* gonna buy out World Pictures?"

"Ronnie seems sure of it. You should see the French Provincial table we just had installed in the conference room."

Ben laughed. What else could he do? Ellen would be unhappy about the records, but maybe it would put an end to the whole sorry mess.

28

Ellen reached out her hand to touch Ben, but all she could feel was cool sheets. She awakened abruptly with a feeling of dread. Was Ben really here last night?

Then she remembered.

He had come back from Milt's office empty-handed, anxious to convince her that she should drop her pursuit of Richard.

She couldn't; she was adamant.

"Well, at least let's not talk about it anymore tonight," he pleaded.

"Okay," she finally agreed. She didn't have the energy to argue with him. She felt completely exhausted.

"I'll take you out to dinner—someplace nice."

"I'm too tired," she said, then, seeing the disappointment on his face, added, "I just want to stay here—with you."

"All right, then." He brightened. "I'll cook. I'll make your favorite dish—peanut butter and jelly." There was a mischievous glint in his eyes.

She smiled, came over to him and hugged him. "You're the best," she whispered.

He made the sandwich, and she forced herself to eat some to please him—she had no appetite at all.

"Tomorrow, we'll have a great day," he promised. "I've lined up clients at the gym in the morning, but I'll come home early, and let's do something fun—take a ride up the Catskills maybe, huh?"

"Oh no, I can't. I have to go back in for another test."

"What?" His face expressed alarm.

"Don't worry—it's just because that stupid MRI was inconclusive."

"Inconclusive? What does that mean?"

"I don't know. They pay a fortune for these space-age machines and then they can't read the results."

"So you have to do it over?"

"No. Dr. O'Brien wants to do a different test this time."

"Like what?"

"Oh, Ben, he gave me some long, involved explanation, but I wasn't even paying attention. I had other things on my mind."

"Ellen, this is your health. You have to pay attention. You can't let this obsession with Jello's death—"

"Okay, okay, I'll pay attention tomorrow. But don't beat me up. I'm too tired to fight."

He took her into his arms then and didn't let go, rocking her like a baby until she fell asleep.

That's the last thing she remembered. But where was

he now? Oh God, it must be late—he'd probably left for the gym already.

She stumbled out of bed and headed for the kitchen—she needed a cup of coffee to get her going.

He had thought of that. The coffeepot was on, and the kitchen table set for breakfast. He had gone to a lot of trouble, put out white linen (brand-new, he must have bought it) and strawberries, milk, cereal. Next to her bowl, he'd left a note:

Dear Ellen, You need the rest, so I didn't wake you. I'll be through by 11 and back to take you to the hospital for your tests.

He had signed the note with a large *B* and drawn a happy face in the top loop and a sad face in the bottom loop. The happy face was labeled *me* and the sad face *you*.

It touched her—he was so caring and thoughtful, not at all the gruff old man he pretended to be.

She looked at the breakfast, but the thought of eating just brought on a queasy feeling. Maybe later. Right now she had to get to the hospital and put into motion the next phase of her plan. No matter what Ben said, she couldn't rest until she saw Richard punished for what he had done.

Fortunately, Mr. Grabowski, the hospital administrator, agreed to see her at a moment's notice. But when she entered his office, she found the normally cheerful man in an agitated state.

"Come in, Ellen, come in—it's good you're here. I was going to call you in myself."

"You were?" She was surprised, but maybe he had heard she'd been ill.

"I wanted to talk to you about Dr. Vandermann." He was twisting uncomfortably in his oversized office chair, which he filled to the brim. "I'm very upset about what's happened."

Ellen was stunned. "You know?"

"Dr. Vandermann left a long letter explaining everything."

"A confession?"

"What?"

"He told you everything?"

"Well, of course. And it's tragic that a young man at the height of his career be forced to make a decision like this. But I must say, I do admire his choice."

"Admire?"

"Choosing between being the chief of staff of this hospital—a position he was assured—and caring for his mother. Now, *that* is a noble gesture."

Ellen sat stupefied.

"And isn't it ironic that the mother of a cardiologist should develop heart disease?"

Ellen's mind was racing; her thoughts were so jumbled she was speechless. The administrator didn't notice—as usual he talked without pause, lest she get the chance to interrupt his monologue: "Fortunately, I came to the office early, read his letter, and managed to get him on the phone just before he boarded his plane for Vienna. I suggested that he bring his mother here. We would give her the best possible care, but unfortunately travel is not possible in her condition. His resignation isn't official, of course, until the board accepts—"

"He resigned?"

"He submitted a letter of resignation, but I am still hoping he will change his mind and take a leave of absence instead. The board doesn't meet until next week."

"Mr. Grabowski—"

"And this is why I wanted to talk to you, my dear. You must help us."

"What?"

"It is well known that you and Dr. Vandermann are friends, if you don't mind my saying so. Please use your influence to persuade him not to make his decision final as yet—for the good of Saint Joseph's." He paused, giving her a chance to answer in the affirmative.

"I can't do that," she said softly.

"Can't?" He didn't seem to comprehend the word.

"Dr. Vandermann and I are no longer friends."

"Oh, oh . . . I see." Apparently, this made more sense to him.

He got up from his desk, not about to waste any more time on a lost cause. "Well, then, I'll have to go to Vienna myself. We cannot afford to lose such a fine doctor." He opened the door for her, giving her no choice but to leave.

"Mr. Grabowski . . ." But he had already turned away from her. Well, there was no point in saying anything now— Richard had fled. "Good luck on your trip." She closed the door behind her.

She could have told him that he was wasting his time going to Vienna—it wasn't likely that Richard would clear out in a panic and leave a map to his whereabouts. But she didn't care what Mr. Grabowski did. Let him run around Europe looking for Richard's mother. He wasn't going to find her—the old lady had died four years ago.

* * *

"Ellen!" Ben called out as he entered the apartment. There was no answer. He stood there, listening for the sound of bathwater running. Silence.

He walked into the kitchen. The untouched breakfast was still there, but lying on top of the cereal bowl was a note from her:

You don't have to take me to the hospital. I'm going in early to take care of some very important business. Be home in the afternoon for a tango lesson. I love you more than ever.

Imitating him, she had signed it with a large *E*, and drawn two happy faces in each of the loops.

Ben smiled. He read it a second time. But what did she mean by "important business"? He hoped that she hadn't devised some new scheme to prove Jello's murder.

As far as he was concerned, the most important thing was that they were together. He found it difficult this morning to be without her, even for a couple of hours.

Her appointment was at noon. He remembered that the doctor's name was O'Brien and that his office was located in the hospital annex. He decided to catch up to her there.

"What can I do for you?" the spindly secretary asked, peering at Ben over her horn-rimmed glasses.

"I'm here for Miss Ellen Riccio. Is she in with the doctor already?"

The secretary hesitated. "Just a second." She pressed the buzzer.

"Yes," came a male voice through the speaker.

"Dr. O'Brien—there is a gentleman here for Ellen."

"I'll be right there."

Ben heard a click and a moment later the doctor came

out. He was a kindly-looking man with a gently wrinkled Marcus Welby face. He extended his hand. "You must be Ellen's father."

"No, but you could call me the next of kin. My name is Ben Jacobs."

The doctor studied him for a moment as if deciding what to say next.

"Is Ellen taking her test now?" Ben asked.

"No, she left a message with my service canceling the appointment, and we haven't been able to reach her to reschedule."

"I don't understand." A deep furrow creased Ben's forehead. "I know she meant to come here."

"I wish she'd kept the appointment—I'm very concerned about her." The doctor's tone of voice underscored the import of his words.

"What's this all about?"

"Didn't she tell you?

"Well, she said she had to have another test, but seemed to take it lightly."

"Hmm." The doctor rubbed his chin with the back of his hand. "Will you come inside for a moment?"

"Of course." Ben followed him into the office. "I wish you'd explain to me what's going on."

The doctor sat down behind his desk heavily and motioned for Ben to take a chair opposite. "Mr. Jacobs, I've known Ellen for a number of years. She is an excellent librarian and a genuinely nice person—"

"I agree she's wonderful, Doctor, but she doesn't take care of herself."

"Well, every patient has his way of relating to his body. Ellen is one of those who doesn't want to be bothered."

"I know what you mean. Just how bad is her anemia?"

"Anemia is not a disease, Mr. Jacobs. It is a symptom of several diseases. Which is why I ordered the MRI. But when I discussed the results with Ellen, it was like she didn't hear me."

"What did the MRI show?" Ben asked, fear beginning to creep into his belly now.

"I can't be one hundred percent sure. That's why it is essential to take a biopsy."

"Biopsy?"

"Yes."

"You mean . . ." the words did not want to leave Ben's lips, "like for cancer?"

The doctor nodded, his kind face full of sympathy.

"I know she's had a bad back, maybe ulcers, anemia even, but—" Ben couldn't continue.

"Unfortunately those symptoms often mask cancer of the pancreas. The MRI shows an enlargement of that organ and a mass around the liver. But I can't say what it is with certainty until I do a biopsy."

"You mean open her up?"

"No, that's not necessary these days. We just insert a long needle into her abdomen, extract a tiny bit of pancreatic tissue, and send it to the lab."

"And they can tell you if she has cancer?"

"Yes, cancer cells show up very clearly under the microscope."

"And *if* she has it," Ben stressed the *if*, not wanting to admit that this could really be, "then you'd have to operate?"

"No, under those circumstances, surgery would be useless."

"Useless?" A flush came to Ben's cheeks.

"By the time this type of cancer shows up it's almost always fatal."

Ben's hands were now shaking. His eyes were boring into the doctor.

"Now, Mr. Jacobs, I don't want to alarm you unnecessarily. I have *not done* the biopsy. I have only the MRI to go by, which is not always accurate."

"How often is it wrong?"

"Well the accuracy of—" He paused for a long moment, then said softly, "Not very often. The MRI is considered better than ninety percent accurate."

"Ninety percent," Ben echoed. "So you are pretty sure this is what she has?"

"Let me stress again, I must do the biopsy first."

"But you already know. That's what you're really saying. You *know*. You just won't tell the patient without double-checking."

The doctor seemed to be weighing his words. "All right, you could put it that way. But it would be irresponsible for me to make a diagnosis of terminal cancer without a biopsy. I sincerely hope that the MRI is wrong."

Ben's jaw clenched. "But suppose it's not wrong."

"Please, Mr. Jacobs, let's not—"

"I have to know what you know! Tell me."

"Mr. Jacobs—"

"Tell me, goddamn it!"

The doctor's voice was very soft. "If the biopsy confirms what the MRI leads me to suspect . . . Ellen may have only six months left."

"Six months!"

"Nothing can be done once the cancer has spread from the pancreas to the liver."

"Why not?"

"Because with the liver compromised, the body has no means of removing its own toxins."

Ben buried his face in his hands.

The doctor leaned over his desk. "Are you all right?"

Ben pulled himself together and looked up at the doctor. "Is there a lot of pain?"

"Well . . . there are many nerve endings around the liver. We can give painkillers, of course, but that won't alter the progress of the disease."

The tension Ben had been trying to keep under control throughout the conversation was now sending tremors through his knotted muscles. Only his voice remained steady, as if removed from the rest of him. "What about radiation, chemotherapy—"

"Yes, that could be tried, but once the liver is involved, treatment of that type would only get her two or three more months at best."

"Can't you do *something!*"

"I'm very sorry, Mr. Jacobs, very sorry, but nothing can be done."

"So you'll just wait for her to die."

"If we had caught it in the pancreas we could have saved her but once—"

"Why didn't you catch it?" Ben jumped to his feet. "She works in this fucking hospital. Doctors see her a hundred times a day, and nobody saw a goddamn thing?!"

The doctor didn't answer. He only looked on with great sympathy as Ben crumpled back into his chair, sobbing.

29

Numb, Ben walked from the annex to the main wing of the hospital. The doctor had let him pour out his emotions until he had nothing left. Now he felt only exhaustion—it was almost too much for him to walk this distance. He was breathing heavily, like a man who had run a marathon . . . and lost.

Normally, he would have taken the stairs to the mezzanine, but this time he opted for the elevator. When he reached the library he stopped in the doorway, taking in the scene in front of him. Ellen, seated at her desk, a bunched up pillow behind her back, was deeply engrossed in some papers in front of her. She looked like a little schoolgirl cramming for her exams. He took a deep breath and approached her.

She raised her head and her face immediately broke out into a smile. "Oh, Ben, see what you think of this—"

She waved a sheaf of papers at him. "I'm composing a report on the whole case, got all Richard's orders from the pharmacy, and I—" Suddenly she stopped. "What are you doing here?"

"I came to see you."

"Oh, you're so romantic, but—" She turned to a doctor who had just approached.

"What is it that you need, Dr. Stevenson?"

"Did the new issue of *Modern Pathology* come in yet?"

"Penny will check for you. . . ." She motioned to the volunteer sorting magazines. Then she turned back to Ben. "Oh, I didn't tell you—Richard's gone."

"Gone?"

"Yes—he put in a letter of resignation, supposedly left for Vienna."

"That's great—you scared him off. You've accomplished your goal."

"Not yet. If I can't send him to prison, I have to make sure he never practices medicine." Her tone was urgent, feverish.

"But Ellen—"

"Sooner or later, he'll want to work in a hospital again—somewhere in the world. And when he does, he will need a reference from Mr. Grabowski, and I'll find out where he is. And believe me"—she pointed to her papers—"that hospital will get this report."

"Ellen, this is crazy. Please give it up. Richard is gone. Jello is dead. *We* are here . . . still alive."

"Yes, but—"

"No buts."

"Ben, don't you understand? I can't let him get away

with this. I *can't*. It's impossible for me to think of anything else."

"I know. You even canceled your appointment this morning."

"Oh, that's bullshit. I know hospital routines. They test you for everything. They have to rule out the worst stuff for insurance reasons. I have anemia, that's all."

Ben just looked at her. She caught his expression. "Okay, okay, I'll reschedule first thing tomorrow."

"No." Ben picked up the phone and put it in her hand. "Now, please . . ."

She shrugged her shoulders. As she dialed, she smiled up at him. "Now that you're here, I'll be too happy to feel sick."

Dr. O'Brien rearranged his schedule to take care of Ellen late that afternoon. Ben sat in the reception room, anxiously waiting, only to be told that the laboratory report would not be ready until the next day.

Ellen didn't seem fazed by any of it, and the biopsy wasn't even mentioned when they went shopping in Brighton Beach before going home.

She babbled on, in that feverish way she had of talking lately, about the detailed report she was preparing. She had hit on the idea of testing Jello's heart, if it was still in Richard's laboratory, for the presence of the drugs she was sure he had used. When Ben wearily cautioned that the presence of drugs did not prove murder, only that Richard had experimented on the heart, she responded as if she hadn't heard him, speculating that maybe the district attorney—once he saw her report—would try to extradite Richard through some international law she was sure existed for such purpose.

That evening they munched on a salad that Ben made with every vegetable known to man. It was as if these vegetables might cause a miracle cure. Ellen didn't have much appetite, but Ben kept urging her on.

With a sigh of relief, he put her to bed to get ready for whatever the next day might bring. Lying beside her, he listened to her even breathing. Finally, a troubled sleep overcame him, too, and he tumbled into the land of nightmares.

He was standing on the bank of the river again, watching his wife flounder helplessly in the turbulent waters. But this time, as her head came up through the swirling current, he saw Ellen's face. And then she disappeared under the water. With a scream of anguish he jumped after her into the river, desperately trying to reach her.

He awoke in a cold sweat.

It was still dark. Ellen was sleeping soundly.

He squeezed his eyes shut very tightly and willed himself to dream again. He wanted it to end differently this time, with Ellen coughing up water safely on the bank, laughing at the minor mishap. But no matter how hard he tried, the image wouldn't come into focus.

He turned over on his back, resting his head on his clasped hands, and stared into the darkness.

How did one pray? He didn't know—he hadn't done it since he was a child. "God," he started, talking silently to the ceiling, "if you're listening up there, please help me."

He waited—maybe some answer would come, some sign that God was on duty.

"I never asked you for anything before," he tried again,

"not even when Betty got sick. But this is too cruel. You let me live this long, let me fool myself into believing that I had it together. Is this your way of making a point? Punishing me for being too wrapped up in myself? Well, it stinks. . . ."

Maybe this wasn't respectful.

He got out of bed and knelt on the floor with his hands folded. "Please, God, I didn't know what it was to be alive until this girl came into my life. She loves me, and without her love, life would be nothing. I'd be a walking corpse. I'm begging you for this one thing, and I'm willing to pay. I'll give up all the time I have left, whatever that is—ten years, fifteen—just *please* give it all to her. Save her. All I ask for me is a couple of years with her. I'm not greedy—I'd take one year. Just let me have her a little while longer. Please, God, I'll never bother you again."

30

Ellen left Dr. O'Brien's office staring straight ahead. Purposefully, she walked out of the annex and went directly to the main wing of the hospital. There was only one place she wanted to go, one person she wanted to see right now.

She took the stairs down to the basement, which had become so familiar to her. When she passed the morgue and saw Gomez wolfing down a sandwich, she almost burst out in the hysterical laughter that lately seemed to be always bubbling up in her.

It didn't surprise her that Sister Clarita was waiting. There was something unreal about the nun—she seemed to know everything that went on in the hospital and she was always there when she was needed.

The little electric coil was already heating water in the chipped cup.

"Tea will be ready in no time," Sister Clarita announced cheerily.

"Thank you, Sister."

Ellen sat down on the trunk; it didn't bother her now that it was really a coffin.

The nun handed her the tea and sat down beside her. "So what is on your mind, my dear?"

Ellen took a sip—she didn't know quite how to begin. Then she blurted it out: "Sister, what happens after we die?"

"We go home, we get to see God again."

"How can you be sure?"

"Aah, that is one of the paradoxes of life—we can never be sure, we can only believe. And this is what is so frightening to most people."

"But you're not afraid."

"No."

"Why aren't you afraid if everyone else is?"

"I believe in the goodness of God."

"I believe that too, but . . . but . . . death is . . ." Ellen was groping for words.

The nun smiled sweetly, almost angelically. "Don't think about death as an end to life, because it is not. Imagine that you are simply taking off your body, like a worn-out old coat. . . . You no longer need it. But *you* continue to exist as you did before—except lighter, happier . . . because nothing weighs you down now, because there is nothing obstructing your view of the other plane of existence which we all sense, but which we cannot see as long as we look through our body's eyes."

Sister Clarita's melodic voice had put Ellen in a trance-like state, or was it the tea? She looked down, the cup was empty, then it was full again. She finished it and stood up. "Thank you, Sister."

"Not at all. We'll talk again, my dear."

She went back upstairs, but she was not ready to return to work. Yet she couldn't go home and face Ben just now. She left the hospital and made her way to the boardwalk.

It was pleasant in the April sunshine. A salty breeze was coming off the ocean, smelling faintly of fish. Frothy waves worked hard to wash the beach clean. Soon all this would be erased from her life. Or would it? Or would she still be here walking the beach, without her "coat," as Sister Clarita put it, invisible to those around her?

As she walked, something struck her leg and she looked down. At her feet lay a red battered rubber ball. She picked it up.

"Hey, lady, over here!" A bunch of boys, probably playing hooky from school, were calling to her from the beach. She threw the ball back.

She removed her shoes and went down to the sand, remembering Ben walking beside her—a routine of so many Sunday mornings. She could smell the pungent, blistered hot dogs she always yearned for, but he never let her eat. Here was where she ran and he chased her. . . . She stopped and rubbed her foot across the sand as if erasing the memory.

She was at the Thunderbolt now. She squinted up at the skeletal remains, silhouetted against the sky filled with woolly clouds. It would be easy to erase this memory now that Jello was gone.

Having come to the point where the boardwalk ended, she put on her shoes and walked out onto the street. People were hurrying along, babbling excitedly to each other. The wail of a siren pierced the rumble of the traffic, a plane hummed overhead, tires screeched. All the sounds of daily life. She reached the subway stop and decided to go home.

But when she got out at Seventh and Flatbush, she still wasn't ready to face Ben. She took a circuitous route to the apartment, skirting Prospect Park, and found herself near the tunnel where Ben had pummeled the young punks on the first night they met. She entered the tunnel, running her fingers along the burnished wood made smooth from thousands of such touches. Caught in a shaft of light were the carved initials they had read together. These she couldn't erase—they looked too permanent. Now she wished that Ben had carved their initials in the wood too— to stay here forever.

Ben was lying on his bed, finishing off his second vodka. He couldn't help it—the tension was too much. He jumped up when he heard the door open, panic rising in his throat, but he forced himself to be calm.

"I'm in here," he called out, as if this was just any other day.

But his panic returned when he heard her footsteps down the hall. Quickly, he moved to the bureau, picked up a pair of scissors, and pretended to be trimming his mustache, a picture of nonchalance.

He could feel her presence—she was standing in the doorway now—but he didn't dare look at her face.

"You want to hear a joke?" she said.

"A joke?"

"Yeah—listen to this: A patient is waiting in a doctor's office for a report. The doctor comes in and says 'What do you want to hear first, the good news or the bad news?'

'Well, Doctor,' says the patient, 'let's start with the bad news.' 'Okay,' says the doctor, 'you have only six months left to live.' So the patient asks, 'What's the good news?' And you know what the doctor says, 'The good news is that I finally screwed my nurse.' "

Ben couldn't even force a weak smile. "I didn't think it was funny when I heard it the first time from Milt."

She came up behind him. Ben's eyes flicked to her reflection in the mirror. She was looking at him with an enigmatic expression that told him everything.

"Oh, I'm so tired," she said.

"Why don't you lie down a while." He put down his scissors and led her gently to the bed, feeling like he was moving in slow motion.

For a long time, they lay quietly side by side, she nestled peacefully in his arms. He had to pee, but he didn't dare move.

She stirred. "I'm sorry, Ben," she whispered. "I didn't want to do this to you."

"To me? To me!" He pulled her tightly to himself.

"I promised not to abandon you."

Ben took a deep breath, "I'm an asshole, Ellen."

She rolled her head over on the pillow, a quizzical expression on her face.

"So fucking worried about getting old. Always me, me, me. How can I go on now without you? I can't, you know. I can't. It's so unfair. You're half my age. It doesn't make any sense. Who's running this goddamn world?"

"But, Ben." She buried her face in the crook of his shoulder. "Wouldn't it be awful if I lived to an old age and never met you, never knew what it was to love you as I do, never had this wonderful love you gave me—nagging me about peanut butter and jelly, teaching me the tango so patiently, carrying the sandwiches down to Coney Island on Sundays. Ben, I wouldn't exchange thirty, forty, or fifty years for that."

"It's not the way I planned it."

"I know, Ben, I know. Me neither. In the library, I was reading books on aging, figuring out how best to look after you, thinking where we might move if you were in a wheelchair."

"You did?"

"Yeah—I had it all worked out."

"But I wouldn't let you take care of me."

"Well, I'm more selfish—I want you to take care of me. . . . Will you, Ben? Will you take care of me?"

"You know I will." His voice cracked.

"Okay."

Quietly, they lay there, listening to each other's breathing. After a while, they both dozed off, lying close together like two inseparable spoons in a drawer. When Ben opened his eyes, the room was dark. Ellen seemed to be still sleeping, her left arm hanging loosely across his body. He turned his head slowly not to awaken her, but her eyes were wide open.

"Let's go out for dinner," he said softly.

"Isn't it too late?"

"No." He nudged her side with his elbow. "Put on your best dress. I'm taking you someplace special."

Speeding along Flatbush Avenue, Ben glanced at the illuminated clock of the Williamsburg Bank tower. It was already after eleven—he'd better hurry or the restaurant would stop serving; the maître d' had reluctantly agreed to seat them if they got there no later than eleven-thirty.

He was determined to bring this oppressive day to a pleasant end. Somehow this was very important to him—it would set the tone for the months to come.

He whipped around the corner at Water Street and, with ten minutes to spare, pulled into the cobblestoned courtyard of the River Café, his headlights glancing off the bright yellow bed of daffodils in the center.

He parked facing the Brooklyn Bridge pylon that seemed to soar endlessly upward, the suspension cables like a gray spider web against the inky sky. He turned off the ignition and for a moment they sat there quietly, the constant hum of the bridge vibrating in the air above them.

"Ready?" he asked.

She nodded.

Going in, they passed a group of boisterous diners leaving, laughing raucously about something.

They made their way across the gangplank to the barge that housed the dining room. Inside, a few patrons were having an after-dinner drink at the bar; a tired piano player was singing Cole Porter:

I've got you under my skin
I've got you deep in the hide of me

He wondered if Ellen was paying attention to the words.

So deep down inside, you're really a part of me
I've got you under my skin. . . .

"Good thing we're late or we'd never get a window seat." He pulled out one of the braided bamboo chairs for her. "This place is booked months in advance."

"Yes, we're lucky." She was wearing a very pretty pink dress, which would have flattered her dark looks if she only wasn't so pale.

"Isn't that nice, Ellen?" He pointed out the window where a huge oil barge was silently gliding past.

She didn't answer. Maybe she noticed the large clump of garbage that was floating beneath their window.

Anxious to lighten the atmosphere—to push away what they were both thinking—he babbled on. He told her about Sarah's friend Brenda and her forays into AA to find a man, about Don and Dawn's second marriage, which was bound to end in disaster, about the new computerized equipment he was contemplating ordering for his gym.

The food came. It was beautifully prepared—the carrots and tomatoes carved into roses and the potatoes into daisies.

"Gee," said Ellen, "it's so pretty I hate to destroy it by eating it." And she didn't.

Ben attacked his Parfait of Tuna and Salmon Tartar with gusto. It was awful—rich and whipped, mixing ten spices too many.

By the time they ordered dessert, everyone had left the restaurant. The oaken clock on the far wall said 1:45. The waiters were yawning.

The Chocolate Marquis was a disaster. He should have taken her to Café La Fontana. Why didn't he think of that? She loved it the first time and the opera music might have been a nice change. . . . Well, he screwed it up again.

Right now, he would do anything to erase the haunted

look in those lustrous brown eyes as she absentmindedly poked with her fork at the leftover dinner rolls.

"Hey, Charlie—"

"What?" She looked up, awakened from some private reverie.

"Ever see *The Gold Rush?*"

"The Charlie Chaplin film?"

"Yeah—you remind me of the little tramp having dinner all alone."

She smiled at last, a weak little smile. "I guess eating with me must feel like that, huh? I'm sorry I haven't been very talkative."

"Oh no, it's not that. I was thinking of that cute bit he did with the bread." He stuck their dessert forks into two long Italian rolls and put them into a little dance on the table. "Look—slow, slow, quick quick, slow."

"They learn more quickly than I did." She smiled again, more warmly this time.

"Nah—you were my prize student."

"Oh sure—probably your only one."

"That's right—the only one." He took her hand, the gloom had lifted.

She squeezed it.

For a moment they just sat still, holding hands, looking into each other's eyes.

Then an idea hit him. "I know what."

"What?"

"Let's go somewhere and dance the tango."

"The apartment?"

"No, no—someplace more exotic."

"Where?"

"Trust me."

31

A billowing wall of dense fog was steadily advancing across the Atlantic Ocean, moving toward shore, toward the bright lights of Brooklyn. It skimmed the surface of the water, traveling on the crests of the undulating waves that rolled up on a sandy beach in a rhythmic pattern, almost in time to the beat of the tango music coming from Ben's car stereo.

Up on the Coney Island boardwalk, Ben and Ellen glided smoothly across the damp wood—slow, slow . . . quick, quick . . . slow.

As they danced, dwarfed by the huge, decaying skeleton of the Thunderbolt, the fog slowly closed in, sending out advance scouts to feel the way with long curly fingers that wrapped themselves around their swirling figures.

Through the gauzy film that now covered all, the lights of the lampposts shimmered softly, their brightness diffused. Cushioned by the fog, the sounds of the city—wailing sirens and bleating horns—receded farther into the distance, growing fainter and fainter, until nothing could be heard but tango.

Ben spun Ellen around, then, as she came back into his arms, he lowered her into a graceful dip. She smiled up at him, and he smiled back. At last they had it all.

The fog was growing heavier and thicker, obliterating everything in its path. Soon they became one dim silhouette floating in space, no longer anchored to the ground.

But they kept dancing, oblivious to the mist wetting their faces, hair, clothes, oblivious to the foghorn moaning a warning in the distance, oblivious that the tape had run out and the music was no longer playing.